STORM

DAWN OF A GODDESS

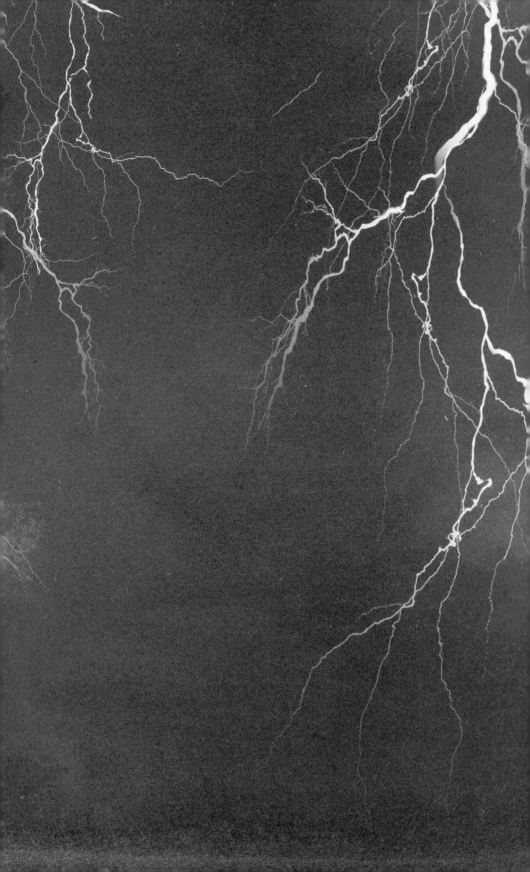

STORM
DAWN OF A GODDESS

TIFFANY D. JACKSON

RANDOM HOUSE 🏠 NEW YORK

© 2024 MARVEL
Jacket art by Raymond Sebastien

All rights reserved. Published in the United States by Random House Children's Books, a division of Penguin Random House LLC, New York.

Random House and the colophon are registered trademarks of Penguin Random House LLC.

Lightning background by LOVE A Stock and lightning bolt by Vitaly used under license from stock.adobe.com

Visit us on the Web! GetUnderlined.com

Educators and librarians, for a variety of teaching tools, visit us at RHTeachersLibrarians.com

Library of Congress Cataloging-in-Publication Data is available upon request.
ISBN 978-0-593-30885-1 (trade) — ISBN 978-0-593-30886-8 (lib. bdg.) — ISBN 978-0-593-81520-5 (int'l ed.) — ISBN 978-0-593-30887-5 (ebook)

The text of this book is set in 11.5-point Berling LT Std.

Editor: Tricia Lin
Cover Designer: Ray Shappell
Interior Designer: Michelle Crowe
Copy Editor: Barbara Bakowski
Managing Editor: Rebecca Vitkus
Production Manager: Tracy Heydweiller

Printed in the United States of America
10 9 8 7 6 5 4 3 2 1
First Edition

To my first Star:
May you always shine bright

ONE

Ororo Munroe stood on the steps of her primary school, little six-year-old fingers splayed, glancing up at the sky, willing the gates to open so she could escape.

A group of girls behind her giggled, whispering in Arabic. She wasn't familiar with the language yet, but their voices echoed in her ear. Just that day, she had asked a teacher to translate the phrase she often heard thrown in her direction during recess, and it now made her want to vomit.

"White jungle monkey," they taunted.

Back straight, eyes puffy from crying in the wash closet, she stared down the street, anxiously waiting for her mother, wondering why she ever thought her hair was something beautiful. It wasn't like the other girls', long silky brown or rich black. It was nothing but a frizzy rain cloud.

She wanted to go home and never leave again. Despite what her parents insisted, this school was nothing like her American school, with its colorful playgrounds and classrooms, where she could wear whatever she wanted. In America, she had chicken nuggets with Tater Tots and cookies.

Here, in Egypt, she had to wear a dark blue jumper over an itchy white-collared shirt. At lunch, she had two pâtés, biscuits, and a slice of flaky date pie. Though, if she was honest, she loved

the date pie. If she was honest, she loved the lessons on hiero-
glyphs and the teachers. She was learning so much.

But the kids . . .

"There she is, Mommy! The freak!"

Ororo winced, peering over her shoulder, spotting two little
boys pointing at her. Pointing at her thick, silver-white hair that
came down to her tiny waist, covering her like a coat.

The boys' mother glanced over, blinking back in surprise.

"My, *what* the devil is that?" she mumbled, hurrying them
along.

Ororo bit her lip, fighting back tears, and combed her hair
down over her face, using it as a shield.

If she was honest, the kids in her school were just like the
ones in America.

"You have eyes like the sky, child."

Ororo startled at the deep voice, looked up through the gate
bars, and gasped, pushing away from it, eyes cast down to the
ground. A large man stood on the opposite side, so large he blocked
out the sun, his beige skin covered in a thin layer of sweat.

"Hello, dear one," he said. "What is your name?"

She shook her head, refusing to look at him.

"Oh, come now, hmm? Surely you have a name."

Ororo studied his shadow on the ground, noticing he was
wearing a hat with a tassel that swung. Her tummy ached, like
the time she'd eaten bad hummus. She couldn't explain it, but
the man's very presence made her ill. She wanted him to leave.

"I'm not allowed to talk to strangers," she mumbled, turning
her back to him.

"Well, that is a shame. I just noticed you crying, and, my,
what extraordinary hair you have." He breathed in deep, sniffing the air around them. His lips smacked. "And your energy . . .
Wherever did you—"

"Ororo!"

Ororo turned to see her mother, face bright, waving at her through the crowd. Someone at the school opened the gate to let her through.

"Mommy!" Ororo shrieked, and ran. She dove into her mother's waist, nuzzling into her stomach, feeling at ease for the first time all day.

"Oh my." Her mother laughed, nearly falling back. "I am so sorry I'm late! Still getting lost in our own neighborhood."

"Hello," the same strange, raspy voice said from behind them. The hair on Ororo's neck stood up. The large man must have followed her through the crowd. "I was just keeping your lovely daughter company. She seemed rather upset."

Ororo buried her face in her mother's coat, and her mother patted her back.

"Would you ladies care to, uh, join me for tea? I insist."

Ororo carefully looked up, only at her mother's face. Ororo didn't like the stranger and she didn't like tea. She just wanted to go home.

Mother smiled at the man. "That is kind, but no, thank you. It is about time for me to start dinner. My husband will be waiting for us."

But the man pushed further.

"Really, I insist," he implored, eyes fixed rabidly on Ororo. "Your daughter is . . . quite extraordinary."

Mother straightened at the comment, gripping Ororo closer. She smoothed a protective hand over Ororo's hair.

"Yes, she is," she said curtly. "Have a good day, sir."

He tipped his hat. "Same to you, madam. Same to you. I'm sure we'll be seeing each other real soon." He turned back to Ororo, an odd smile on his face. "Goodbye for now, dear one."

Mother pulled Ororo along, scurrying down the busy street

toward home. Ororo looked back. The man had disappeared into the crowd, yet she had the lingering sense that someone was still watching.

✕

When they finally reached home, Ororo threw her backpack down by the door and sighed. The world inside their home made sense, while everywhere else did not. Mother made her way to the kitchen to put away food from the market. Ororo pushed her hair back from her face and glanced toward Daddy's office. She knew what she had to do.

She scuttled past the living room, where Daddy sat in his favorite leather recliner. Quiet as a mouse, Ororo crept into his office, slid open the top drawer of his desk, and grabbed her prize. She padded across the hall and into the dark bathroom, the floor tiles cool against her feet. Flicking on the light, she looked up at the mirror, chewing the inside of her cheek. Yes, this would do.

She climbed up to the bathroom sink and stared at her reflection, noting the determination in her features. With a deep breath, she tugged at a chunk of her hair . . .

"*Ororo Iqadi Munroe!* What on earth are you doing?"

Ororo's blue eyes flared in the mirror with her arm frozen, a pair of black scissors held taut to her silver-white hair. *Caught.* She winced. How had she not heard her mother coming?

"Goddess help me with this child," Mother called to the ceiling. She stomped into the narrow bathroom, snatching the scissors out of Ororo's hands.

"Have you lost your senses?" She glanced back into the living room. "David, do you see what you daughter is attempting to do?"

Ororo let out a *hmph* in frustration. "Of course he does, Momma," she said, climbing down from the sink. "He has *eyes*."

Daddy held in a laugh. "Well, she certainly has your Kenyan pragmatism," he quipped before returning to his book on African theology.

Mother narrowed her eyes at him. "And your American stubborn foolishness."

He took off his glasses and winked. "Touché."

Mother couldn't help but smirk in response. "So silly."

Ororo frowned. "What does prag-maz-tism mean?" She hated not knowing things. Hated feeling like she was missing out. Her mother always said that even as a baby she'd stayed up until morning, never wanting to miss a thing.

"Never mind all that," her mother muttered, dragging her out of the bathroom and into their colorful living room filled with art, books, musical instruments, gemstone-colored pillows, and plush Turkish rugs.

The early-evening breeze billowed through the curtains of their top-floor apartment that faced east, giving them a view of the Giza pyramids in the distance. It was why they'd picked the place. Daddy wanted to wake each morning and be reminded of their great leap to Cairo.

Mother sat on the leather sofa, placing Ororo in front of her so she could look her daughter square in the eye.

"Ororo, tell me: what on earth would make you want to cut your beautiful hair?"

Ororo wrung her fingers. "Because you and Daddy don't have white hair. You have normal hair."

Mother's eyes softened. She glanced at Daddy, who softly closed his book.

"Sweetheart," he said, "there's absolutely nothing wrong with your hair."

Ororo took in her parents, one by one. Both her mother and father had dark copper skin with brown eyes. While her father had jet-black hair he kept cut low, her mother had tightly curly brown hair.

Ororo's own white mane stopped at her waist, like a cape draped around her back, and her eyes were a clear blue ocean. *White jungle monkey.*

"No one else has it," she cried, tugging at her locks. "Why do I have to look like this?!"

Mother smiled at Ororo, reaching up to tuck a lock of white hair behind her ear. "You know, there are many women in my family who have hair and eyes just like yours."

Ororo blinked in surprise. "Then where are they? How come I've never seen them?"

Mother hesitated, her eyes holding a strange sadness. "It's . . . hard to explain."

Ororo's eyes filled with tears. "The other kids make fun of me. They call me a freak, and I don't want to be a freak."

Mother wrapped her arms tight around her daughter. "Oh, sweetie. I know it's hard to believe, but your hair— It just means you're special."

"But I don't want to be special. I want to be like everyone else."

Mother laughed, wiping Ororo's tears away. "My dear child, you were not meant to be like everyone else. You were meant to shine like the brightest star."

"I don't care!" Ororo cried, stomping her foot.

"Sweetheart, have I ever lied to you? Do I not always tell you the truth?"

Ororo thought of all the times her mother had carefully explained things to her. About how plants grew and flowers bloomed, and how stars were made. She nodded twice.

"So, trust me when I say one day soon, you'll learn that when you are born different, it means you were meant to be part of something different. Something way bigger than anything you could ever imagine. A dream so big that it may scare you." Mother smiled mysteriously. "That's when you learn just how brave and powerful you can be."

Ororo pushed a strand of hair out of her face and sniffed. "But why do I—"

A sudden boom made her mother jump to her feet. The sound rang through their apartment. Ororo tensed, the back of her neck prickling.

"What's that noise?" she asked, gripping Mother's waist.

Daddy slowly stood, facing the balcony.

"Mommy? What is that?"

"I'm . . . I don't know." Her mother's arms tightened around her. "David?"

Daddy stared out the open doors, squinting into the darkness. He gasped as orange light filled the room, growing brighter, the noise deafening. He spun around, racing toward them.

"Get down! Get down now!"

"What's happening?" Ororo screamed, gripping her mother.

"David?"

"DOWN!"

Mother yanked Ororo to the floor, throwing her body on top of her baby girl's. Daddy curled himself around them as the room shook with a violent jolt, dust pluming. Her mother screamed. Then the roof and floor collapsed all at once.

✕

Ororo peeled her eyes open at the sound of something churning nearby.

"Mommy?" she moaned. "Daddy?"

Blackness surrounded her. She couldn't tell which way was up or down. She tried to move her arms, legs, and head. She could feel everything, but she somehow could not move. As if she were trapped inside a tight black box.

She listened for her parents' voices, but nothing rose above the noise. Her little hands reached and patted around her body, hitting splinters of wood and metal . . . then something soft. She gripped it and tugged.

A shirt. An arm. A hand. A hand she would know anywhere.

"Mommy," Ororo gasped, yanking harder.

The hand felt cold, stiff. Her stomach dropped, and the blackness began to swallow her.

"Mommy!"

Desperate, Ororo beat against the trappings of her box, clawing at everything, wheezing breaths, her lungs heavy.

"Help! Help me," she cried. "Mommy, I can't breathe, I can't breathe. . . ."

She shouted, fought for what felt like hours. No one came.

As the smoke slowly cleared, light began to slip through the cracks of the black box, and Ororo wiggled and saw what was holding her in place. A huge metal beam pinned her to the ground. And as much as she pushed, it wouldn't budge.

"Goddess help me!" she finally cried. And with all her strength, she pushed the beam enough to free her leg and scoot back, bumping into something soft. She froze.

Daddy.

"Daddy," she whimpered, shaking his shoulder. "Daddy. Please wake up."

A few feet away, she could now see her mother's arm, sticking out beneath the crumbled bricks and concrete.

"Please, Mommy, please," she sobbed as a drop of light poked through the rubble. She frantically clawed at it, digging herself out of the stone, concrete, and wood, desperate for freedom, desperate to escape. Darkness crowded her, threatening to swallow her.

She pushed. And pushed. Until finally the sky came into view through a small hole above. She crawled out, whimpering, knees scraping against the hot concrete. Before she could find her balance, her hand slipped. She tumbled out of the hole, rolling down hot metal, tiny fires, and sharp rocks, until she landed in a sobbing heap on the ground.

But she was out. She was out of that dark place.

She took her first staggering breath, her lungs heaving, smoke and screams surrounding her. Hands bloody from digging herself out, she shakily used them to help her stand, then turned to face a towering plane propeller.

TWO

Face covered in soot, clothes ripped and bloody, Ororo picked her way through the hot rubble, coughing up smoke. She took in her surroundings.

Mountains of sharp tan rocks mixed with bent metal sheets and rods surrounded her, pockets of fire scattered throughout, the heat suffocating. She could barely see through the ash.

It was as if the world had exploded and she was the only one left alive. But she couldn't be. There had to be others.

"Hello?" she called, tears streaming down her face.

She spotted movement in the distance and inched toward it, praying someone would help her, help her parents, before she noticed other children emerge from nearby. Their clothes were worn, their faces careful—they didn't seem to be looking for help like her. She stared, dazed, as they popped out of their hiding spots, wandering through the rubble, picking up whatever they could find.

Ororo stumbled, limping away from the crash site. Emergency workers had begun digging through the destruction, moving debris and helping injured people up. But no one tried to stop her as she wandered. She was just another kid in the crowd. Her feet led her down a nearby alleyway as a mob of people tried to push past her for a better look, peering at where her home once stood. While others were running toward the terrible bad thing, she was drifting away.

"Hey! You!"

Ororo whipped around. A boy stood on top of a crumbled piece of concrete. He was older, maybe by a few years, and dressed in dirty jeans, a black shirt with a brown scarf wrapped around his neck, and gray sneakers. His jet-black hair was pushed back and tied in a small ponytail.

"Never seen you around," he said with a curious expression. "Who are you?"

Ororo rubbed her arms, backing away. "Please . . ."

He cocked his head to the side. "What's wrong with your hair?"

She trembled. What *was* wrong with her hair? Her mother had never truly explained. And now her mother was surrounded by hot darkness. Her legs started to feel numb, a chill overtaking her.

"It's . . . it's . . . just this way," she said through chattering teeth.

The boy blinked in surprise. "You're American." He looked back at the crash. "Wait. Were you on that plane?"

She shook her head.

"No," she whimpered, eyes filling with tears. "We were home. My mother. Daddy . . ."

The words didn't seem real. She must be dreaming, she tried to reason with herself as her body swayed.

The boy glanced back at the crash site and the onslaught of people gathering.

"Do you have any other family?" he asked softly.

Ororo thought hard. She didn't know of anyone else. It had always just been the three of them. And now her parents were gone.

She shook her head.

He whistled through his teeth. "Damn."

That was when it truly hit: Ororo was all alone. Where would she go now? Where *could* she even go?

"What's going to happen to me?" she wondered out loud.

"Well. Nothing," the boy said. "You're one of us now. You'll be in the streets, with the rest of the kids who don't have parents."

Ororo shivered, blinking furiously, thinking of the kids she saw digging through the remnants that were once her home. She thought of the kids she often saw panhandling on her way to school.

How would she eat? Where would she live?

She started breathing harder and harder, her lungs struggling. The boy jumped down to stand in front of her with a torn expression, mumbling Arabic under his breath. He gave her another once-over.

"Maybe . . . I may have someone who will help you. But you'll need to pass the test. All of us do."

Ororo shut her eyes and took a big gulp of air. ". . . Test?"

"Yeah. I'll show you. But first—" He pulled the long brown scarf off his neck and handed it to her. "Here. Wrap up your head."

"Why? I'm not Muslim."

"You don't want to draw so much attention to yourself," he explained. "Do you?"

Ororo hesitated, but quickly realized: if no one knew what her hair looked like, maybe they wouldn't treat her so differently.

She looked at the boy, taking in his wary expression but kind eyes, as if he knew what she was feeling.

Slowly, she nodded and took the scarf. She wrapped it around her head as best she could, trying to stuff her hair inside.

"Here, let me help you. At least until we find someone who

can really show you how to fix it right." He stepped closer and turned her around, tenderly tying her hair back. "I'm Moche, by the way. What's your name?"

She struggled to find her voice. "Ororo."

Moche stepped back, admiring his work. "Not bad." He took her hand and tugged her down the alley. "All right, come on. I'm taking you to my boss, Achmed El Gibár. He'll know what to do with you."

X

Time blurred in the weeks that followed. Before Ororo knew it, staying with Achmed, Moche, and the other boys like him almost felt normal.

She still couldn't stay inside for too long. The walls always seemed to shift and move closer. She slowly became more comfortable stepping inside, but only during daylight hours. At night, she still preferred the outdoors, where the ceiling could not cave in on her.

It had been just shy of three months of living with them when Ororo found herself following Moche through unfamiliar busy streets. She had never been to this side of Cairo, and certainly not without her parents. The thought of them, stuck under that rubble, in that dark place, still made her chest go hollow.

"Where are we going?" she whispered.

"Remember that test I told you about? It's time."

Dread filled her belly. "What? But . . . I'm not ready."

"Boss says you are, so you are." Moche glanced back at her with a grin. "Don't worry, I'll go easy on you."

Moche led her through an open-air bazaar filled with Egyptian people bartering goods, toward a small back alleyway, making a hard left. He slipped through a narrow hole in a boarded-up door. Inside, the building lay largely in shadow, filled with rotted wood and machines covered in dust. Pigeons fluttered above, raining down feathers. Streams of sunlight slipped through the cracks in the covered windows.

"What is this place?"

"One of the old silk factories," Moche explained. "This is how we move through the souks. Come on."

But Ororo's feet were frozen, eyes widening at the falling ceiling beams and burnt furniture. The floor looked like it would cave in at any moment.

Trapped. She would be trapped, under the rubble. Again.

"I . . . it's too dark in here," she gasped, suddenly unable to breathe. "We . . . we can't get out . . . no light . . ."

She struggled to explain, struggled to find the words as panic flooded her trembling body, dust circling as her vision blurred.

Moche shook his head. "Ro, you can't live outside forever! This is the fastest way to get through the souks. And we're not talking a stroll. You gotta move like you have somewhere to be, always." He clapped a hand on Ororo's shoulder. "It'll be okay, watch. Ready? Go!"

Moche took off through the abandoned building, hopping over broken chairs, skating around discarded tables like he was made of air. Ororo pushed her legs to keep up, holding her breath as the walls seemed to close around her, fighting against the desperate need to close her eyes and block the raging panic. The desperation made her move faster, strides almost matching his. Moche glanced over, as if proud, before slowing near a broken window, climbing out onto the roof of the next building.

"See?" he said. "Easy. Best way to travel and give security the slip."

Catching her breath, Ororo let out a small, relieved laugh. Following Moche, she climbed down a stack of wooden crates leaning against the side of the building and peered inside a narrow window. On the other side was a packed bar filled with tourists and Egyptians alike, drinking red wine, snacking on dates. A man in the corner played a flute over the heated discussions and laughter.

"You see that white man over there in the brown jacket?" Moche whispered.

Ororo followed his gaze, spotting the jacket across the room. Despite the commotion, the man focused solely on his book, taking casual sips of dark beer.

"All you have to do is take that wallet in his left pocket."

Ororo blinked up in shock. "Take it. You want me to steal?"

He snorted. "Oh boy, are you green. Yes! Steal that man's wallet."

The most Ororo had ever stolen in her short life was a piece of candy out of her mother's purse, earning her a brutal scolding and lingering shame. She shook her head, hot with alarm.

"I can't. I'll get in trouble."

"Not if you don't get caught. But you have to snatch it quick. Walk in the front door, then out the back, and run down the alley. Don't stop for anything."

Ororo wavered. "This is really what Achmed wants me to do?" He had taught her about picking locks, but he never mentioned anything about taking what wasn't hers.

"Of course. Nothing in life is for free, and we all must pay our way somehow. If you can pull this off, Boss will take you in for good. He only takes in a special few of us, and we're his children." Moche shrugged. "Otherwise, you'll be stuck on the streets with the other kiddies, digging your next meal out of the trash."

Ororo shuddered. She had seen other children rummaging in garbage while out shopping with her mother. Watched her father give coins to the kids begging outside the gates of the museum. She didn't want to be one of them.

Ororo looked back at the man in the bar, still reading. "But . . . why him?"

Moche rolled his eyes.

"Boy, I have to teach you everything, don't I? Okay, let me give you some tips. You have to, what I call, read the room, to pick out your best target. Look around, what do you see, what do you hear? See his watch, how nice his blazer is? He has money. When he ordered, he had an American accent. . . ."

Moche went on as Ororo examined the man again. Could she really do this? But what choice did she have? It was either be with Achmed, Moche, and the other boys, or be in the streets . . . alone.

"Okay." She sighed. "I'll do it."

"Good. Meet you on the corner at the end of the alley. Remember, don't stop."

"Move like you have somewhere to be," she said, repeating his mantra.

Moche patted her shoulder and took off.

Ororo swallowed hard, setting her eyes on the wallet sticking out of the man's pocket. She glanced at the exit on the other side of the bar, a few feet away. Could it be that simple?

Be brave, she heard her mother say. But wasn't bravery doing the right thing? How could the right choice feel like she was about to do something wrong?

She edged toward the door of the bar and slipped inside. The room was so busy that no one paid any mind to the small girl who had just walked in, and she slowly made her way through the bustle, eyes trained on the man in the brown jacket. He set down his glass of beer, fishing out the wallet, unaware of the girl stalking him like prey. She watched as he flipped through a thick stack of dollar bills before calling over the waiter.

Moche was right about him, she thought. But if the man was preparing to pay his bill, then he would be leaving soon. It was time to act.

Heart thrumming, Ororo tiptoed behind him, little fingers splayed. No one looked her way. For once, she was invisible. Eyes fixed on the man, she held her breath, feet moving double-time. In one quick move, she snatched the wallet and speed-walked toward the door without flinching.

A wave of adrenaline rushed through her body. She had done it, she was brave. A smile bloomed over her face. . . .

And then the world went quiet. Something didn't feel quite right. The room around her was almost mute.

Her skin prickled. She glanced to her left, fidgeting with her headscarf. Maybe someone had seen her or spotted her hair.

It was then that she noticed a waiter at the bar, his eyes unmoving, coffee steaming out of a pot suspended in midair. She turned to her right to find a couple stuck midstride. In the corner, the flute player's cheeks were puffed, but no sound came out.

The entire room had frozen around her.

Is this some kind of joke? she thought.

"This is not a joke, young lady."

Ororo spun around. The man in the brown blazer stared directly at her as he slowly stood up. Ororo couldn't move. Though she wasn't frozen like the rest of the room, fear kept her rooted in place.

He smiled as he approached. "I believe you have something of mine."

Ororo gripped the wallet in her hand, tears of shame exploding.

"I'm . . . I'm so sorry. I'm . . ."

"It's all right," he said, bending to meet her eye. "What is your name?"

She hesitated before croaking out, "Ororo."

His eyes fell on her headscarf. "That is quite a beautiful name."

Ororo tucked an invisible stray hair back in place, glancing around the frozen bar. "How did you do that?"

He smiled. "My name is Charles Xavier. I'm a professor."

"My father was a professor," she blurted out. "American, too." In that moment, thinking of her father, a wave of humiliation hit her. What would he say if he saw her like this? What would he want her to say? "I'm sorry I took your wallet! I . . . I . . ."

"Hmm," the professor noted, then closed his eyes. He frowned as his lashes twitched and fluttered, almost as if he was thinking too hard for his brain to handle it. He let out a loud exhale. "Ohhh. I see. You've been through something quite terrible, haven't you?"

He opened his eyes, now full of pity, and patted her little hand.

"But your mother was right. You were meant to be part of something bigger. And this"—he tapped the wallet—"isn't you."

Ororo clutched his wallet, guilt an immense boulder on her shoulder.

"You are destined for something far greater," he continued. "But the only way to learn that is to go home. Your real home. That is why I . . ."

His mouth opened but quickly closed before his head snapped up, like a gazelle that has just realized it's being hunted. He looked past Ororo, eyes widening at something unseen.

"What is it? What's wrong?" Ororo asked.

He jerked with a wince, gripping the side of his head.

"Ororo," he said through gritted teeth, "it's time for you to go."

She struggled to find her tongue. "But . . ."

"Keep the wallet," he groaned, struggling through some invisible pain she could not see. "I'm sure you'll give it back to me someday."

Footsteps echoed behind them. A sharp, cheery whistle cut through the silence, the melody somehow pleasant yet eerie.

Someone was coming. Ororo glanced at the rest of the room, still unmoving. Chills crept down her spine.

"Run along now," the professor whispered. "Hurry. And hide. Don't let him see you."

Him? she thought. But her fear spoke loudly, and Ororo didn't waste a beat. She ran out the exit, but stopped short at the sound of a deep voice she had heard before.

"Why, you are not what I was expecting at all."

Heart thudding in her ears, Ororo's curiosity spiked. Her senses told her *run . . .* but she couldn't help herself. She had to know.

Ororo tiptoed back to the door, peering inside. Who was the "him" the professor wanted her to hide from?

On the opposite side of the bar, a large man in a crisp white suit stood at the entrance, the sun shining behind him. Dark purple glasses covered his eyes, and the tassel on his burgundy fez swayed with his every move. Ororo squinted, racking her memory. She knew this man from somewhere, but where?

"I'm sorry to disappoint," the professor said. "And you are?"

The man glanced around the frozen room, amused. "I sensed a presence . . . an incredibly powerful energy nearby."

"Well, there is no one here but us."

The large man laughed. "Are you so sure?"

The professor motioned at his table, and the large man joined him, his white suit gleaming. He removed his glasses to reveal dark, unreadable eyes.

"It is not you I'm in search of, my new friend," the large man declared, scanning the motionless bar. "Though I am thoroughly impressed with your talents. But this person . . . this person is beyond both of us. Might you be hiding this person from me?"

The professor seemed unfazed by the threat. "I would do no such thing. But if such a person existed, what would you want with them?"

"I would want what any self-respecting businessman would want," he said with a wet laugh.

"Ah," the professor said, sipping the last of his beer and setting it down on the table. "So, you must be the Shadow King."

"Indeed. And you, you are not from around here."

"I make it my business to know of others with . . . special talents."

The Shadow King slammed a large hand on the table, causing the empty glass to rattle, and Ororo jumped. *"You know of me,"* he bellowed, *"and yet you dare come to Cairo and not make your presence known?"*

The professor sat, unmoving, as the two men stared at one another. Ororo's pulse raced, her every nerve alight with panic. She took a closer look at the table, eyes skipping over the professor and the Shadow King. Wildly, she sensed a silent conversation was being had, words exchanged but never uttered.

Suddenly, the professor's eyes turned a glowing red, almost like bright Christmas lights. Ororo stopped breathing.

"No," the professor groaned. "Stop." He snapped his eyes closed, frowning hard. He held two fingers to his temple. The large man let out a yelp.

The professor's eyes returned to brown.

Ororo slapped a hand over her mouth to keep silent.

"We will not battle here, my friend," the professor barked. "We should continue this conversation of the minds in the Astral Plane."

"If you insist," the Shadow King hissed.

The two men went silent again, their eyes closed, mouths taut. Sweat dotted their furrowed brows, their facial expressions morphing from pleasant to anguished to surprised.

Ororo's eyes jumped back and forth between them. She had expected them to leave, to go to the astral place the professor had mentioned. But they remained motionless.

The rims of the Shadow King's eyes glowed red. He shook with a choking grunt before going ghostly white. Then he slumped, face falling flat on the table with a heavy thud.

The room unfroze, people shifting, moving, and breathing again as the large man lay dead on the table.

Ororo watched in horror, shock flooding her body. Then, before the professor could turn, she spun around and sprinted down the alley, bumping into carts and people in a haze.

What have I just seen?

A hand shot out. She shrieked as someone yanked her around the corner.

"Hey! You got it!" Moche's voice broke her out of a trance. "That was fast."

Moche slipped the wallet out of her hand and counted the cash inside, whistling through his teeth.

"I knew that'd be a good score. Whew, this is a lot of money. I'm going to keep some, or the boys will get jealous that you stole a good score from them. You can't be too good from the start. You need to build up." He finally looked her in the face and frowned.

"What happened? You look like you've seen a ghost."

But Ororo didn't know where to begin.

THREE

Nine Years Later

American tourists are so predictable.

They always carry a thick wallet with all their credits cards and cash in their back pockets or at the top of their open purses, just waiting for anyone to snatch it from them. In the busy souks, they don't even feel me brush by them, scooping their contents with ease. Tourists come in search of things they can put in their homes to prove they've been to Egypt—incense, rugs, and pillows. I've stolen too many of their wallets, cell phones, watches, and jewelry to count.

In this sprawling capital of the world's most famous sandbox, there are many souks, or street markets to Americans. But none are as beautiful as the Soor el-Azbakeya, otherwise known as Azbakeya Wall or Book Heaven, where there are endless rows of cafés and over a hundred secondhand bookshops. Our crew has our typical souks we frequent, like Khan El Khalili. Fridays are reserved for Souq al-Gomaa. With so many people from all over the world, it's easy to score there.

But me? I like a challenge. And Book Heaven is where I'm typically found.

I learn a lot about people and their taste from their wallets. Some carry photos, random fast-food receipts, or business cards in hidden pockets. But they always carry a crisply folded twenty-dollar bill. As if hiding it away will keep them from spending it. It always tickles me.

The group of tourists I'm scoping out today sound like they are from the Deep South of America. Their tour guide, Kadir, gives me a quick nod as he leads the group past. He is on the boss's payroll as well.

I shift my scarf forward. Not Muslim, but I still wear a hijab. Helps me blend in. My silver-white hair isn't exactly good for this line of business.

As Kadir leads the large group, the first to approach them are the kiddies, their hands cupped, begging for change, impressing them with a few English words.

As the tourists fawn over them, I fly through the group easy. I'm not a short girl, but I keep a low profile, my hair always covered, moving quick. An innocent bump of the shoulder here, waiting for a laugh there. Sticky fingers as I snatch wallets, coin purses, maybe a camera or phone before slipping into alleys, out of sight, a ghost in the dust.

I notice one of the new kiddies panhandling on the corner, watching the others clean house. He's not the best. Gun-shy and skittish, just as I was. I drop a coin purse in his hand and give him a wink before disappearing down the road.

Where do I carry my own wallet? In the inside pocket of my harem pants.

X

"Ah! I knew I'd find you here."

Perched on a tall stool in the back, I look up from my book

on modern philosophy as Moche strolls into my favorite book-shop, tossing a quick greeting to the owner, Muhammad, as he makes his way over to me.

The Fahmy and Co. bookshop is only a narrow strip, maybe the size of one of those white tourist vans, stacked from floor to ceiling with books, a lone light bulb overhead. Dust covers the floor, peppering the pages. There's no organization to the shelves. You could find a book about Iran next to a romance novel, but I know where mostly everything is filed. Muhammad spends most of his time meticulously organizing the vintage newspapers, prints, and posters bursting out the shop's entrance. The walls vibrate as the train rumbles underground, and you can barely hear yourself think.

I look up, glancing past Moche as I hear a call to prayer from outside the store on a staticky speaker, the sky a light peachy-pink as hectic foot traffic crams the streets. Is it time to go already?

"Shouldn't you be working?" Moche asks, leaning against a shaky table of sun-faded books.

I shrug, turning back to my book. "Letting the boys catch up to me. I've scored more than enough."

He raises an eyebrow. "Oh really?"

Always so suspicious. I reach over to my sack and toss it in his direction.

"Yes. Really."

Moche takes out five wallets, two digital cameras, and an iPhone, whistling through his teeth.

"No one likes a show-off, Ororo," Moche chides with a grin, but in some ways his teasing has a certain percent of truth to it. He makes these little remarks whenever my take exceeds the entire group's. Proud and humbling in equal measure.

I lick a finger and turn the page without looking up. "You told me last week to go easy on the boys, and I am. I could've gotten twice as much."

On most afternoons, once I'm done with my scores, I find myself back down at el-Azbakeya, settled with a book and a cup of burning-hot tea. The bookshop keepers know me well, pointing me in the direction of academic literature, world travel, and books on herbal remedies. Books my father would have read. I sometimes wonder if we may have studied the same text. If he watches me from the beyond with pride.

Moche shoves my scores back in the sack, taking in the bookshop with confused curiosity.

"Why do you always hang out here? You've probably read every book ever written by now."

"Books are familiar friends."

"So is money," he jokes.

I close my book and swing my legs around.

"You know, I can teach the kiddies how to read. Maybe start a school for them."

He laughs. "They read money good enough."

I shake my head. Moche has always kept his eyes on the prize.

"You think Achmed would approve?"

His thick black eyebrows shoot up. "No. And you'd be foolish to ask. We have a business to run. Speaking of which, come on. We have one more stop to make before home."

I tug on my headscarf, making sure there are no flyaways. Moche smiles as he helps.

"You look fine." He laughs. "Can't see a thing."

He says that whenever I'm worried about my mane threatening to expose me. I don't mind having my hair out in front of Moche. He's seen me at my worst. But no one else has ever laid eyes on the white beast in years, and I'd like to keep it that way.

I follow Moche down the road, weaving through traffic and dodging speeding cars in a city that doesn't believe in stoplights. If Achmed El Gibár is my boss and father figure, then Moche is very much my big, and sometimes annoying, brother. Moche is much taller than when I first met him as a child. He's no longer all gangly arms and legs, and now has more the body of a young man, with dark olive skin and jet-black hair he still ties in a small ponytail. He's always in a uniform of forest green tunic over khaki pants. His shoes look like they've been through five world wars.

We dodge traffic in another roundabout, Moche taking a hard right. This isn't the usual way back to the pickup spot, where the van is parked to take us all back home.

"Where are you going?" I ask.

"Hakim said a tour bus just dropped a group who left their bags near here."

"At this hour? Tah! They're just begging for it, aren't they?"

Moche nods. "Boss wants us to check it out. It'll be an easy score. Wrap up the day on a high note."

We take the back alleys, talking about our scores for the day and funny people we've clocked, until we reach one of the old silk factory buildings at the far end of a street, the tall wooden door cryptic and ancient.

"This way," Moche says, pushing it open with his shoulder.

"They're in here?" I ask, trying not to sound skeptical. Why would a group of tourists drop their bags off here with no security? Even the silliest of Americans wouldn't do something so foolish, would they?

"That's what Hakim told me. Their bags are on the third floor. But we don't have much time. They're doing a sunset dinner cruise. Belly dancers and all that."

I look around, my skin prickling. I'm pretty sure the building is abandoned—plus, we hardly ever go after places this quiet. None of this makes any sense.

"Are you sure?"

Moche laughs, pushing me forward through the thick red curtain. "Come on, you. Stop being so paranoid."

We move fast up the stairs until we reach a landing with a red curtain blocking another door hiding behind it. He jiggles the handle. Locked.

"It's here?" I ask again. Hakim *has* to be mistaken. This location is too specific, too far away from any quick exits.

"Yeah. Can you open it?"

I pull a short metal knitting needle out of my hijab. "Tuh. Of course I can."

I drop to my knees to examine the lock while Moche eyes the hall. I dig the stick into the keyhole and press a hand to the lock. Boss taught me long ago that you can feel for a weak spot through the wood.

"Hurry up, Ro," Moche whispers.

"I just started," I snap.

He fiddles with his jacket buttons. "Well, I would've had it done by now."

I turn to glare at him. "Then why aren't you doing it?"

Moche stutters. "W-well . . . I . . . just hurry up."

There's a scratching sound behind the door, and I fall back on my butt with a gasp, the needle firm in my grip. "What was that?"

"What?" he says, whipping around.

"I just heard something!"

"Woman, are you serious? It's probably some rats. You scared or something?" Moche casts another glance down the hall, gesturing quickly at the door. "Come on! Let's get out of here in case the belly dancers finish up too soon."

My stomach tenses, still uneasy. I could've sworn something was moving. But I take a deep breath and lean back in.

Focus, Ororo. You must focus. Concentration is key.

That's what Achmed would say if he was standing over me. Always stay ready and focus on the task, no matter what. Concentration is key to survival. When you focus, you can do anything.

The lock clicks. Bingo.

We exchange a quick glance, a silent understanding of what to do next. The clock starts on our three-minute window. That's all we allow ourselves. The goal is to run in, grab any jewelry, money, and electronics, as much as we can fit in our pockets, then slip back out.

The door creaks open, the room pitch-black. We shuffle inside, my breath catching in my throat as I feel around for the light panel.

"Are you sure this is the right room?" I ask, heart racing. It'll be impossible to find what we need in the dark.

"What's with all the questions?" Moche snarls from somewhere in the room.

"Well, it's just . . . you know I don't like—"

"SURPRISE!"

A deep voice shouts behind me as an arm swoops around my waist.

"AH!" I cry and jump, grabbing the arm. I tumble forward, pulling my assailant onto the floor and placing my foot on his neck in one swift move.

"Ro, wait," the voice begs, choking at the lack of oxygen.

Lights pop on and I glance down at my victim.

Hakim.

"Um, surprise?" he croaks. His light copper hair complements his hazel eyes, which always feel full of mischief. He holds his hands up in surrender.

"Happy birthday, Ororo!" The room explodes with red, purple, and green lights as my ten brothers come out of their hiding spaces with face-splitting smiles. I quickly adjust my hijab, making sure it's still in place after my scuffle.

"Oh!" I laugh and offer an arm to help Hakim back to his feet, glancing at the ceiling draped in ragged gold satin curtains, the windows blacked out with papyrus paper. "Today is my day?"

Hakim rubs his neck, groaning. "She almost killed me."

"Then I taught her well," Moche says with a laugh, clapping his back. "And almost is not enough."

My mouth waters as I survey the banquet of food laid out on a long table—kebabs, kofta balls, semsemia, and baklava, even sodas. Food we never have at home. Our typical dinner is plain ful medames with bread, water, and hot tea to fill our bellies before bed.

I shake my head. "You didn't have to do all this."

"We know!" Moche proclaims. "But Boss said we could. Let's eat! I'm starving."

We sit on floor pillows and the boys dig in, loading up their small plates. Someone turns on a speaker with a playlist of Arabic hip-hop, Afro trap, and some American music. I feel a grin tugging at my mouth. We don't have many nights like this. Our group is only allowed one birthday celebration a year, so really, this day belongs to all of us.

The yearly birthday celebration always reminds me of family dinners from when I was a child. There was something Mommy used to make for me that I can never remember the name of. It was white like my hair, doughy yet solid, and sat like a big snowball on my plate next to stewed meat and fish. I've searched and searched, but never see it in any restaurant windows in Cairo.

Some days, I let myself imagine life from before my parents died. Walking through the streets of New York, sitting in movie theaters, eating hot dogs, playing in the parks . . . flying on planes?

Daddy reading bedtime stories . . . Mommy dancing in the living room. . . . . It all feels so far away, like a dream. Was any of it real?

I blink back the thought, glancing at the head of the table, and catch Moche staring at me. We exchange a look, his dark eyes boring into mine, and I know what he would say: *Stop all that thinking of the past. It won't bring money into our future!*

I clear the lump in my throat and adjust my hijab. With it being my birthday, there will be more eyes on me tonight, and I need to make sure not a hair is out of place. The boys have never seen my hair, and I fear the day my brothers learn just how different I am. The day they realize how much I don't belong and they consider me something to be thrown in the streets.

But until that day, we're a family. And watching my family feast like kings warms my heart.

Moche whistles, then raises a bottle of purple Fanta. "A toast! To Ororo. The one who keeps us on our toes."

"The one who scores the most," Omari says, laughing loud and easy. Omari wears a tan shemagh, his black eyes matching his black hair. Sometimes I catch him dabbing a little cedarwood musk on his chest, slicking his wavy hair back with water. I've even seen Moche borrow some oil from time to time. It's not hard to see why Omari is the ladies' man.

"Not always," Moche corrects, throwing me a wink, and I roll my eyes.

"The one who knows exactly what the weather will be!" Bassel says with a little nudge. He's the sweet and curious one of my brothers, his light green eyes twinkling. Today he's dressed smart in a plaid shirt, and it adds to the charm of his ears sticking out a touch.

"Ah yes! Which reminds me, Ororo, what's the temperature?" Moche asks.

I chuckle before licking my finger and pointing it up in the air. "Ummm . . . about twenty-three degrees."

The boys whip around to little Amir, the youngest of the crew. Amir tips up his brown-framed glasses, pulls out a flip phone, and presses a few buttons. The boys lean in, enraptured.

"Twenty-three exactly!"

The table erupts with cheers, everyone high-fiving me.

"How do you do it?" Amir laughs. "Tell us your secrets."

I shrug with a smirk. "What can I say? It's a gift."

"Oh boy," Hakim says. "Here comes that American cockiness."

I stiffen, managing a smile. They don't mean anything by it, but they never quite let me forget that I'm not one of them.

Being the only girl doesn't help. Always the butt of jokes. I have to work extra hard to prove myself, prove that I belong, prove I am more than what they see. Even if the perfection kills me.

"Remember that day she said there was going to be a sandstorm and two hours later, a sandstorm appeared?" Bassel asks, passing around a basket of warm flat bread.

"Or that time she called the flood?" Amir adds.

"It wasn't a flood," Omari challenges. "It was just some heavy rain."

"There were cars underwater!" Hakim shouts. "We could've floated back to Garbage City. Gosh, I also remember how green little Ro was back then. She couldn't even score a cell phone if it was sitting right in front of her."

I narrow my eyes and take a sip of cola. "And now look at me? Running circles around you."

The boys roar with laughter as Omari reaches for another kofta ball.

"Hey!" I shout, shooing his hand away. "Don't eat everything! We should bring some back for the kiddies. They're probably starving."

The table groans. "Ugh, this goddess," Hakim jokes.

"All right, everyone, how about a little game?" Moche offers.

"What do you have in mind?" I ask.

Moche digs under the table and procures two wooden boxes—one black, one brown—each with a unique padlock hanging off the clip. Delicate designs are etched into the wood, and Moche sets them on the table with a solid *thunk*.

The boys gather closer, whispers surging.

"Where did you find these?" I ask, tracing a finger around their intricate carvings.

"Boss sent them."

"Ah. So not much of a game. More of an assignment."

Moche winks. "Always on the job. So, who's up for it? Whoever unlocks their box first wins a bag of dates." He dangles the sweet treat in front of us, and all around, eyes go wide, mouths watering.

Hakim slams down his bottle of Fanta. "I'm in."

"Me too," I say eagerly. "It's my day, after all."

"Pick your box."

Hakim and I stand shoulder to shoulder as the others gather around us. "Ladies first," he quips. Always challenging, always judging. But I'm never one to back down from a fight.

I square my shoulders and raise an eyebrow.

"I'm no lady," I snap, jutting my chin at the boxes. "You pick."

He shrugs. "Suit yourself."

He grabs the mahogany box, leaving the black.

Moche smirks at me. "Amir, start the countdown."

Amir readies his phone and adjusts his broken glasses. "Good to go!"

Hakim takes out his weapon of choice—a large paper clip—as I pluck the knitting needle out my scarf.

"Sixty seconds. Okay, and go!"

Hakim hunches over his box and immediately goes to work

as the boys cheer us on. I rotate my box with a smile. Achmed used to give us these types of boxes when we were little, practicing and testing our skills. He even made us work on locks blindfolded. Once he realized I had mastered every challenge he threw my way, he would send me out to unlock random storage units and apartments, digging through jewelry boxes and expensive trunks, bringing back whatever I found.

"Thirty seconds!"

I set the box down and slip my needle in. The lock is not complicated once you find the right angle to tackle it from. I could have this open in five seconds if I really wanted to.

I glance at Hakim, his eyebrows pinched, face flustered as he struggles with his lock. Across the table, Moche stares at me. Just me.

No one likes a show-off, Ororo.

I swallow, fighting my instincts, and pull my hand back slow, dragging my needle around the lock aimlessly.

"Ten seconds!"

Hakim clicks open his lock and the boys cheer, congratulating him. He grabs the bag of dates off the table victoriously. He grins and offers me one.

"Better luck next time, little American girl."

I fake a laugh and sip my soda as Moche gives me a knowing smirk.

FOUR

In the center of Manshiyat Naser, or what people call Garbage City, on a bed made of tarps and old afghans, I roll up my sack with the few items I own, using it as a pillow as I gaze at the stars. From here, you can see the twinkling lights of Giza, the pyramids sleeping giants on the horizon. The city is quiet yet thrums with energy.

People call it the Garbage City because it is just that, a mini city full of garbage as far as the eye can see, towering as tall as some buildings, lining the streets and making them so narrow that cars or trucks can't drive through. Thus, most take to the streets on foot. And with no streetlights, at night it is like walking through a pitch-black cave.

Kiddies, old women, and desperate men sift through the trash daily, finding anything they can eat, or sell, or turn into toys. Most of the buildings are abandoned relics of a once-thriving neighborhood, now half-finished or crumbling from past fire bombings and riots.

Near the center of Garbage City is the Villa—what I like to call our headquarters, while others just call it home. The Villa is one of the few buildings with running water, though the electricity is dicey. The roof provides the most privacy, and it's where I spend most nights. With it being too hot during the day and most of the boys being afraid of heights, up here I can let my guard down more than I can anywhere else in the city. On the floors below, my brothers sleep in corners on makeshift cots, spread out so if the place is ever raided, we can escape easily. But despite the conditions, Boss says it's safer for us here. We don't really have to worry about police raids, since no one comes to this part of Cairo.

Each day, we hand over our scores to Achmed, who calculates our earnings, deducts our boarding, then pays us a few pounds—which, if you save up, is just enough to buy yourself something from the market. Anything else we own is "found" in the streets.

I use my earnings at the fruit stands on ripe bananas, crisp apples, juicy oranges, sweet melons, and tart pomegranates. Sometimes I treat myself to some mahshi for lunch, greedily devouring the roasted peppers stuffed with spicy rice.

I would have loved some dates tonight.

Little American girl. It always comes off as a slur. To the boys, I was adopted by this city. I wasn't born of it, so I'll always be an outsider.

You would think I'd be used to being ostracized. Having white hair is not just different—it's weird. And in this world, different and weird are never warmly welcomed. I learned that as a child, the way kids would stare, point, ice me out of games, and call me names. It was clear that my hair and I were not a welcome sight. I wasn't wanted. Around then, Daddy had just accepted an offer to teach in Cairo. Mommy had promised life would be different in Africa.

But coming here was just more of the same. More kids who didn't want anything to do with me. When one journeys to the market to shop for oranges, one does not pick up the bruised, damaged, or deformed fruit first. One looks for what is perfect, what is familiar, what is known. Anything else is garbage.

That's why it's so important that the boys never know what's under my scarf. Learning of the pain that loneliness can bring only made me more hungry, more desperate, more determined than ever to be seen as normal.

I slip off my hijab and unravel my white braid, letting my hair hang off my shoulders, falling to my waist. It's so long now. I've only cut it a few times, with Moche's help, of course, burning any trace of it in garbage bins. Sometimes I see the snow-white strays in the bathroom drain or on the floor in the great room and sweep them away, pretending they don't exist. That the real me doesn't exist.

I rake my fingers through the knots and sigh, the air heaven on my scalp.

There are some days I wish to truly be invisible. My hair wouldn't be a problem, I could live as free as the doves that flock over the pyramids in Giza. Soaring and untouchable. Moche and I once visited, paying for tickets to walk among the great ruins. Moche was excited to ride the camels up the peak to see the perfect view of the three pyramids. His camel gave him an awful time, grunting and smacking, walking anywhere but on the path it was supposed to tread, and Moche almost fell off its back a few times. My camel bowed gracefully, walked with pride, and didn't want to leave my side.

That was when I noticed the doves, how they flew in sync like a choreographed dance. They had each other, they had family, they knew who they were, their purpose.

Now that I have my own flock, with my brothers, I will stay with them no matter what.

In just a few hours, everyone will be up to start their day. The old women will come to retrieve their laundry hung on clotheslines across the roof, the boys will be taken to the souks in search of our next hit, and the kiddies will be sifting through trash for treasure. Another day in Garbage City.

Another birthday. Another year older. Another mark in time without my parents.

Tears prickle as I pull out the old thin wallet from my secret pocket. I don't have a picture of them. But I do have the wallet and ID of that strange American who made time stand still. I always keep it with me. It's a reminder of that day. A reminder of a life I had before this one. I examine the ID in the candlelight for the millionth time. Charles Xavier. His eyes stern, steady, and focused, as if he is still watching me.

You were meant to be part of something bigger. "Bigger" seems like such a relative term. Garbage City is huge. Egypt feels like a world within a galaxy. What else could there be? I think of the streets below, with kiddies rummaging through its contents. Is this what my mother intended?

The nearby ladder shakes. Someone is climbing up, fast. I quickly shove the ID and wallet away before Moche's head pops into view, a blanket tucked under his armpit.

I lean up on my elbow. "Did you give the food to the kiddies?"

He rolls his eyes. "Yes, I've fed your stray kittens."

"I wish you wouldn't call them that," I mumble, slumping back onto my blankets.

He stares at me for a moment, face aglow from the candle.

"Your hair is getting long again," he says. "I can help you cut it if you'd like."

I huff, braiding it back into its tail as Moche sets up his bed parallel to mine.

"I wouldn't have to cut it all the time if you'd just let me chop it super short like I want to."

"No, Ro, you can't! What if all your strength is in your hair, like the story?"

"You mean like Samson in the Bible?" I laugh. "Where'd you hear that fairy tale?"

He plops down, smirking and yanking off his worn sneakers.

"There must be something to it. You survived a plane crash, after all. Your hair must be filled with magic."

My fingers stop moving as the color drains from my face, the building ripped from under me.

In an instant, his smile falls. "I mean . . . well, I didn't mean . . ." He tears his eyes away and sighs. "It's chilly tonight, yeah?"

We never talk about the night that ripped my world to shreds. We lock the memory in a safe so it never feels air. The less I talk about it, the farther it feels. I take a deep breath, deciding to ignore the foot he shoved in his mouth. He meant well.

"It drops one degree and you'd swear it's about to snow," I say.

"Snow!" he exclaims. "Don't speak such evils. I couldn't even imagine."

"It's not as terrible as you think."

"You remember it?"

I remember everything. My parents taking me to the park, teaching me how to catch flakes with my tongue and make snow angels. The way the snow twinkles in the light.

Moche lies on his back, staring up at the stars. When we were younger, I would always ask about his parents, what they were like, what happened to them. He had to have memories, too. But Moche would just shrug with a childish grin and say, "The only parent that matters is the money I make."

Will I ever have his temperament? Will I ever *not* question what my life would look like if Mommy and Daddy were still with me?

"Well . . . maybe one day I'll go to a place that has snow," he announces, all serious-like. "But not right away. There are other places I'd much rather see first."

I twist to my side. "So if a bag of money were to drop from the sky, where would you go?"

"Ha! New York," he says. "We should visit your homeland, of course. Then Hollywood. Paris. Rome. London. Japan. Then come back here."

"What? Why, when there's so many other places you can be?"

He waves off the notion. "You're mad. Nothing can be better than home." He yawns. "Besides, work is here. That bag of money will run out soon enough."

I lean up on my elbows, gently wading into the waters. Moche may be the brother I'm closest to, but we've always wanted different things. The boys are the reason I am here, not the work. "There's nothing . . . I don't know . . . *more* you want to do?"

He laughs. "Why, when I'm so good at what I do?"

I push further. "But you don't have dreams? For something . . . bigger?"

He gazes up at the stars, smiling. "Yeah. I do." He turns on his side to face me, eyes shining like black onyx. "My dream is for us to take over and be the new boss. You can train up the kiddies and I'll negotiate new tour traps. We'd run the whole city! What about you?"

I blink, sipping a bit of air before giving him a fake smile. "Yeah. Same."

He gives a sharp nod, as if it's already decided. "But one day, we will score big enough to take that trip." He sighs with a grumble. "Maybe then you'll tell me why we must sleep on this roof and not in a cozy room with four walls."

Even the thought of four walls makes me shudder. "It's too stuffy down there. And Hakim snores like a donkey."

"Better than waking up covered in sweat and dust."

"You could always stay downstairs," I offer.

"And leave you alone? Never!" He laughs, and I see that boyish glimmer in his eyes. "I always have to keep my eye on you."

"Like an annoying cat." I snort, then stare up at the sky. "I just like being closer . . . to them."

Moche nods, as if he understands what it's like to lose your whole universe.

"You know," he starts, twiddling with the ends of his shirt. "When you marry, that man will eventually see your hair."

"You mean *if* I marry. And by then, I'll have enough money to keep bottles of henna nearby at all times. He'll only know me as a jet-black beauty until I'm old and rightfully gray."

I laugh but Moche only shrugs, not meeting my eye, lips twisting to the left. "Or not. I don't know, he may love it as it is. He may find it . . . beautiful."

"Tah! You mean before or after he goes running into the desert to get as far away from me as possible?"

I sit up, rolling my hair into a low bun before working on securing my scarf. I always sleep with it on, just in case anyone decides to come up here in the middle of the night. But from the corner of my eye, I catch Moche staring again, as if he's staring through me, his mind far off.

"What?" I ask with a nervous chuckle. "What's wrong?"

He blinks up in surprise and clears his throat.

"Uh, nothing," he says, giving a weak smile. "So. Did you like your party?"

I think of the boys dancing at the end of the night and laugh. "It was okay."

He beams, blows out the candle, and rolls over, his back to me.

"Thanks for letting Hakim win," he says with a yawn.

I burrow in my blanket. "I don't know what you're talking about."

FIVE

The smell of moss and wet leaves tickles my nose. Raindrops kiss my cheek as I stir, my surroundings bleeding through the edges of sleep.

Wait . . . rain?

My eyes pop open and I find I'm no longer on the roof, but lying in a soft bed of thick emerald vines, surrounded by giant trees, their braided roots shimmering, snaking out toward a glittering stream at my feet. Teal bioluminescent algae flickers on the seafloor, lotus flowers twirling on the surface like ballerinas.

I shoot up, gripping the moist earth beneath me. My hair drapes down my back, long and flowing. I gasp, immediately searching for my scarf, but it is nowhere in sight. The misty wind flutters through my strands, curling around me.

I haven't worn my hair like this since I was a child.

The sounds of the rainforest are almost deafening. Frogs, beetles, birds, baboons, leopards, elephants . . . there's an overwhelming kaleidoscope of noises. Above, the stars are twinkling diamonds spinning closer to earth, the sky a brilliant royal blue and purple. I stare, awestruck. I've never seen anything so beautiful in my entire life.

Where am I?

The hair on my neck prickles. I'm not alone.

"Ororo."

I spring to my feet and spin around, heart racing. At the base of the giant tree stands a tall old woman in a glowing turquoise silk dress, her thin wrists, neck, and ankles adorned with gold cuffs. Her skin is the color of freshly wet soil with deep wrinkles, her long white hair braided over her shoulder, reaching her waist. Eyes a twinkling crystal blue-gray.

Blue eyes like mine. Hair like mine.

"Do not be afraid," she says, though her lips do not move. I startle, and she smiles warmly. "Yes, Ororo. I can hear what you're thinking, too."

A whimper escapes me as I stagger back. Her accent feels . . . familiar, her voice like wind chimes.

"I'm dreaming," I mumble, then laugh aloud. "That's what I get—too much soda before bed. This is a dream."

The old woman's head ticks to the side. "Is it? Or is it time for you to finally see who you really are?"

Her words *thunk* hard against my chest. Even my dreams are challenging me, questioning who I am, as if I don't belong.

I want to wake up, need to wake up. But she reminds me of someone, her essence strangely familiar.

"I know who I am," I shoot back, my neck tensing. "I'm Ro."

Her eyebrow raises. "You are more than a street urchin."

Who is she? And how— "H-how did you . . ."

"Your spirit is awakening," she says, her head tilting to the sky, palms facing upward. "I can feel it, sense it. I never would have found you, otherwise. It is time, Ororo."

The forest stirs, the vines coming to life like giant worms, the earth quaking. I surf the wave as the ground rolls beneath me, then fall to my knees on the soft bed of moss and tiny yellow flowers.

"Time?" I snap. "For what?"

The woman raises her arms, lifting her hands to the sky.

Then her eyes change as she blinks, turning to thick white foggy pearls, not a drop of color in sight. My tongue stills, knees frozen to the ground.

This isn't a dream. This is a nightmare.

The wind picks up, swirling around the forest with the force of a powerful tornado. I grip hold of a nearby tree. Something in the back of my mind tells me I should run, but I can't look away.

"Time to come home, Ororo. Come home!"

Home? What does this woman know of home? The only home I've known was ripped away from me.

Irrational tears spring up before I can stop them. "Where is home? How?"

But the old woman can't hear me over the powerful gusts. Animals' screams echo through the forest. Unsteady on my feet, I reach for her as bolts of light burst from her hands, rippling toward the sky. She mutters more words at me, words I have a hard time hearing over the shrieking wind, her hair flying in every direction. But she seems unbothered, more relieved, a small smile on her lips.

She's causing this storm; she's tearing down this beautiful forest. *She's* doing it all!

"You are more powerful than you know, Ororo Iqadi Munroe. More than you can ever dream."

I feel it then in my bones. *She's a madwoman! A witch! A sorceress! And she's going to kill me.*

I hold on to the tree, the wind picking up speed, leaves, branches, and pebbles blinding me. The trees begin to wave, their bark cracking, twisting in the fury. The storm rages, tearing through the forest, sweeping up anything in its path. I bury my face, gripping hold of the trunk until I feel her hand on my shoulder, trying to yank me away.

"No, please," I cry. "No!"

"Storm . . . Ro! Wake up . . . storm!"

43

Moche's voice cuts through, and I lift my face.

"Huh? What?"

He shoves my shoulder, harder. "Wake up! It's a sandstorm. Run!"

The pebbles in my dream were still slapping my face. I flip onto my side, my legs wobbling, barely conscious enough to grab my pack as sand particles scratch my cheek.

"Hurry! Get inside!" Moche orders from . . . somewhere. I can hardly see or hear him through the whipping sand. Thunder drums the sky, lightning breaking through the pitch-black night. This is no ordinary sandstorm.

Am I still dreaming?

I grab hold of my scarf, pulling my shirt up over my neck, covering my nose and mouth. The storm snuffs out all light. Panicked voices echo from down below. I fight through darkness, careful with my steps, trying to remember the dimensions of the roof. One wrong move and I would go flying to my death.

"Moche! Where are you?"

"Get to the ladder!" he shouts, seeming a million miles away. "I'll get our things!"

I swing my arms left and right, wind tearing through my hair and clothes, until I touch the first sheet of the hanging laundry and follow the clothesline straight to the ladder. I take it down, jump through a broken window, and race through the hall. But the storm is powerful; the sand keeps chasing me, like a swirling black mass in the air. I run harder, toward the open apartment with the one working shower. I burst through the bathroom door, click on the ticking florescent bulb, and stop dead in my tracks at the image in the mirror.

Wild white hair. A surrounding storm. The old woman . . . is me.

And my eyes are white like snow.

A scream rips through my lungs.

"RO!" Moche calls from somewhere down the hall, followed by more voices calling.

NO! He can't see me like this!

I shove the door closed and lock it, returning to the mirror. White foggy orbs stare back at me.

"No!" I scream, dragging fingers down my face, body trembling. I'm awake now. I'm awake. But my eyes are *gone*.

The grim dusty green walls begin to vibrate, as if something is coming, something big heading straight for our home. And the howling wind outside . . .

It sounds just like the engine of an airplane.

My heart, lungs, brain . . . everything stops working in that moment. I'm a shell as the bathroom shrinks to the size of a tin can. I back away, lose my footing, and fall over the edge of the claw-foot bathtub, floundering as the walls begin to cave in.

My lungs can't draw enough breath. So obsessed with my eyes, I didn't realize I've trapped myself inside a bathroom-shaped coffin. My hands scramble, reaching for anything to grab hold of. That's when I feel it—a static shock growing in my palms, sizzling like oil in a pot. It should burn, but it feels cool to the touch.

Am I seeing things, or is there light in my palms?

"Oh Goddess . . ." I hear myself mumble as the room whirls, my vision blurring. I can't breathe. This must be the last moment before I go blind. *My eyes!*

"Ro? You in there?" Moche calls, banging on the door. "Open up!"

A sob is stuck in my throat. I grip my chest and wheeze in painful bits of air through closed lungs, and it feels like blades nicking at my esophagus. Is the ceiling falling? Is the building crashing down? Will I be in the dark again?

"What's wrong?" I hear Achmed's voice outside the door.

"I think something happened to Ro! I think she's having another nightmare."

Pounding on the door, but my heart is louder. I need air, I need to get out. But I also can't let them see me this way. I wrap my loose scarf tight around my face and hair, trying to become invisible.

"Hey, I think the storm has stopped," I hear Amir say. "What's going on with Ro?"

"Ro? Open up!" Moche shouts, pounding on the door again. "The storm is over!"

It can't be over. It just started. I can still hear the wind in my ears. The plane is coming for us. And my eyes, my eyes . . . what happened to my eyes!

I cover my face and tuck into a ball, waiting for the void to take me. Maybe then I'll finally see my parents again.

Something hits the door. Once, twice, then the wood explodes.

"Ro!" Moche screams, jumping into the tub with me. "Ro, are you hurt?"

I wrap my arms tight around my face and shake my head. "Go away. Please!"

Moche's hands are all over me, checking for injuries. "What's wrong? What happened? Did sand get in your eyes?"

"Please, just go away," I sob.

"Let me see," he insists. "Look, on the count of three, I want you to open your eyes."

I can't. I don't want them to see my eyes. I don't want to have another thing different about me. And how can I score anything blind? They'll kick me out, I won't survive, I'll be all alone.

"Please don't make me," I cry, trying to wiggle away from his voice. "Please."

Moche grips my hands tight. "We need to try. Ready?"

I shake my head, trying to fight him off. But he's much bigger, stronger. "No, please, no."

"One. Two . . . three!"

Moche tears my hands away, examining my face, his thumb pushing my eyelid open. I snap it back shut, coughing up a sob, my body trembling. This is it. He'll never speak to me again. White hair is one thing, but this will be too much.

Moche lets out a relieved breath.

"You're fine," he mumbles, patting my knees, and I can almost hear the fear melt out of him.

I shake my head. "No. No, I'm not!"

"Look for yourself."

I open one eye and meet his dark browns staring back at me. Staring as if nothing has changed.

"Hey, you," he whispers, lightly gliding a finger down my arm. "You're okay."

Impossible.

I jump up and lunge for the mirror. Frantic crystal blues stare back at me from a tear-soaked face. No whites, no cloudy fog. I touch my red cheek with trembling fingers and catch Achmed staring at me in the mirror. His face is expressionless, and he's dressed in dark khaki pants, an orange turban, and a navy tunic, with a long white beard and one shiny gold hoop earring.

His stern eyes make me swallow hard. I readjust my scarf before turning to the door. Everyone is behind him, eyes wide, waiting.

"But . . . I . . . I . . . saw . . ."

Achmed sighs and turns to the group. "All right, everyone. Back to bed. Sunrise is in just a few hours."

SIX

My hands look like they always did, but now they feel different. Like they were attached to the wrong body. A body I don't recognize anymore. I keep flexing my fingers, eyeing my palms. But they stay normal, no glowing light to be seen.

All morning, the boys joked that I was losing my touch. "How could our very own weather girl not tell us a storm was coming?"

While the city cleaned up after the surprise sandstorm, perched on the rooftop, I surveyed the damage. Laundry, blankets, and books were strewn all over the roof, and the people below worked on clearing the streets of trash that had been knocked over.

There wasn't a scratch on me. But it felt like I'd been hollowed out and then patched back together with rubber glue. I could still hear the wind howling through my ears with the faint whisp of the woman's voice . . .

Come home.

A tingle in my hand makes me jump. It feels like my palms hold the vibrations of a plucked violin string. I tighten my fingers into a fist.

I scroll through my memories, trying to place that woman's

face. She wasn't familiar, but we had the same frosty blue eyes, the same bone-white hair.

And she knew my name. My full name. No one knows that, not anymore.

Of course she did, idiot. It was just a dream.

But it felt so real. And I can't shake the feeling that I knew that woman from somewhere.

In any case, I don't have time for dreams or nightmares. I take a shuddering breath and dust off my hands, trying to revive the nerves I lost in the night, and head for the souks. It's time for work.

Running through the narrow alleys, there are murmurs of the lack of tourists today, likely turned off by the violent storm and deciding to stay inside the walls of their fancy resorts. Tours are canceled and Nile cruise ships are docked. Which means fewer people frequenting the shops.

No matter. I love a challenge. Besides, I need to work. I need to feel something as close as possible to normal.

I scan the street for my first target. There's an old couple with Australian accents, debating over the price of a pair of gold lanterns. The man's cargo shorts have large pockets, large enough to hold the fat wallet I see sitting on his right hip.

I charge forward with laser focus, but the man turns, faster than I expected, and in my frustration, I run into a nearby cart of fake jade statues.

"Damn it," I growl, stomping my foot, and a shock of breeze whips through the streets, startling everyone. People yelp, clutching their belongings, and I freeze in place.

Did I . . . ? No. No way.

Now the tingling in my fingertips feels stronger somehow. I wring my hands and run in the opposite direction. Maybe some coffee is the cure. Or maybe something stronger.

I make it all the way to Fahmy and Co. in a daze, finding Muhammad just rolling up the gate and pulling out a stand.

"Good morning, Ororo," Muhammad says. "Did the storm wake you?"

I swallow, smiling shakily as I shuffle past him and into the shop. Maybe the lack of sleep is getting to me.

Nothing a book can't fix.

✕

I blink, moss tickling my nose as I lie face down on what I thought was a comfy pillow cushioning my cheek. The moist forest air is such a change from the dry desert.

I sigh and sit up, gazing at the purple sky, the twirling stars, and palm my temples. "Not again."

Another night in the forest. The fifth night in a row. Tiny glowing red ants march across sparkling grass blades. Pink fireflies weave through luminous plants. Jumping orange fish splash in the tiny pond to my left. My hair floats and coils around me like I'm a mermaid underwater.

Though I never asked to be here, I have to admit that it's breathtaking.

"I see you, daughter," the old woman's voice whispers. "I see you. And it is time you see who you are as well."

I spin around, looking for the old woman. Almost hoping I'd see her this time, just so I could give her a solid piece of my mind. After four nights, I'm tired of the riddles with no answers.

But tonight the forest is darker, chillier, and this time I'm alone.

"You are never alone," the voice whispers, and then she begins singing a song. A familiar melody echoes around me.

"Where are you?" I shout. The sky turns, faster than the earth, as the wind kicks up.

"Follow your heart. Let the Goddess lead you back to you, kipenzi. Come home. Come home where you belong."

A tunnel of wind falls into the pond, swirling into a waterspout that towers high above the forest. It leans, threatening to come crashing down on me, and I scream, throwing my hands up.

The waterspout stops and bows as if I'm a queen, water streaming up the wave from the pond and then dripping to the grass by my feet.

"What the . . . ?" I stumble right into the pond, plunging into the darkness, water drowning my scream.

I jump up and I'm back on the roof of the Villa, sweat dripping down my face, clothes sticking to my skin.

Moche stirs in his bed, rubbing his eyes.

"What's up?" he grumbles sleepily. "Something wrong?"

"Nothing," I say, out of breath, reaching for my hijab. "Go back to sleep."

His eyes close as he quickly drifts back.

But there will be no rest for me tonight. Nothing could make me return to that forest again. I wait until I hear his steady breathing before slipping on my shoes and climbing down the ladder. Maybe a walk through the streets of Garbage City will help me iron out my frazzled nerves so I can try to figure out what the hell is going on with me.

At this hour, it should be quiet. But outside the Villa, I spot three little boys sifting through the fresh trash, added by the city that doesn't care.

"Hey," I say, walking over to them. "Kiddies? What are you doing out here? It's three in the morning."

The boys' eyes shift to one another, their lips dry, faces gaunt. No one speaks. But the littlest one's stomach growls like a passing truck.

My heart breaks. Careful to compose my face, I struggle to smile.

"Here," I whisper, opening my wallet and peeling off a few dollars I made the night before. "Go home and buy some food in the morning."

The kiddies give the money a wary glance, lips pressed together.

"Don't worry," I insist. "I won't tell the others."

The kiddies nod, letting the oldest pocket the cash, and scramble back inside the building. I watch them run, my heart heavy.

This is no way for children to live.

But I've lived like this . . . most of my life. I just don't know how to explain to Moche or anyone that as much as I love my brothers, I wouldn't wish this life on anyone, especially children. They should be free to experience joy and the love of family. Not fighting for their life, trying to crawl out of a dark hole. . . .

A small collective pattering of feet tears through the streets in my direction. I freeze, waiting to see who else could be up this late at night, just as two stray dogs come trotting out of the darkness, their tails wagging. I cough out a trapped breath and smile.

"You again?" I laugh as they circle me. The dogs in Garbage City have always loved me. Moche calls me the dog whisperer, the way they all seem to gravitate toward me. I give the tan one a good scratch behind the ears. "Okay, pups. You can walk with me."

We stroll the quiet street in no particular direction. I stuff my hands in my pockets, my mind still racing. It feels good to walk. My legs need the exercise and I need the air, no matter how pungent the rotting trash is.

Come home.

Now I'm hearing her while I'm awake. That breathy voice

feels so real, so familiar, as if she's sitting right on my shoulder, whispering in my ear. But what home is that woman talking about? After Mommy and Daddy, the Villa is the only home I've ever truly known.

There's also the fact that she looks like me. Her hair, her eyes, and even her smile. . . . And the song the woman was singing, it was in Swahili.

My mother's language . . .

Mommy would hum something similar in the kitchen while making dinner. A song about a Goddess she used to mention. Now I wish I had paid more attention to the words.

I have never thought much about my mother's homeland. Daddy said we would visit it, since we were moving to the continent. He wanted to take me to the elephant orphanage and to feed the giraffes. Mommy wanted me to have a true home-cooked meal and learn more about the Goddess.

Now I know nothing. All her history, gone.

Come home.

These dreams have to mean something. They have to be a sign of some sort. Perhaps I can find an interpreter—I've heard of dream interpreters in some bazaars. But even if one could help me with the riddles, what would going "home" look like, if *this* is not my home?

I'm so caught up in my own thoughts, turning the idea of home over and over again, that the shooting pain takes me off guard.

"Ow," I mutter, hands flying to my stomach. It's not a cramp, but something similar. A strange tugging sensation.

I must be getting sick, I think. A tummy ache like when I was a little girl. Maybe Achmed still has some of that medicine he once gave me when we had fish that didn't agree with us.

Yet, I'm not tired. I'm still walking. Or more like I'm being pulled in one direction. I stop resisting the pull when I realize I'm walking in soft sand.

"What the . . ."

I whirl around and see the city in the far distance. Somehow, I walked straight into the desert. I don't even remember leaving Garbage City.

My blood stills. I pinch my arm, confirming that I'm wide awake. How did I drift so far without noticing?

One of the strays rubs against my leg, begging for attention.

"Yeah, I don't know how—"

The sight of the strays leaves me speechless. It's more than two dogs. It is nearly twenty, all different shapes and sizes. Their reflective eyes locked on me, tails wagging.

They all followed me out here and I didn't even notice. Am I sleepwalking now?

"Come on." I sigh, turning back toward the city. "We're going home."

X

"More?" Muhammad exclaims.

I nod. "Yes. Please. I'm dying."

Muhammad shakes his head, pouring my third cup of coffee for the afternoon after another sleepless night. Every time I close my eyes, I find myself back in that forest. The dreams won't stop coming, so I just won't sleep. Problem solved.

Except a whole new slew of problems has begun. I'm practically falling asleep standing in the souk. My eyes blur, and the caffeine makes my hands too jittery to slip into unsuspecting pockets. So I sit in the bookshop, flipping through old *National Geographics*. Yet I can still hear the hum of that woman's song, like a ghost haunting me.

Could I be possessed? Cursed somehow? But how and when?

All I know is that everything changed after my birthday. And I need it all to go back to the way it was.

Come home.

"Ororo!"

I jerk back at the booming voice, hitting my head on the shelf, and a stack of books rains down. Moche storms into the bookshop with that look in his eyes that he saves for the boys when they act up.

"Why don't you say it louder and tell everyone my name," I snap as I clean up the mess I've made. Did I mention that the lack of sleep has also made me . . . moody?

Moche snatches a magazine out my hands and slams it on the table, dust blooming.

"What's up with you? Why aren't you out? Two tour buses passed through, and you didn't hit either one of them. What's wrong?"

My stomach tenses, and I reach up to readjust my scarf.

"Nothing's wrong," I say, trying to act normal, despite my shaky hands.

Moche sucks his teeth. "You can fool everyone else, but you can't fool me. I know you. You've been acting weird ever since the sandstorm. What's up?"

I breathe out some anxious air, struggling to compose my face. He's right. He knows me. Which makes lying to him that much more complicated.

"I told you, I freaked when sand got in my eyes. That's all. I'm fine."

I angle myself away, hoping he won't notice my burning cheeks, hoping my defensiveness will dissuade him from asking too many questions. But I can feel his eyes bore into my back.

"You're off your game," he warns, his hands on his hips like a disappointed father. And I hate that. I hate that I am disappointing him. It doesn't happen often.

Which reminds me . . . it *doesn't* happen often. I'm the best in the business, so to speak. Better than the rest of the boys. Even he can't deny that. Can I not have an off day or two? Or five?

I whip around to face him. "Has that ever happened before? I've brought in more in one day than some have in a week!"

The anger melts out of his eyes as he sighs. "Look, I'm not here to fight."

"Tah! I beg to differ," I retort, crossing my arms.

He shifts back on his foot and straightens, as if bracing himself.

"I'm just telling you," he starts with a hard swallow, "that you're short your daily take. And if you don't bring in . . . well . . ."

I take a deep, painful breath. "You'll kick me out? Is that it?"

Moche's face, a war of emotions, cracks, his voice softening. "Ro, I'm . . . just worried about you."

But I see the truth in his expression. Despite everything, I'm still expendable. It won't matter what I do or say. Something inside me threatens to crumple, but I won't let this break me. I won't let anyone see me break.

I straighten my spine, blood now boiling, throw the book aside, and shove past him.

"Ro, wait! Where are you going?" Moche snaps.

"To get my game back!"

X

My next target looks as tired as I feel. He and his wife are dressed like European explorers in their ridiculous khaki vests with the millions of pockets and matching hats. The type that cost a lot of money, or so Moche has told me. Spending the day exploring the pyramids in this blazing-hot sun has drained them of any energy. They make the perfect easy prey.

Fighting a yawn, I move closer, pretending to be a part of the crowd, just a normal citizen shopping for fresh spices.

But inside, I feel something roped around my stomach like a thick rubber band, trying to yank and pull me away from the souk, threatening to snap my skin if it doesn't get its way. My feet are anxious for a long walk, and I'm itching to find out where. . . .

No. I have to keep going. I have to do this. Achmed has kicked out boys for less. They're the only family I have left. I can't let them down.

I steel myself as I go in for the attack, the man's wallet in clear view, but just as I reach it, I notice two policemen rounding the corner.

"No," I gasp, blood draining from my face.

A tingle in my right arm rips down into my fingers as a searing static explodes from my hand that's still on the wallet. Before I can manage to pull away, it zaps the tourist like a stun gun.

He screams with a jerk, falling to his knees, his wallet catching on fire in his pocket.

"Ken?" his wife says. "Ken? Oh my God! What happened?"

Ken slumps on the ground, his body shaking as if seizing. She drops beside him, holding his head in her lap, frantically patting out the fire with her purse. And all I can do is stare in stunned silence as Ken's eyes roll to the back of his head.

The wife glares up at me and screams. *"Help!"*

The police turn in our direction and spot me standing over the couple.

"Shit," I mumble, and sprint away.

"Hey! You! Stop!"

I take off through the souk, dodging tables and shoppers, hopping over displays. The police follow, close on my heels. Closer than they've ever been before. Sweating out my coffee, I leap for a nearby ladder, catching enough air to swing myself up. The air swoops beneath me like a strong breeze.

"Get back here, you!" one of them shouts from below, but I'm already out of range.

Keep moving, I scold myself. No time to think. Only move. I dart across the roof, hopping over to the next building, my heart pounding, one hand holding my scarf in place. I've only been chased by the police once before, not long after I first joined Achmed. Can I outrun them again?

Adrenaline pumps through my veins, and despite my exhaustion, I'm fast, and I know these streets like the back of my hand. I scale down the side of the building, weaving across the street, and slip into the metro tunnels, heading for my second home. When I see Fahmy and Co., I slip through the door, my heart hammering in my chest.

Nibbling on my nails, I pace inside the bookshop, trying to slow my breathing, trying to work out what happened. What I can't seem to explain to even myself.

I . . . electrocuted that man in broad daylight.

This is not a dream. This is really happening.

Panic bubbles up, my mind swirling, yet I keep picturing that forest, with the waterfall, and the woman. The woman who looks like me.

It might be paranoia talking, but all of this must mean one thing: a curse has been put on me. There's no other explanation.

I don't know why—it's not like I have any enemies—but it doesn't matter. All I need is to find whoever did it and get them to undo it before anyone finds out. I'm already a black sheep of the group—I don't want to be a leper on top of it. I just have to stay calm and handle this in the most logical and practical way possible.

She certainly has your Kenyan pragmatism. . . .

My heart stops. Kenya. My mother's family was from Kenya. All the women had my eyes, my hair. Which means . . . that woman and the forest must be in Kenya.

If they are powerful, then maybe they will know what's happening to me and how to fix it.

But . . . how do I find them?

"Ororo! Where have you been? I've been looking all over for you."

I hold my breath before turning to him. I don't want anyone to know what I've done, but Moche . . . he's good at keeping secrets. I'm sure he'll know some doctor or witch who can help me find a cure. I exhale slowly.

"Moche . . . I think I'm in trouble."

He shakes his head, grabbing my hand and leading me out. "Save it. We got called in for a meeting."

"Meeting? Right now?"

"Yeah, come on. Amir is spreading the word. Everybody has to swing back."

But it's the middle of the day. He would never call us all back this early unless . . . oh no.

"Is, um, Boss okay?"

"It wasn't Boss who called the meeting," Moche says as we climb into a waiting van.

"Then who?"

I give Moche another glance, but his mouth is set in a thin line, his eyes on the road ahead. And without another word, the van speeds us toward Garbage City, my secret thick in the air between us.

SEVEN

When we pull up, there are three shiny black town cars parked in front of the Villa. Moche eyes them warily as we enter and head up to the great room. My head is spinning, trying to imagine what could be waiting for us when I haven't even processed what happened with the tourist earlier.

The great room is on the top floor, where Boss hosts all our meetings. It's unfinished, like most of the building, except it has high ceilings with exposed beams, broken framing, glassless windows, and a giant gaping hole in the corner, where, if you're not careful and trip on the scrap supplies, you can easily fall several stories. Toward the back, down the narrow hall, is Boss's office, with the red door.

As we enter, I see the boys standing in a U shape, facing four giant men in sharp black suits. Between them is a shorter man in navy.

I follow Moche into the crowd, the room tense and muggy, and we join the lineup with the rest of the crew.

"What's going on?" Moche mumbles to Hakim. "Where's Boss?"

Hakim fidgets with his collar, as if worried about making a good impression. "I have no idea. No one has seen him since breakfast."

"Who are these guys?" I ask, trying to tone down my panic. "Police?"

Bassel shakes his head, his face pale. "I don't know. They were here when I came in. Wouldn't answer any questions. Just told us to gather everyone up."

I take in the men walking around our home like they belong. Boss never lets adults in the Villa when he's not present. He keeps our location mostly secret, barely lets us talk to strangers, always wary of others' intentions.

I swallow hard. Something has happened.

The whispers die down as navy suit walks forward, his hair like black ocean waves, light gray stubble on his jaw. Despite his eyes hidden behind dark sunglasses, it feels like he is looking directly at me.

"Hello, friends," he begins. "My name is Farouk."

Though his voice is scratchy, it also seems familiar, but I can't place it. I fidget with my scarf, not wanting a hair to fall out of place.

"I'm sure you are all wondering why I've called you here today."

Moche glances around the room at the boys, then steps forward, chin raised. "Where is Achmed?"

"Ah. The brave one," Farouk says, as if amused. "You must be second in command. I am sorry to inform you that unfortunately, your boss has been detained by the police. And he has put me in charge of your care."

The room explodes in confusion. Achmed arrested? How? For what? And who is this stranger he has never mentioned before?

"I'm sure you have a lot of questions, as do I," Farouk continues, pacing in front of us. "Many, many questions indeed."

There is something about his motions that feels unsettling. The way his steps seem hesitant, like he's not used to his own feet. His strides are too long, arms loosely flailing when he turns. I glance around, wondering if anyone notices. But the boys stand frozen, eyes wide in fear. Poor Amir, he looks so small. Too small to be caught up in this mess.

"You see, I was visiting a friend in the hospital," he continues. "When I overheard a very peculiar story . . . of a tourist who had been electrocuted while out in the souk. His wallet was on the ground, burnt to a crisp. It seems someone was trying to steal it from him."

The boys murmur to one another, and I forget how to breathe.

"What does that have to do with Achmed?" Moche asks, and I can sense his frustration.

Farouk takes in the room, waiting for silence.

"I'd like to have a word with each of you. In private. Until we get to the bottom of this. Starting with . . ." He waves a finger around and points to Hakim. "You."

Hakim flinches, glancing at Moche as if looking for permission to move. Moche nods at him.

Two of Farouk's men step forward and take Hakim to the back room. The meeting room remains silent.

Minutes tick by like hours, my heart drenched with guilt. Because I screwed up and brought this upon us. I, somehow, got Achmed in trouble—my mentor, the very man who has sheltered me all these years.

Time seems to pass both too fast and too slow, as one by one, my brothers are called. They interrogate each one of the boys until I'm the last person standing.

"You," one of the men bellows, pointing to me.

Steeling myself, I lock eyes with Moche. His hands roll into fists as he watches them lead me away.

We walk down the long, echoing hallway before the two men shove me inside the office and slam the door shut.

"Hello, Ororo. Very lovely to meet you at last."

Farouk sits in a lone steel chair in the middle of the room, his legs crossed. I can hardly contain my shock. All of Boss's stuff has been removed, as if he never existed. On instinct, I look back at the door, then to the two windows behind him. Achmed hired builders to install locks on the windows to secure the stash of goods. Sunlight beams through the bars, casting split shadows on the dusty floor.

"Well," Farouk coaxes. "Can you not say hello?"

I can hear Moche's voice in my head. *Play it cool, Ro.* Watch my smart mouth and temper. Men don't like that, especially not the powerful ones.

I keep my distance. "Hello."

Farouk tilts his head and studies me for a long, silent moment. With his eyes hidden, I can't tell what he's thinking. But standing closer to him, his very presence makes my skin prickle.

"Do you know what happened to the tourist today?"

His voice is like ice; the room almost seems colder with him in it.

I shake my head and rub my arms, riddled with goose bumps.

"Really?" He chuckles, uncrossing his legs. "Someone said they remember seeing you in the souk, being chased."

I shrug. "That is normal in this line of work, don't you think?"

He cranes his neck back to bark a laugh. "I suppose so. My, my, you have grown up so splendidly."

I keep my face even, trying not to give away my terror. He knows me. But I have no clue who he is.

"You know, I've been looking for you."

My stomach does a little flip, mouth going dry. "You have?"

"Yes. You knew my brother, before he . . . died."

I struggle to bring up any memory of someone I knew who passed away, but no one comes to mind other than my parents. Though his voice is familiar, nothing else about him is.

"It has taken me a very long time to make it back here," he

says, voice drifting as he glances down at his lap. "Luck just happened to strike at the right moment."

I fidget with my scarf, trying to shake the feeling that he can see my white hair, with some sort of X-ray vision. What would stop him from telling the others?

I swallow and continue to play along. "Well . . . how can I help you?"

He crosses his legs, face darkening. "There is a man looking for you. A Professor Charles Xavier. Do you know of him?"

The wallet burns on my hip, but I manage to shake my head. "No, I don't know anyone by that name."

Farouk seems to see right through my lie, and he continues as if I didn't say a thing. "Ororo, do you remember what happened in the bar that day?"

My mouth goes dry. I remember everything. . . . The room freezing, the glowing red eyes, the way the large man fell forward, dead . . .

"Sorry," I say with an uneasy laugh. "I think you have me mistaken for someone else."

Farouk pauses for a moment, taking me in. He rises to his feet, and there it is again—his unsteady steps. There's something *off* about him. Perhaps he's had too much wine; maybe that's why he thinks he knows me. He regains his balance and sets his attention back on me.

"Ororo, I believe you are in need of mentorship . . . and protection."

"Why do you think that?"

"Don't play coy with me, girl. I know what ails you," he hisses. "I can feel the chaos brewing inside you. A power like something no one has ever seen before."

My throat closes, but I keep my poker face. *He knows somehow.* I swallow, letting out a light chuckle. "I'm quite hungry, but not much more than that, I'm afraid."

He removes his sunglasses, keeping his eyes closed as he wipes the lenses clean with a crisp handkerchief, his face relaxed as if he is worried about nothing.

"Today in the souk, you almost killed a man just by touching him. You are not so foolish as to believe that you don't possess something . . . special? I can see it clear as day, shimmering off you like heat waves." He says it so matter-of-factly, his tone so flippant, that I struggle to keep my shaking hands still. This man is mad. I have no special powers . . . and yet, something *is* happening to me. Something I can't explain, a sickness of sorts. But how does he know that?

"Professor Xavier killed my brother, knowing you were watching him," he says, his voice smooth. "He is very dangerous. And he's looking for you."

He replaces his glasses before I have the chance to meet his eyes. And somehow it feels purposeful. Like he doesn't want me to see. My stomach jerks, that tugging sensation, feet desperate to run, as if my body wants to be anywhere but here.

"If he gets his hands on you, he can do great damage," the man continues. "Use you for your powers. Cause great pain. Hurt the ones you love." A sinister grin crawls across his face. "But if you come with me, you will be welcomed in my family. I will provide you protection. And I will teach you all that I know. You will be safe." He leans forward, hands pressed together. "Don't you want to feel safe?"

Keep him talking, Ro. I hear Moche again. Everything has a cost. He wants something.

"And then?" I squawk.

Farouk laughs, deep from his belly. "Whatever you want, dear one. We will use your powers to protect us from the professor and his evil schemes. You and your little friends out there . . . we will rule over Cairo. Together. You'll have more money than you've ever imagined." His smile drops, chin dipping downward.

"But we don't have much time, child. This power you wield . . . can be dangerous if in the wrong hands. People can be hurt. But not your people, if you stick with me."

Sweat builds under my scarf as my mind races. How would he know about powers . . . unless he has them, too? Unless he's using them right now, digging around in my thoughts?

My fingers tingle, and I curl them into fists. I still don't understand; it was *his* brother who seemed to want to hurt the professor. How do I know that Farouk is not the same? Just another madman after me.

And yet, what if he's right about the professor? What if he is the real evil one? I think back to his kind eyes that day, his willingness to give me his wallet. But really, I know nothing except what I made up in my head. I could be wrong about him.

I think of Moche and his dream, all the places he wants to visit. I think of the kiddies, the way their bellies would be full every night. Farouk could give it all to us. But there's something about him that makes it feel like there are a thousand beetles crawling across my skin.

My palms itch, and I fold them behind my back. "I . . . I need to think about it."

The corners of his lips tighten. He takes a cigar out his jacket, studies it a moment, considering, then lights it up. "There's not much time. We only have until the next worm moon."

I raise an eyebrow at the comment it seems he almost didn't want to admit. The next worm moon? Why not say a few days or weeks? What does the moon have to do with anything? But I consider his action, his tight movements, and he doesn't have much of a poker face. He's holding something back.

"And if my answer is no?" I ask.

His eerie laugh bounces against the cement walls. "Then nothing, dear one. Everything will be as it was. While we're in this room, time is standing still."

Mind scrambling, I bite my lip, looking back at the door, toward the great room where Moche and the boys are waiting for me, wishing I could be near them, just to feel safe again. I haven't felt this uneasy since that day in the bar so many years ago.

Standing still . . .

I turn back to him. "How do you know about what happened to your brother?"

Farouk tips his head to the side. "What?"

"If your brother died in the bar but you weren't there, then how did you know that I was there? The room was frozen. No one saw a thing except me. And I never told a soul."

Farouk pauses, but his face seems to darken behind his glasses.

Powers. I cough, taking a shaky step back as I nearly suffocate in the smoke-filled room.

Farouk sighs, as if suddenly bored of the unsaid game we are playing. "The choice is yours, Ororo. Don't you want to belong to a real family? One that can truly protect and love you?"

Something tugs at my stomach again.

Come home.

The voice blares like an alarm, and I know right away I want nothing to do with the man.

"Thank you," I say, keeping my voice steady. "But I already have a family who can protect me."

Farouk smiles. "Very well, then. The choice is yours."

Despite his pleasant demeanor, I sense the danger simmering beneath his taut skin. This is far from over.

He walks to the door, holding it open for me. "After you, dear one."

Hesitant, I slowly walk past him, but not before looking right into the space behind his glasses, seeing his glowing red eyes.

The same eyes that strange man had in the bar.

I swallow and give him a warm smile. "Thank you."

Farouk walks behind me as I lead the way, my mind racing to make sense of it all, eager to find Moche. I need to warn him, and somehow plan our escape.

Farouk's cheerful whistling slices through the air, and my blood runs cold. I gulp, glancing back at him in momentary shock. He simply smiles and carries on his tune. That sharp and pleasant yet eerie melody I would know anywhere.

That whistle . . . those eyes . . .

My bones turn to noodles as a horrifying realization hits me. It's him. It's the Shadow King . . . but in another man's body? Is that possible?

Heart racing, I can barely breathe as Farouk, the Shadow King, follows close behind.

As we enter the great room, Moche jumps to his feet, taking a visibly relieved breath. The rest of my brothers stare at us. All I want is to scream for everyone to run. But I have to play it cool. I have to—

Farouk grabs the back of my head, tosses me on the floor like a piece of lint. My knees hit the concrete and I skid forward.

"Ro!" Moche shouts, running toward me.

"What are you doing?" Hakim screams.

But Farouk's men stop them from coming any closer. Farouk kicks my side and I scream, pain shooting up my back.

"Leave her alone!" Amir cries.

"She's just a girl! She doesn't know anything," Bassel snaps, outraged.

"This is the rat who got Achmed arrested!" Farouk shouts, grabbing me by the collar.

I wheeze, gripping my burning side, and shake my head. "What? No!"

"She gave up Achmed for her own freedom. The very man who raised you."

The boys stand around in collective confusion. Moche lunges for me, but the boys hold him back. In the chaos, I see the fear in his eyes and resolve to be strong.

"It's not true," I yell, tears streaming. "I would never do that! Achmed is like a father to me!" I point at Farouk. "You know me. You don't know him!"

"You've all known she was never one of you," Farouk snaps. "See for yourself!"

He nods at one of his henchmen. The tall balding man stalks toward me, locked on my head.

My hair!

My stomach sinks, filling with dread, and I stop breathing. Before I can scramble away, he reaches his large hairy hand and yanks at my hijab. I grab hold of the scarf, my neck stiffening. From the corner of my eye, Farouk stands by with a satisfied smirk. He knows this is my worst fear, my worst nightmare, coming to life.

"No! Please, no!" I scream, desperation taking over. I'm on my back, legs swinging at his groin and stomach, slapping his arms, hands, face, frantically trying to fight him off. But I'm powerless against his strength as the thought of what comes next strangles me.

They can't see! They can't know!

The man shakes me around like a rabid dog, jaws locked on its prey, and pries the scarf from my fingers, casting it aside with a grunt. My hair falls out of its messy braid, rolling down my back, and I let out a screaming sob so painful it burns my throat.

There are audible gasps as the room freezes. The boys stare, pure shock in their eyes. I keep my own eyes down, my chest heaving deep, shuddering breaths as I try to block the image of their horror from being burned in my mind. Naked, exposed, humiliated, I stretch my arms out, blindly feeling around for my scarf, the ground wet with my own tears.

All these years, I shielded them. All these years, I kept them in the dark. But now . . . but now . . .

Silence. Instead of the shock and ridicule I had always expected, the room is somber, like the moments before a funeral. I want to drown myself in the quiet. I can't look at their bleak faces, the pitiful stares. This isn't what I expected, what I always imagined, which somehow makes it that much more unbearable.

Moche hesitates, then makes the first move. Followed by Hakim, then Amir.

"What are you doing?" Farouk barks.

The boys form a ring around me, linking arms, until I'm surrounded by a tight circle, their backs shielding me. Amir reaches behind and hands me my scarf, with the needle wrapped in it. Something in me recoils—the scarf was ripped off my head by that man, and I want nothing to do with it anymore. But I have no other choice.

I grab it from Amir. "Thank you." I sniff.

Farouk scoffs. "She's not Muslim!"

"She deserves respect all the same," Moche snaps.

I twirl my hair around the needle and quickly stuff it securely back under my scarf.

Moche glances over his shoulder at me, face blanched, his eyes unsure.

"I'm okay," I whisper. It's a lie, but I need us both to hold it together to get out of this mess.

"If you are done with your theatrics . . . ," Farouk hisses, then nods at his men. "Take her away. We'll deal with her later."

Chaos erupts as the boys try to hold the line, but the men charge into the circle, pushing the boys aside. Amir reaches for me as one of the men scoops me up and drags me back to the office, Farouk following close behind. I hear Moche shouting my name as a door slams shut.

They throw me on the floor and I spin around, hot tears spilling.

"What do you want!" I shout.

"My offer still stands," he says plainly. "Leave these street urchins to starve. We have the world to take over!"

"No! Never!"

He shrugs. "Suit yourself. You'll have plenty of time to reconsider as you sit in here and think. Let's say, until the next worm moon, yes?" His features split in a snarl. "And what you won't give me freely, I'll take by force if I must."

Farouk turns on his heel and storms out of the room. His men follow, locking the door behind them. My breath quickens, palms sweating as the walls close in. Pulse racing, I cover my mouth, holding in an earth-shattering sob. I'm too shaken to worry about what he'll do to me. After all, the worst has already happened. The boys have seen my hair. I've been outed. Violated.

Focus, Ororo. You must focus.

Even with the room empty, being in Achmed's office brings back so many memories of all the lessons he taught me, all his wisdom. The way he would stand behind me as I worked on a complicated lock with a ticking clock beside me.

Concentration is key to survival, he would breathe. *When you focus, you can do anything.*

Focus. I need to get out of here and rescue the boys. They don't know who they are up against. I am not entirely sure myself, but I remember the look on the professor's face when he told me to run and hide, and now I know why. The Shadow King is a monster, hungry for power. And he'll take it by any means.

I stumble to my feet and glance at the door. I could open the lock easily, but I would be walking into an ambush, caught within seconds.

I glance at the window. Achmed always said that to save

yourself, you must run alone. *Whenever you're about to be caught, scatter and hide. Wait until the coast is clear, then return home. Better one caught than all caught.*

I know this building better than the Shadow King and his men. Better than anyone. But it doesn't feel right, leaving my brothers.

Come home.

"Stop it," I whisper, slapping my ear. Now I'm positive I am losing my mind. I take a deep breath and wait until I can no longer hear footsteps pacing outside the door before slipping the needle out of my scarf.

Sixty seconds. That's all I got.

I rush over to the window and grab the padlock. I twist my needle in until it pops and clicks, then opens. The gate creaks as I slip out, balancing on the crumbling ledge. I look down and immediately regret it. My legs threaten to give out as I eye the traffic below me, six floors down.

"Oh Goddess," I whimper, gripping the building tighter, my vision blurring. No time to stop and think. I shuffle to the corner and grip the thin copper pipe that snakes along the side of the building, testing its strength. Will it hold? No time to check.

Sweat dripping off my face, I climb down, the metal crunching and squeaking under my weight, threatening to give at any moment. But it doesn't reach the bottom, stopping at the third floor. If I jump from this height, I'll break both of my legs.

I consider climbing back inside. But what if they're waiting for me? What if Farouk changes his mind about giving me time once he finds out about my escape?

"Jump."

I jolt at the little whisper coming from below, and I look down at the street. The three kiddies from the other night push a wide bin against the wall, right under me.

"Jump. Jump, Ro," they whisper, waving me on.

"Oh Goddess," I mutter, glancing up at the sky, and I let go of the pipe, holding in a scream. Wind whistles past my ears as I fall, landing in the bin of empty plastic bottles. I swim through the trash and tumble out, head snapping back up at the window.

No one saw me. For now.

"Thanks, kiddies," I whisper, and they give me a solemn nod. Then, keeping low, I race into the shadows.

✕

When it's nightfall, I use the cover of darkness to climb out of my hiding spot beneath a damp cardboard box. Four dogs sit outside, their backs to me. As if they're keeping watch.

"Good boys. Stay," I whisper, and scramble into the streets. I don't know where I'm going, but I know I have to get far away from the Villa. The highway is too visible, Farouk's men might be at the market and the souk . . .

Before I have time to make a decision, I find myself walking, my feet leading me in one direction. Something is pulling me again, the trembling rubber band about to snap. I don't know whether to trust it, but it's better than doing nothing.

I can't let the Shadow King take me. He knows more about what's going on with me than I do. And whatever is going on, he's trying to score big. I think about the dead man in the bar and shudder. I'm sure this is a score that I won't survive. No matter what, I'll never work for him!

I turn the corner and gasp at the figure standing in the middle of the road.

Moche.

He spots me with frantic eyes and charges toward me. I choke

out a sob and dive into his hug. He grips my back, pulling us behind an old rusted car filled with soda bottles. We squat down,
checking our surroundings.

"I was so scared," he whispers, hugging me again. "I thought
they were going to kill you. Are you okay?"

I nod and grab his hand. "Come on. We have to get out of
here!"

I try to yank him, but he stays rooted.

"I can't, Ororo," he says, shaking his head.

"What? We have to!"

"I can't just leave the boys. Who will watch out for them?"

"But . . . I can't stay here," I say, my voice rising in pitch.

Moche's eyes are frantic. "Why? What do they want with you?"

I pause. How do I explain to Moche what the Shadow King
is when I'm not even sure myself? And even if Moche understood, what could he do? How would he look at me, knowing
what I did to the tourist?

Knowing that I'm broken . . . a freak. I can't bear the thought.

"They . . . think I'm something that I'm not. I'm . . . sick.
There's something . . . wrong with me."

Moche listens, trying to understand. "Is what that man said
about Achmed . . . true?"

I glare at him. "You know it's not."

The light leaves Moche's eyes. "Then what are you going
to do? We can try to hide you, but his men are combing the
streets. We can't hide you forever."

The tugging at my stomach again. *Come home.*

It's as if the woman is standing right behind me. Her voice is
laced in the wind.

I stare out in the distance. The dreams, the whispers, the
burst of light in my palms, what the Shadow King wants . . . it's
all connected.

I bite my lip. "I think I know what I must do to cure this . . . bug that I have. But I think the cure might be in Kenya."

Moche blinks, baffled. "Kenya?"

I can't believe what I'm saying, either. But as I said it out loud, nothing felt more true.

"That's where my mother's people are from," I try to explain. "If I can find them, maybe they'll be able to help rid me of this. Then I won't have anything that man wants. He'll leave us alone, and we'll be free."

Moche rubs his hands together, thinking. "Are you sure this is the only way?"

"No," I admit. "But I have to try something. And like you said, I can't stay here and hide forever."

Moche takes me in for a moment, then nods. Quickly he digs in his pocket and pulls out a wallet.

I wave him away. "Moche, no, don't."

"Here," he says, lumping a ball of money into my palm. "Listen carefully. Take the river down to Luxor. It's busy, lots of tourists with fat pockets. Get what you need. Then make your way to Aswan, to the harbor. There is a ferry that will take you to Sudan."

My eyes widen. "How do you know all this?"

"Listen!" he snaps, shrugging out of his jacket and passing it to me. "The ferry only leaves twice a day, noon and midnight. Do not miss it. After that, you'll have to make your way to Kenya from there." He looks me in the face, eyes more serious than I've ever seen them. "Ro, if this man can find you in Cairo, he can find you in any city. Stay off the main roads. Avoid indoors, sleep outside if you must—you're good at that. Don't talk to anyone until you reach where you are going. Keep your head down and your eyes sharp."

As I slip on Moche's jacket and struggle to commit every

detail to memory . . . it all suddenly dawns on me. Leave Cairo? I've never been anywhere else on my own. What if I fail, and I never see him again? I heave a shaking breath as I take him in, my brother who's always looked after me.

As if reading my thoughts, he pulls me in for another hug. "You'll be okay, Ro. Like you said, you're twice as good as the rest of us. Just hurry back to where you belong. I'll be here waiting for you."

He pulls the hood up over my hijab. My chest tightens, trying to hold back tears. He grips me by the shoulders, searching my face.

"You can do this, Ro," he says, pushing me down the alley. "Go. I'll distract them."

I nod and run, only turning back once to Moche watching me leave.

EIGHT

I never imagined leaving Cairo. Not without my family or my brothers. I'd seen so much of the world through books, never thought of seeing it with my own eyes. Alone.

With the money Moche loaned me (a *loan*, because I definitely plan to pay him back once I see him again), I am able to secure passage on a small cargo sailboat with a handful of strangers. Even as it pushes off from the dock and I watch the lights of Cairo disappear behind us, I have trouble believing that it was all real. Boss arrested? The Shadow King after me? The boys seeing my hair . . . leaving Moche. . . .

The Nile River gently rocks the boat, lulling most passengers to sleep. But I'm wide awake and alert, leaning against the mast post.

The sharp scent of the water tickles my nose. The last time I was on the water, Moche, Hakim, and I snuck onto a felucca, taking a night joyride up the river toward the Qasr El Nil Bridge, passing all the fancy hotels on the riverbanks. Despite the ache in my chest, I feel a small smile at the edge of my lips. Achmed was so mad when we got home late that night. He always cared about us.

Now he's in jail, the boys are trapped with a monster, and it's all my fault.

I hiccup a breath to keep from crying. No time for tears. I need to keep my wits about me. Focus, Ororo. Focus.

"Not much wind, long night ahead," the old crewman at the helm says to no one in particular as he stares up at the sails. "No moon, either. You can really see how beautiful the stars are. It never gets old."

I fidget with my hoodie, trying to keep my face covered, as I gaze up at the mainsail, the Milky Way twinkling above. Even as my world crashes around me, I wonder what it would be like up there with the birds and the planes. How odd, that I still always want to fly, even knowing the destruction it can cause.

A strange tingling sits in my palms, and I try to rub it away. The air in my lungs is icy, and the rocks at the bottom of my stomach weigh my entire body down. I can still hear that woman's voice, following close.

Come home.

I grit my teeth. Home is with my brothers. Not some fantasy forest. The quicker I find answers, the quicker I can get back to them.

I glance up at the sail, squinting as I think back to the sudden breeze in the market.

As long as I'm cursed, maybe I can make it work for me a little. Seeing that it's ruining my life, I don't think it's too much to ask. *Maybe . . . I can help speed things along.*

Tentatively, I raise my palm to the sky and hold it there. And hold it. And hold it. . . .

Nothing.

"Tuh," I spit. This is ridiculous. But the dreams and this crazy stuff happening to me with the lightning and the wind . . . it all has to be connected. I just need to find the source of it. I need to find the old woman in Kenya and get rid of this curse once and for all.

Then I'll be free to go back to Cairo. Yes, the boys have seen my white hair, but I can make up some story about that. Look at the way they stood up for me when Farouk ripped off my hijab, how they sheltered me. They must love me. Everything will go back to the way it was.

Resolve seeps into my bones and I'm up on my feet, looking for the crewman. "Sir, do you have a map? A big one."

✗

Soon as the boat touches the dock, I jump off and make my way to the nearest tourist trap. I have to re-up on money, then find a bus to the Aswan harbor. From there, I'll have to travel through Sudan, then Ethiopia, until I reach Kenya.

The problem is the lack of transportation. Most of the countries are landlocked, and Moche said to stay off major roads and keep out of cities. So the only available options are buses, hitchhiking rides, and walking. This journey could take weeks—weeks of hiding, running, watching my back. If the Shadow King can make himself look like a different person, if he can hide in some other man's body . . . if he can survive *death*, then who knows what else he is capable of.

Even in my panicked state, I can appreciate how stunning Luxor is. In the East Bank, the streets are wide, bright, and clean, flanked by tall, arching palm trees. The hotels are more classic in design, cruise ships docked along the river. There is way less traffic, and the buildings seem well maintained. I doubt they have anything close to a garbage city here.

The West Bank is home to the Valley of the Kings and the Valley of the Queens, with tombs dating back thousands of years. Here, tourists from around the world stand on lines to see where King Tut is buried. Colorful hot-air balloons soar over sprawling farmlands. All the places I've read about and heard tour guides mention are just beyond my reach.

But this isn't a sightseeing day. I'm on a mission.

Down the road from the Luxor Temple, I make my way to the frenzied market, a combination of tourist shops and gro-cers. Makes me instantly miss home. I move quick, plucking two wallets in the bustling market. I stop and buy myself a new hijab as soon as I have the chance, toss the other one away with the memory of that disgusting man's touch. Out of habit, I scan the crowd, always searching for someone, anyone, who remotely looks like me. Copper-brown skin, long white hair, crystal-blue eyes . . . but there's never anyone else.

Up a few yards across from a hotel, a crowd of locals gath-ers around vendors baking fresh aish baladi. Some warm puffy bread and tea will help soothe my nerves before the long trip to Aswan. Elbowing through, I pull out some change just as the hair on my arms raises to the sky. That tingling sensation in my palms reaches up my neck.

Come home.

Something feels off. Scanning the crowd, I straighten my scarf and force myself to back away. A gasp escapes me as I run right into a rock-hard chest.

"Did you have fun on your little night cruise?"

I spin around and face the deep voice. The man is tall, with dark olive skin and thick curly hair. A navy polo over khaki pants. No one I recognize. But he knows me. I can sense it in his smirk. I swallow and paste on a smile.

"Sorry. I don't know what you are talking about," I say coolly, backing away from his reach. But I run into another man, just as a third corners us. They are like triplets in uniforms.

"Ro, is it not?" the first man asks, laughing at me as the sec-ond leans closer.

My muscles go rigid, mouth dropping open. The man leans forward.

"Scream," he whispers, touching his side, "and I will cut your throat."

My insides riot in response, but I remain composed, chin raised. I will not let these henchmen sense my fear. But how did they find me? How did they know?

The third one grabs my elbow, roughly leading us away from the crowd. No one notices as I stumble down the street, surrounded by three men. So much for Moche's advice. Captured within hours of leaving him. He'll be so disappointed.

We turn a corner, heading down a narrow alley. The first man walks ahead, stops in front of a building, and opens the battered metal door. It creaks open, revealing darkness beyond, silence as the men move to shove me through.

My breathing picks up. Without thinking, I dig my heels into the ground. The stone walls of the alley begin to cave in, the door a black hole. . . .

"No," I whimper. "No, I can't go in there. Please, no."

"What is the matter with you!" the third henchman barks, shaking me.

"Let me go," I beg, reeling back, realizing I would rather be stabbed in the heart than walk into some unknown building and be buried alive. "Let me go! Just let me go!"

The first henchman rolls his eyes and slams the door. "Stop all this. The Boss just wants to talk to you."

I flail like a dying animal, using my entire body weight to slip out of his grip and thump on the ground. My palms sting like a thousand tiny needle pricks, and the cool sensation gathers in my chest, builds in my veins as the second henchman reaches to grab me.

It's happening again.

"NO! Wait, let me go! Please!"

It takes two of them to capture me, holding both of my arms as I kick wildly, trying to keep them away. They don't understand I could kill them, like I almost killed the man in the souk. They don't know what I can do.

"I believe the young lady said to let her go."

We all turn to a deep voice behind us. A boy, tall with a slender build, stands at the mouth of the alley.

"Who are you?" the head henchman snarls.

The boy shrugs one shoulder. "No one of importance."

He grunts. "Well, move along, then. This is none of your business."

The boy tips his chin at their hands gripping my wrist. "Not until you let her go."

The henchman rolls his eyes and turns to his partner. "Get rid of him."

And before they can move, the boy somersaults past, landing a firm kick on the man holding me. I jump out of the way, back against the wall.

The men stand frozen and stunned. Then the first henchman looks at his crew. "What are you waiting for? Get her!"

The boy tosses his sack aside and shouts something I can't understand before fly-kicking the other two men in the face. The feeling in my palms fizzles out as I press against the wall. My heart slows as I stare in shock. Who is this boy, and what are these moves?

The henchman narrows his eyes. "You are from Wakanda?"

The boy stands alert, his eyes laser-focused.

The henchman laughs. "You know, there were rumors that a young prince was said to be out traveling. Funny that I should find you here . . . with her." He glances at his crew, who are slowly getting up from the ground, rubbing their jaws. "Boys, we're going to make this a two-for-one special!"

The boy spins to me. "Run! Now!"

I don't wait. I sprint for the road, but just as I clear the alley, I glance over my shoulder.

The boy is like a carnival acrobat, flipping, kicking, and punching anything in his way. The whole display is mesmerizing. But just as he knocks out one man, another manages to land a hard strike to the boy's stomach. He crumples as the leader slams him to the ground.

They kick and stomp the boy as he grunts. I double back, unsure of what to do. Do I just let these men pummel a stranger, one who tried to help?

And then the setting sunlight catches off the leader's flint as he raises it in the air.

"NO!" I scream, running toward them.

I don't know how it happens. All I intended was to push the man away. But before I even make it near him, a blinding white light explodes out of my palms, sending the leader flying into a stone wall, cracking it like a crater. Dust and debris scatter. Smoke sizzles from the man's back as he slumps, landing face down on the ground.

For a moment, everyone stands in stunned silence.

But then the boy springs to his feet and leaps onto the last henchman, knocking him out cold. The boy crouches low to the ground, readying himself for another attack. But there is no one left.

He limps toward me. "Are you hurt?" he says, panting.

I blink, still trying to shake off my shock. The leader lies motionless, his body crumpled at an awkward angle. "I . . . I killed him."

"He would have killed me," he says, kicking his knife away. "But are you okay?"

A startled laugh bubbles from my lips. "You just got your ass whooped, and you're asking *me* if I'm okay?"

He pauses to examine the men. "Yes. I suppose I am."

"I'm fine. But you—"

"I am fine as well. Just a scratch."

He glances down at the man I pounced on, at the black burn marks on his back, and raises an eyebrow at me.

"How did you . . ." He swallows his words, eyes landing on my hands. My blood freezes.

Oh Goddess. He saw everything.

"Well. Got to run," I spit out with a wave. "Nice meeting you!" I turn on my heel and bolt for the road.

"Wait!" the boy shouts, chasing after me. "Where are you going?"

"Somewhere I have to be."

"May I offer you a ride?"

"No, thanks!"

"It is the least I can do," he insists. "For saving my life."

What is with this boy? I thought he'd be long gone by now. "It was nothing. Besides, I'm going pretty far."

"So am I."

I stand at the crosswalk, looking both ways as the rubber band inside me stretches, pulling harder. I glance up at the sky, the clouds turning pink and orange.

Wait, what time is it? The last ferry for the day leaves at midnight. I might miss it if I don't find a bus to Aswan soon. Or . . . or. . . .

I turn to the boy, really taking him in for the first time. For someone who just finished whooping butt, he doesn't look too bad. His eyes are bright, warm, and knowing, and his face is kind. His thick jet-black fro is cut short, picked out slightly. Though he's leaning heavily on one leg, a fresh cut bleeding from his forehead, he stands tall, shoulders pulled back.

He looks . . . nice. Nice enough, anyway. Besides, he hasn't run for the hills yet. And he did offer me a ride. "Can you take me to the Aswan harbor?"

He smiles. "Where are you headed?"

I roll my eyes. Why does he have to be so nosy? I don't have time to argue, so I get straight to the point. It's not like I'll ever see him again.

"Kenya." It seems far enough to persuade him otherwise, so I can get going. But his eyes only sparkle.

"I am traveling that way, too," he says, scooping up his cast-aside sack. "We can travel together."

"Ha! I don't think so. I just need a ride."

"Look, you do not need to tell me . . . everything." He glances over to the burnt henchman in the alley, and I wince. "But, perhaps we should consider sticking together."

"Why?"

"Whatever happened back there, well, it scared you. But it also saved my life. Clearly someone is after you. And others may know who I am, and will be after me, too." He cocks his head, eyebrows raised. "But, if we work to protect each other, we could both make it back home in one piece."

I glance at the sky again. Somehow, the Shadow King knows I'm still in Egypt. He must have spies all over the country. No way I can take regular transport and not be spotted. And it'll take me weeks on foot. Hitching a ride would be the fastest and safest way to Kenya.

But . . . who is this guy? And why is he not running scared? My eyes narrow. "He called you a prince."

The boy checks his side. "That he did."

"You don't look like a prince."

He grins. "I will consider that a compliment."

I search the alley. "Where's your royal caravan?"

"I'm traveling light."

"You have a car?"

"A motorbike."

Even better. I won't be cramped inside a tin box with wheels.

"Okay," I say, brightening. "Lead the way."

He grins, heading back toward the alley, then stops short.

"Wait. What is your name?"

"Sarah," I say without skipping a beat.

He gives me a pointed look. "If this is to work, we should start trusting each other."

Moche would say I'm a great judge of character. Right now, my gut is telling me this boy fights good, but is as green as okra. I doubt he'll try to pull one over on me.

"Ororo. You?"

He smiles, offering his hand. "My name is T'Challa."

X

T'Challa's bike looks like it was made from junkyard scraps, held together with pieces of tape and a prayer.

"Are you *really* a prince?"

He notes my skepticism and grins.

"I am trying to keep a low profile," he says. He removes the tarp and stands next to the bike, like a proud toddler with a freshly made mess.

I've seen camels in better condition. I'm not sure if this thing will make it down the street, let alone the four hours to Aswan. But he readies himself, tying his sack to the back of the bike before hopping on, jumping to start the engine.

"Come," he says, offering a hand.

I wave it aside. "I got it," I say, and climb on behind him.

T'Challa adjusts his seat and looks over his shoulder at me.

"You are going to have to hold on to me."

"I have good balance. I'll be fine."

86

"Safety first," he counters, making it clear he won't move. My eyebrows twitch. He's green but not a pushover, which means I'll have to respect his boundaries.

"Okay, okay," I say, snaking my hands around his waist to hold on to his—surprisingly—rock-hard stomach and squeeze close. "Better?"

"Uh, yes." He clears his throat. "Better."

It suddenly dawns on me, the proximity I have to an absolute stranger. But at least he seems nervous about me being so close, even a little on edge. A good sign. He knows not to mess with me.

And with that, he kicks up the stand, revs the engine, and peels out.

We take the scenic road down the East Bank of the Nile, neither of us speaking as we ride toward the water. The city is beautiful, and I hate to admit it, but I feel more at ease on T'Challa's bike. Unexpected traffic adds hours to the journey, and nightfall cools the air around us a little. For the first time since leaving Cairo, I feel like I'm able to take a breath.

When we finally reach the docks, T'Challa runs his bike up the ferry ramp, making it just before the ferry sails away. The ship is in the same condition as his bike, taped and glued together with spare parts, rusted on the sides, and I try to hold in a cringe. I wouldn't be surprised if we start to sink in the middle of the night.

As T'Challa talks to the porter, I survey the scene. Now that we've stopped moving on land, I feel like I'm on display, waiting for the Shadow King or his men to pop out of hiding. I tug at my hijab, shifting from one foot to another. Could I be so lucky as to escape without him knowing?

The boat rocks, and I plant my feet to keep my balance.

"I got us two first-class tickets," T'Challa says. "They only had one cabin left."

"First class?" I squawk. "Are you crazy? I don't have that type of money!"

"Consider it a gift, after saving my life," he says, smiling.

I square my shoulders. Of course the one boy I need to rely on would be an arrogant donkey.

"Look, I'm not a charity case. I can pay and make my own way."

He nods. "Understood."

I roll my eyes. "Okay. Now we need to scope out the ship."

"There are only farmers and fellow countrymen on this ship. I'm sure it is fine."

"You don't know that, and— Wait . . . where is your bag?"

He frowns, thumbing over his shoulder. "I left it on the bike."

"You *what*!"

I don't even wait for an answer. I sprint down to the holding deck, and, just as I thought, a shadowy figure stands over the bike, hands on the bag.

"Hey!" I scream. The figure looks up and scurries away to the main deck.

T'Challa rushes to the bike and opens his bag. He digs around and exhales. "Everything is still here."

"What were you thinking?!"

He holds up his hands. "It was an error in judgment."

"Never, ever leave your bag unattended! That's, like, Life 101."

He huffs, untying his sack. "I was distracted." He looks pointedly at me. "Any other lessons I should know?"

"Yes. Starting with checking the perimeter."

He narrows his eyes. "Where are you from?"

No one needs to know that. I dodge the question. "Does it matter?"

"You do not act like other girls. It is like you are always on some sort of high alert. Are these war tactics or street tactics?"

"Are women not allowed to be strategic in Wakanda? I bet you don't even let women in your army."

He smirks. "Fine. We shall do it your way."

We begin our walk around the ship, side by side, as the lights of Aswan fade behind us.

"Eyes open," I instruct. "Not everyone is who they seem."

"I do know how to scout properly," he says, his tone amused.

"Yes, but do you know how to read people?"

He frowns. "What do you mean?"

I scan, and tip my head toward the right.

"That man over there by the stairs . . . What do you see?"

He shrugs. "Just a farmer in a gray tunic."

"Take a closer look. See his glasses? Brand-new. Clean-shaven. And he's wearing an expensive watch under that long sleeve. He's most likely a businessman, traveling, like you." I point to an old woman on the other side of the ship. "Or how about her?"

"Her? The grandmother?"

"Yes, but where is she heading? Looks like most of her belongings are in that old carpetbag. But look how she keeps checking over her shoulder. Definitely stole something and is on the run."

He chuckles, eyes dancing. "And if you were to look at me like this, what would you see?"

I eye him up and down, from his fine posture to his street clothes to his arms crossed over his chest. "You? Well, I see . . . I see a boy trying to be a man. Wearing clothes that don't quite fit like he is used to. His hands look soft, his nails too clean. He comes from wealth, but he's embarrassed by it. So he's out with commoners, probably has to live up to his father's dreams, maybe taking over a shop or something."

T'Challa's face falls.

"Am I right?" I ask.

"You . . . are somewhat correct," he says, gazing out to sea.

I hesitate. Must have pushed a little too hard.

Play it cool, Ro. He is not the enemy.

"Looks like the ship is good," I offer. "And no rain tonight. Just a bit of breeze. Think we're safe for the evening."

"Well, now that *that* is settled," he says, holding his breath, "shall we see about our quarters?"

We take a set of stairs down to the lower deck, and quickly, I begin to question how much I need to sleep on this ferry. The small ship has even smaller quarters, and I can feel the walls squeezing in on me as I drop down to the deck below, my head nearly touching the ceiling.

"It's very . . . cramped down here." I can barely get the words out through my squeezing windpipes. With each step, my breathing quickens, becoming shallower. I glance at T'Challa, but he keeps walking calmly, studying each room we pass. I drag myself a few doors down, where T'Challa uses a key to open room 20.

Inside, the narrow room has bunk beds to the right and a window the size of a small bean pie. My feet won't let me take one step inside.

"Well . . . this is . . . nice," he says, painting on a strained smile. Clearly not up to his royal standards. I would find it hilarious if the sight of the tiny room didn't give me severe heart palpitations.

Too small . . . too small . . .

"I'm . . . going to sleep on the deck," I croak.

"The deck?" T'Challa says, as if disgusted. "But there are perfectly good beds right here."

Vision blurring, I shake my sight straight. It doesn't matter that I'm in mortal danger and this boy is offering me a safe haven. I refuse to explain to a stranger how the thought of stepping inside that tiny room makes me feel like I'm being crushed to death inside a soda can.

Don't panic. Not in front of a prince.

"I'll be fine." I bow my head. "Your Highness."

T'Challa purses his lips as I shut the door behind me and run up the stairs. As soon as I'm outside, I take a violently deep breath, trying to slow my heartbeat.

On the deck, passengers sprawl out, taking up every square inch of the floor. I step over sleeping bodies, light shining off their glistening skin, and make my way to the hanging lifeboats, where there is a small amount of free space.

Using Moche's jacket as a pillow, I lie down and gaze up at the stars, the boat rocking softly, water lapping against its side. I haven't slept for more than a few hours in days. I should be exhausted. But I'm wired, and now that I'm alone, my mind flies back to what I did to that henchman in Luxor. How light bloomed . . . no, sparked in my hand.

And then the way he lay still in the alley. My heartbeat stutters at the memory of the tourist in the souk, seizing. The blinding light that shot out from my palms.

But that's impossible.

I keep repeating the phrase to make it true as Farouk's words haunt me. . . . He was right. That the tourist in the souk nearly died when I touched him. That the henchman in Luxor *did* die.

My stomach plummets to the bottom of the sea. I couldn't let him kill T'Challa, the boy who saved me, but I never meant for anyone to die. I stare at my palms, before burying my face in them. What kind of monster am I turning into?

It's getting worse. Whatever this is. I still have no idea where I'm going or what I'll find when I get there. I still don't know if there even *is* a cure.

But I have to try. Moche and the boys, they need me.

"I did not mean to make you uncomfortable."

I peer through my fingers and find T'Challa standing over me, his expression mournful.

"Uncomfortable?"

"Yes. You are a girl . . . I mean, woman. You would probably prefer your privacy than to be trapped in a room with a strange man. My apologies. I was not thinking of your feelings."

Well, at least he's not completely oblivious. I sit up and lean against the lifeboat. I've grown up living with twelve smelly boys, so privacy is a laughable concept. But I don't want him to know the real reason I prefer the outdoors. I'm not ready to talk about that yet—with anyone.

"It's beautiful tonight," I offer, trying to change the subject.

He joins me on the floor, following my gaze toward the stars.

"Back home, in Wakanda," he says softly, "there's a cliff I like to sit on to look at stars like this. I used to think, there is no place in the world like this. Then I found there are many places that stars look beautiful from." He sighs. "Still, there is no place like home."

"Hmm," I muse, massaging the tight muscles in my palms. I feel that way about Cairo. Even Garbage City has its moments. "So, tell me, what is a prince doing riding around on a bike fit for . . . well, no one, really?"

He glances at the floor and chuckles. "What do you know about Wakanda?"

I think back to the geography texts I've read in the bookshop. "Only that's it's a ridiculously small country with not much to offer."

He folds his hands. "Yes, we like to appear that way. We are very private people." He chuckles. "I'm on a walkabout."

"A what?"

"It is a tradition to walk around this great continent and meditate on the meaning of being king of our nation."

"Except you're not walking," I counter.

He laughs. "Well, it *is* the twenty-first century."

"Then why not fly?"

"I wanted to experience . . . life, firsthand."

I can understand that. I think back to my conversation with Moche. About that feeling of wanting to see and do more. Wanting more. "Where have you been so far?"

"I started in South Africa, rode up the west coast to Namibia. Then Cameroon, Nigeria, Ghana, Liberia, Senegal. Then I made my way east to Egypt. I was planning to stop in Kenya and then Tanzania before heading home, even before meeting you."

My mouth drops open. I can't even play it cool and contain my shock. He's been everywhere! Did he see Mount Cameroon or the African Renaissance Monument in Dakar? What was the city of Lagos like? I have so many questions about every place he's been, but one point sticks out in particular.

"So, you're going to be a king?"

He stiffens. "It is my destiny. But . . . it is also quite complicated."

"Mmm. Family drama," I say with a nod. "I get it."

T'Challa cocks his head to the side. "Technically speaking, yes." He juts his chin in my direction. "What about you? What is your destiny in Kenya?"

"Tah! Who said I have one?"

"Everyone has one."

Come home.

The woman's words reverberate against my eardrum. Her voice is louder now, and I swallow, taking a moment to steady myself.

"Maybe not me," I respond to T'Challa, feigning confidence.

"Then what is in Kenya that has you so desperate to escape?"

I try to keep my tone nonchalant. Despite what he saw, I don't want him knowing too much about my mission. He's still a stranger, and I'm not sure if I can fully trust him just yet.

"My mother's people are from there. I'm looking for them."

He raises an eyebrow. "Are your mother's people like . . . you?"

I zero in on his meaning. "Maybe," I say slowly. "Not sure."

He leans his head back and closes his eyes. "Well then, I hope you find them."

Several silent moments pass. I smack my lips. "That's it? That's all the questions you have?"

"I am trying to respect your privacy," he says with a knowing haughtiness.

Unbelievable.

Against my better judgment, something inside me gives way. "You and I just saw freaking lightning—or *something*—burst out of my hands, and you're not the least bit curious?"

"Oh, I am very curious," he says, a playful smile on his lips. "But?"

"But . . . I do not want you to run away."

"Tuh! I'm not scared. Of anything!"

T'Challa remains silent, giving me the same knowing look that's starting to grate on my nerves.

He's playing me.

"Look," I say, turning to him. "We need to set some ground rules in order for this trip to work."

"All right," he says, facing me, seemingly humored by my determination.

I count off on my fingers. "One, we need to stay off the main roads and out of major cities. We can be spotted, and we can't have anyone on our trail."

He strokes his nonexistent beard, then nods. "All right."

"Two, no hotels or luxury cruise cabins," I say, waving around at the ship. "We could be spotted."

He shrugs. "Outdoors is fine by me."

"Three . . . you need to keep the nosy questions to a minimum."

He cocks his head to the side and squints.

"What?" I ask.

"So . . . are we really not going to address, how do they say, the elephant in the room?"

I hold in a shudder. He's seen me do . . . *more* than anyone has. But I can't just spill my guts to a complete stranger.

"Fine. I'll give you two questions per day."

"Per day?" he balks, wounded.

"Okay, three. Any more and you're pushing it."

"I suppose I can live with that. For now, until you trust me enough to change your own mind."

Hmm. He isn't as pushy or demanding as I would think a prince would be. I study him, and despite the lightness in his words, his eyes are open and serious as they meet mine, and there's a strange feeling in my chest. Somehow, in the moonlight, with the waves gently splashing against the boat and the wafting smell of seawater, this stranger can truly see me, maybe even more than Moche ever did.

"Now," he starts, his voice low. "As for our route . . ."

He glances around the ship, checking to see if anyone is watching. When the coast is clear, he scoots closer, then touches the black beaded bracelet on his wrist. A light purple hologram map appears, floating just above his hand.

I nearly fall off the boat.

"What is that?" I gasp, trying to keep my voice down.

"These are kimoyo beads," he whispers.

"That is . . . I mean . . . *what?*"

The corner of his mouth tips up into a proud smirk. "Wakanda is the most technologically advanced nation in the world. We just like to keep it a secret."

"So why are you telling me?"

"I have seen your secret." He meets my eye. "Now you have seen one of mine."

I can't tell if this is an olive branch or a trap. Because if I ever told anyone about Wakanda, he could certainly expose my whole, uh, dilemma.

It's insurance, a smart tactic. Guess I can't call the boy stupid, no matter how green he seems.

He waves away a screen and a topical map pops up. Licking my lips, I take in the glowing details, tempted to reach out and touch the light. That bracelet is probably worth a fortune. Off that alone, the boys and I could eat like kings for weeks.

"I thought you were keeping it low-key?"

"I am."

"That phone bracelet thingy could teleport you back to your home country!"

"We tend not to teleport," he says matter-of-factly.

I scoff. "I was joking."

"Oh," he mumbles, as if confused.

Is this guy serious?

"This is the only piece of technology I have on my person, serving more as a tracking device, a locator. It was the only way my family would let me take this journey alone. My mother is quite overprotective."

Well, there goes that idea. Wouldn't want to help a kingdom track us back to headquarters. Bad for business.

New pieces falling into place. The easy smile. The sure confidence. . . .

"So Wakanda isn't just huts, cattle, and farmland," I say. "I mean . . . you really are like a *prince* prince, aren't you?"

He squirms. "I suppose I am."

Why is he acting all nervous all of a sudden? He can't expect me to behave normally. Who on earth randomly runs into a prince? He's probably used to all sorts of attention. Used to people throwing themselves at his feet.

He's going to learn quick that that's not me.

"Tuh! And you're taking this trip to see how the other half lives?"

"Not exactly. But I am learning a lot."

I roll my eyes. "I bet."

"Really, this is no different from a cellular device," he insists, trying to downplay the fancy gadget and failing badly.

"I wouldn't know," I grumble, lacing my fingers together.

"You mean . . . you have never had a cell phone before?"

I narrow my eyes. Could he at least try to mask his shock?

"Not all of us have tasted life with your silver spoon."

"Gold."

"What?"

"My spoon," he says with a smirk. "It is gold."

I let out a laugh and he smiles. A blinding smile that makes my stomach flutter.

Oh no. Absolutely not, Ororo.

No matter how cute he is, I need to keep this relationship professional. I'm on a mission, and he's a means to an end who happens to be royalty. I need to keep my emotions in check and not fawn over him like some lovestruck groupie.

"Anyway, back to what you were saying. Our route."

"Right. The ship lands in Wadi Halfa. So we shall head down through Sudan, toward the capital, then to Ethiopia, until we reach Kenya."

"How long will it take?"

He reads the map again. "Depending on the conditions of the roads and weather, we should be able to make it to Nairobi in a week's time."

I frown. "Why Nairobi?"

"Whatever you are looking for, it would be wise to start in the capital and work your way out to the surrounding areas."

That's a good idea. I didn't even think of that.

"Sounds like a plan."

The prayer bell rings. Men rise, washing their hands and feet before setting out their mats.

T'Challa turns to me. "Do you need a moment to pray?"

"I'm not Muslim."

He takes in my scarf but doesn't ask any questions. Curious but not disrespectful. I kind of like that.

And with his fancy beads . . . maybe this trip won't be so bad after all.

NINE

The morning sun blazes down on the small, dusty town of Wadi Halfa, the desert mountains in the far distance, peppered with cactus plants and skinny trees starved for water. As the boat eases into the dock, I steel my nerves. It's not lost on me that this is my first time out of the country since my parents died. I'm equal parts terrified and excited to explore. My mother always said I had my daddy's adventurous spirit. I think back to that time, a time I barely remember now, when I was excited to move to Cairo and explore all that Egypt had to offer. Whatever happened to that girl?

Focus, Ororo, focus. There's no time to think of the past.

Adjusting my hijab, I go belowdecks and find T'Challa unchaining his bike from the rack. If all goes to plan, with his map thingy, we'll be in Kenya in a few days. But I still have to keep my wits about me. The Shadow King must have learned of our run-in with his men by now. We may have just a few hours' head start. Who knows how far his reach goes.

"We need supplies before we set out," I say, tying Moche's jacket around my waist. "The farther south we travel, the hotter it gets. It's already forty-nine degrees."

T'Challa nods in agreement, bending to secure his pack, muscles peeking out of his T-shirt. I look away, cheeks burning.

"I read that there is a small outdoor market not too far from the port," he says. "We can go there."

Perfect.

We deboard and weave through the throng of taxis and shipping trucks, following the paved road into the town, made up mostly of old stone buildings painted robin's-egg blue, yellow, and sand. Businesses catering to exports. Most of the men are dressed in tunics and kufi hats, the women in long skirts and hjiabs, their skin ranging from dark chocolate to almond.

T'Challa turns down a side street and parks in front of a grocer. The market is nothing like the souks in Cairo. It's the length of a mere three blocks, with a scattering of vendors selling Egyptian souvenirs, clothes, household items. This place can't have more than a hundred people on its best day. I even spot a vendor yawning over his morning coffee.

There won't be much to score here, I think bitterly as I hop off the bike. But there must be something, people traveling through here, heading for the ferry. Only way I'll be able to properly scope out a good target is if I lose the dead weight.

I turn to T'Challa. "Meet you back here in twenty minutes?"

T'Challa blinks with a frown. "Do you not want to shop together?"

"I work better alone."

He hesitates before nodding. "Okay. I will be waiting by the bike."

We split up, which isn't hard to do, given the market is maybe half a mile long. I buy a canteen, a mat, a silk scarf, another T-shirt, and a small book bag, filling it with apples, dried apricots, nuts, bread, and seeds. By the time I'm done, I only have five dollars left from the money Moche gave me.

I adjust my hijab. I need a new score. Of course I could have just snatched the supplies I needed, but I have a rule about stealing from my own people. Tourists are my favorite targets.

The market buzzes with mostly locals, but luckily, there are a few tourists in the mix. One in particular, a backpacker, is trying to use his phone to help translate a shopkeeper's offer.

I stand next to the man, putting on my best fake accent. "May I help?"

I do a quick translation, pointing him in the direction of the bus depot, all smiles and laughter, then scurry off . . . with his wallet in my bag. I'm only a few feet away when a hand grabs my elbow, yanking me back.

In my panic to fight, I lose balance, thumping right into the firm chest of my kidnapper.

T'Challa.

His eyes flicker above my head then back to my hands.

"Did you just steal that man's wallet?"

"Say that any louder, why don't you?" I hiss, shoving past him. He stands in front of me like a human wall.

"Give it back," he snaps.

"Why?"

He huffs. "What do you mean, why? It is not yours! And it is the right thing to do."

How did he even know. . . .

My eyes narrow. "Were you following me?"

He blanches, stumbling over his words. "I . . . just happened to be nearby."

"Yeah, right." I snort. I try to sidestep him, but he steps with me.

"I am not going on this journey with a criminal."

I reel back. "A criminal? Look, just because you've had a gold spoon in your mouth all your life doesn't mean you know anything." Leave it to a prince to judge the rest of us from his high horse. He has no idea what it's like out on the streets.

"All I need to know is that you should not steal from anyone. It is immoral."

I glance over my shoulder, spotting the backpacker in the distance. I throw up a hand at T'Challa. I *have* to get to Kenya. I should've known I couldn't trust him to understand.

"Fine. I don't need you. I'll take the bus."

I spin around on my heel, but he's already in front of me.

"How can you be so flippant about this?" He crosses his arms, his eyebrows raised. "Do you do this in Cairo as well?"

I purse my lips. I *really* don't need this right now. "Look, he's just a tourist. Probably doesn't need it as much as I do."

"I don't care," T'Challa says, stepping forward. "Give it back."

Does this boy think he can intimidate me?

I narrow my eyes and square my shoulders. "You can't tell me what to do!"

"No, but I will not assist a thief," he growls through clenched teeth.

I stiffen, the words cutting deep. And the way he's looking down at me like I'm nothing but dirt on the bottom of his shoe. . . . Anger begins to boil like tea in my belly.

"You know what, I bet it's easy for you to stand there and judge me. While you sit upon your golden throne, looking down on every country except your own." I think of the kiddies back home, think of the many nights I've gone hungry just so they can eat *something*, and my hands ball up into fists. "Some of us *need* to steal so we can survive. Do you even know what it's like to have to survive? To be out on the street? To have the world after you?"

T'Challa balks, opening his mouth to respond, but frowns. He glances around, and I'm distantly aware of the air chilling. A pressure builds in my chest, climbing to my throat.

"Ororo—"

"To have to beg for scraps, to dig through garbage, to starve?"

"Ororo . . . stop it!"

"Stop what!" I snap.

He points up. Above us, dark clouds the size of boulders roll in with the wind, lightning flickering inside. The market comes to a standstill, and all around, people look up, baffled by the sudden change. I gape up at the sky, heart in my throat.

"You need to calm down," T'Challa whispers.

My stomach lurches. "I . . . I . . . I'm not doing it!"

He looks up again. "I think you are," he says calmly. T'Challa grips my hand and pulls me around to the back of a building. "Try to relax."

"Relax?" I scoff. "I don't know how!"

He's talking to me but eyeing the sky, as if waiting for it to fall.

"Think of something . . . peaceful," he says in that same measured tone. "Or anything that makes you happy."

I struggle, coming up empty. A good score? No. Playing with the kiddies? No. My birthday party, maybe . . . but then there was that sandstorm.

Everything has been marred by sadness. When's the last time I've been truly happy?

With Mommy and Daddy . . .

The air charges, the wind picking up speed, knocking over makeshift tents and wooden tables. I can hear people in the market crying out as objects clatter, setups are destroyed, the storm catching everyone off guard.

"Okay, that is not working." T'Challa thinks hard, rubbing his hands together. "Uh . . . shall I tell you a joke?"

"A joke?" I echo, feeling myself about to tip over the edge. "Right now?"

"Yes! Okay. What do you call a lion who swims?" He pauses for dramatic effect. "A sea lion."

I blink up at him, his eyes glimmering.

"Or how about . . . what is a lion's favorite day to eat?" He smiles. "Chewsday."

There's a long pause before I unwillingly snort.

"That was . . . the worst joke I have ever heard," I say with a laugh. "Just awful. You have no game at all."

"I have . . . game," he says defensively, arms crossing.

I blow out air. "*Pfft*. Not with those corny jokes. It's pitiful."

His mouth twitches into a half smile, and he glances up. "Well, it worked. See?"

The sky is back to a beautiful blue, not a cloud to be seen.

"Yes, it did," I mumble, not wanting to admit it. Not wanting to believe what I have just done. The thought makes my spine stiffen.

It's getting worse.

"It appears I will have to store up many jokes for this journey," T'Challa quips.

"Please, no more. I beg you," I say dryly, trying to hold back a smile. Moche would have cracked so many jokes on this guy. . . .

Thinking of Moche, I swallow. I wonder how he and the boys are doing. Are Farouk and his men still hanging over them, or have they left now that I'm gone?

In any case, I can't stay in one place for too long. I give myself a shake and refocus. "Someone probably saw all of that. We need to get out of here."

T'Challa studies my face before giving me a nod, and we hurry back toward his bike before anyone can give us a second glance.

X

As planned, T'Challa takes the more scenic routes, with rough, often unpaved roads, and extra-long stretches between towns and villages. With sprawling rocky desert land on either side of us, it feels like I'm flying through another planet. The sky seems so big without being blocked by massive buildings, the roads wide with so little traffic.

T'Challa pulls over at a small stopover town, consisting of three short stone buildings on the side of the paved road. One donkey outside turns curiously in our direction.

"What are we doing?" I ask as he climbs off the bike. I eye the street warily. Though it's rather quiet now, I'll never forget how quickly those three henchmen appeared out of nowhere. I shiver, despite the heat. "We should keep going. It's not safe to stop!"

"We need to rest," T'Challa retorts. "And eat. I am starving."

He motions to a hole-in-the-wall with tables and chairs, the smell of burnt meat wafting through the open windows. I stiffen and adjust my hijab.

"I'm not going into a restaurant. There could be cameras in there!"

He points to three donkeys hitched to carts parked out front, curiously craning their necks in our direction. "There are not even cars here! We are almost in the middle of nowhere."

"Almost is not enough." I cross my arms, rolling my neck. "I am not going inside there, so you can forget it!"

He sighs. "Okay." He motions in the other direction, toward some storefronts and people milling about. "Looks like there are vendors across the street."

I dip my head mockingly. "That's more like it, my king."

He purses his lips. "Don't call me that."

Say what you will about the prince, but he doesn't utter another word about my paranoia. He goes with the flow without much fight. We purchase some food without incident, and soon we're back on the road again. I breathe a sigh of relief as we leave the town behind us.

Our first campsite is a few kilometers from the little town, in the savanna, under an acacia tree. We snack on cured meats and oranges, laying our mats out six feet apart. The sun is setting, but we don't light a fire. Can't risk the attention from people or curious creatures.

The backpacker's wallet is a gold mine. Five hundred dollars, credit cards, and two ticket stubs. Apparently he is from Cincinnati, Ohio, and is twenty-five years old.

T'Challa stares at me as I comb through the wallet, his eyes hard.

"Something on your mind?" I say, challenging him.

"I just don't understand how you can do something . . . like that."

Not this again. "You don't have people who are hungry in Wakanda, do you? Or poor? Or homeless?"

He shakes his head. Is that even possible in this world?

"Well . . . what would you do if you did?" I ask.

"We would provide for them. Food, shelter, whatever they need so they don't have to resort to unlawful acts."

I scoff. Must be nice. "Well, that's Wakanda. The rest of the world doesn't operate that way. And if you weren't living under a rock, you would know that."

T'Challa rubs his hands together.

"What if it did, though?" he asks seriously. I lean on an elbow and face him. What's this boy on about now? "What if the world was perfect? Would you still want to steal? What would you do?"

My tongue sticks to the roof of my mouth. It wasn't so long ago when I asked the same question of Moche, before everything happened. Before everything fell to pieces.

To be honest, I haven't thought of a future without Moche and the boys in it. And who would hire a girl like me? The idea is almost laughable. No education. No parents. Not even a real home.

"I don't know."

T'Challa lies on his back. "Maybe you should consider other options."

"Well, do you have other options besides being king?"

He stiffens, then takes a deep breath.

"I believe I am owed answers to certain questions, as promised."

Change of subject. Of course. But a deal is a deal, and I'm not one to back down from a promise.

"Okay, fine," I huff. "Ask your questions."

T'Challa sits up eagerly.

"Back in Luxor, what did it feel like? When the light shot out of your hands?"

I sigh. I've been trying not to think about it. Trying to pretend it didn't happen. But I guess it's better that he's curious rather than running scared.

"It . . . felt like thousands of little pricks in my fingers. It didn't hurt, it just . . . surprised me."

"Like static electricity." He mulls this over. "And today, at the market, did you feel anything when the clouds were turning?"

I think back but can't remember feeling anything except anger.

"It felt . . . cold. But I wasn't uncomfortable."

"Did you eat or drink anything out of the ordinary? A different food or herb you've never had before?"

I think of the spread at my birthday party. I guess someone could have put a curse on the food. . . . But everyone ate everything, and no one else is going through this. Just me.

"No."

"Hmm. That's very interesting," he mutters, folding his hands in his lap. You can practically see the mental wheels turning. His gaze is steady as it meets mine, his brow furrowed. A smile plays at his lips, and I shift.

"What are you doing?" I snap.

He glances up. "Trying to figure you out."

I raise an eyebrow. "But why aren't you more, I don't know, freaked out by all this crazy stuff?"

He chuckles. "We have our own 'crazy stuff' in Wakanda. I feel very at home with you."

My breath hitches as I stare at him in the moonlight. He feels at home . . . with someone like me? A wave of warmth wraps around my bones.

Wait . . . moonlight!

My neck snaps up at the crescent moon. *Until the next worm moon,* Farouk said. T'Challa follows my gaze.

"Not yet full. Still beautiful."

"Whhh—" My thoughts trip over themselves, my heart speeding up. "What kind of moon is that?"

T'Challa's lips twist. "I believe it is a regular moon. Are you into moon cycles?"

"Yes," I lie. "Do you know when the next worm moon is?"

He chuckles. "Tell me, you do not believe in those silly superstitions, do you?"

"What do you mean?"

He tips his head. "The closing of portals, and so forth."

I gulp hard and keep my voice even. I have no idea what he's talking about, but I can't have him knowing too much about what's going on with me, why someone like Farouk is after me. Not when I don't even know what's going on myself. "No. I am just interested."

He sighs. "Well, I believe it's the next cycle. So, next month."

So I have a little over a month to get to Kenya and find a cure. That isn't much time. I glance over at T'Challa and catch him watching me.

I flip on my side, turning my back to him. "Good night, T'Challa."

"Is . . . that your way of telling me you are done talking?"

"Yes."

He chuckles. "Then good night, Ororo."

X

The pull of the rubber band snaps me awake. I blink up through the branch of the tree, dawn making the sky a swirl of pink and blue, and for a brief moment, I am lost, forgetting the last forty-eight hours.

Then I remember I'm not on the roof in Garbage City. I'm in Sudan, an entirely different country, with a boy. Not just any boy—a *prince*.

But this is no fairy tale. Far from home, on the run, this is more like a nightmare.

I take a deep breath, the air balmy and thick. It will be hot today. I snuggle my face into Moche's jacket. It still smells like him, like home.

Come home.

The tug of that woman's voice . . . feels as if there's a war within my body I'm not ready for. But the quicker I make it to Kenya, the quicker I'll find answers. Something has to explain why all of this is happening now. I readjust my scarf, making sure not a hair is out of place before sitting up and glancing over at T'Challa's mat. Empty. I jump to my feet.

"T'Challa?" Did he abandon me? I *knew* all of this would scare him off. What if he runs back and tells someone? For all I know, the Shadow King might already be on his way.

Heart thumping, I scan the savanna, only to exhale with relief. Over near the tall reeds, a body dances about, his voice chanting. T'Challa has somehow found a crooked stick that he has sharpened into a spear. He thrusts it through the air as he moves with acrobatic kicks and flips. His invisible opponent would have been dead several times over.

I make my way to him, wading through the reeds. As I draw closer, I see that he's lost his shirt, skin covered in sweat. I gulp, trying to focus on his movements instead. "What are you doing?" I ask, my voice cracking, keeping a short distance between us in case that stick flies out his hands.

"Training," he says without looking at me. "I exercise every morning."

"I see." I watch him for a few moments more as he trains, his muscles glistening in the early morning light. I clear my throat. "What else do you do?"

His body stutters, thrown off by the question.

"What do you mean?"

I shrug. "I mean, for fun?"

"I . . . well, we do a lot of things. But between training, lessons in weapon proficiency, and other national matters, my time is taken."

"So, you do . . . nothing, is what I'm gathering?"

He gives me a look. "Not nothing. In school, our studies are quite rigorous between sport and training."

I cross my arms, looking over my shoulder toward the road. "I wouldn't know anything about that," I mumble.

T'Challa tilts his head. "You mean you have never had schooling?"

My defensiveness stirs. "Hey! I'm well read, thank you very much. Just because I didn't go to fancy schools doesn't mean I don't know anything."

T'Challa pauses to take me in, then nods. "Let us find you some breakfast. Maybe it will help your mood."

I jerk back. "Are you calling me cranky?"

He smiles. "You have a splendid way of hearing the things you want to."

That charming, beautiful smile almost disarms me. Almost.

I look away as T'Challa puts his shirt back on, and then we return to pack up our camp.

"It'll be extremely hot today," I say, rolling up my mat. "It hasn't rained around here in days."

T'Challa nods without looking at me, as if he was deep in thought.

After securing everything on the bike, I carefully make sure we leave no trace of our presence before we continue on our way.

We don't ride for too long before we come across the next village. This one has more people than the last, bustling in the early-morning hour. My shoulders tense up as T'Challa slows, weaving through the small crowd as we approach the center of the village. We stop at the gas station to fill up, then head to the local market in search of breakfast.

"So you have really never been to school?" T'Challa asks as we sit at an outdoor café, eating ful medames with hard-boiled eggs and flatbread. "Then where did you learn how to read?"

I roll my eyes and sip some tea. "Why is that so hard to believe? Some of us didn't have the opportunity that you did."

"Did you ever want to go to school?"

Thoughts of school try to creep in, of the short years I spent on playgrounds, trying to make friends with the cruel kids who made fun of my hair.

I swallow the *yes* sitting on my tongue and square my shoulders. "You don't always need school. You can learn a lot from just books."

"But you are so well-spoken. I just assumed . . ."

I slam my hand on the table. "Are you really trying to say that people who didn't go to school can't be well-spoken?"

T'Challa fumbles over his words but remains speechless.

I scoff. "Unbelievable. My parents taught me how to read, okay? My dad was an important professor. He was a *brilliant* man!"

Both of T'Challa's eyebrows rise, face taut with an *aha* expression. I flinch, knowing I've already said too much. What is wrong with me?

"Well, naturally, you adopted his capabilities," he says, casually peeling an orange. "If your father was a professor, I find it hard to believe you are of the streets that you claim."

"The streets raised me."

"But that is not where you come from," he counters in a knowing tone. "The streets didn't teach you to read."

I stiffen and turn to the market. "We need to get going," I say, slinging my bag over my back. "Need to grab more snacks for the road ahead. It'll be hot today, but cooler later this evening."

T'Challa follows me in silence as I purchase some water, apples, oranges, and bananas, doing my best to ignore his presence. So the prince made a point, but he knows nothing about my past. Nothing about all I had to do to survive. And yet I can't help but feel a tingle of pride.

He thinks I'm brilliant, like Daddy.

On the table next to the fruit cart sits a variety of mini Egyptian statues—little pyramids, falcons, Anubis figurines, and sphinxes. The typical souvenirs you find outside most major spots. The vendor probably thinks he can make a few dollars selling them here. I start to walk away, but something on the table catches T'Challa's attention, and he strolls over to the old man.

"As-salaam alaikum, friends," the man says. "Welcome!"

T'Challa picks up a small black panther, palming it in his hand.

"Ah! These were handcrafted by my brother," the vendor says. "He worked many, many hours on it. Made from the finest black obsidian, mined in caves of Luxor, outside the Valley of the Kings."

T'Challa turns it over, mesmerized. "How much?"

"Twenty," the old man says.

T'Challa nods. "I'll take it."

"Hang on," I say, stopping him from reaching for his wallet, and look the man square in the eye.

"Five," I say, keeping my tone even.

The old man narrows his eyes.

"Ororo," T'Challa whispers. "The man said twenty. That is more than fair."

"Ten," the man counters.

"Five," I say again. "And you're lucky to get away with that."

The man grabs the panther out of T'Challa's hand, shaking it in my face. "Young lady, this here is precious stone!"

I scoff. "Really?"

I snatch it out of his hand and bang it against the edge of the table.

"Hey! What are you—"

The panther cracks, crumbling, revealing its white grainy interior, the black paint chipping.

"See?" I say. "Sandstone."

The man straightens, giving me a once-over, then shrugs, wraps up another panther in pink newspaper, and hands it to T'Challa.

"Five."

"Make it two for our trouble," I warn.

As we walk off, T'Challa stares at his package. "How did you know?"

"Tuh, I can spot a fake from a mile away? Handmade, my ass. Most of his junk was made on a factory line in China. Besides, no price ever spoken is the final price."

T'Challa considers this, and I pause.

"Please don't tell me you haven't at least tried to negotiate for anything during your journey?"

T'Challa remains quiet, and I let out a laugh.

"I cannot believe you go exploring the world and let people rob you blind."

"Well, they must have needed the money."

"Don't we all," I say, thinking about the backpacker's wallet in my pocket. How excited he must have been to be going to Egypt. For the first time, I think how horrible his trip will be once he realizes he has no money or identification. My stomach twists with guilt.

"We should keep moving," I say. Staying in one place, shopping for souvenirs—it's almost asking for trouble, and my nerves are prickling.

T'Challa reaches for my arm. "Come now. We have time, Ororo."

"No, we don't," I state, yanking my arm back.

"Why are you in such a rush, anyway?"

What is it with all these questions? What reason do we have to stay here? I cluck my tongue impatiently. "I need to get to Kenya so I can return to Cairo."

"Why?" he presses.

Frustration wells in my throat, but I recognize it for what it truly is. It's helplessness, as I think of my brothers back home, taking the heat from Farouk's men for me.

I glance behind us, scanning the crowd for anyone suspicious, then turn back to T'Challa, this green boy who can fight, this stranger who said he feels at home with me.

Why is he so curious all the time? And why do I always feel the need to tell him the truth?

I let out a groan. "My brothers . . . they're in trouble."

His eyebrows knit. "But I thought you said you had no people."

"They're not my real brothers, but they're family all the same. We're a part of the same . . . crew."

"So they are like you? Pickpocketers."

I raise an eyebrow. "Not all of us were born in a castle, Your Highness."

He bristles, waving a hand. "Is it going to be this tense between us the entire journey? If so, I must ask: When are you going to stop pretending to be something you are not?"

"What does that mean?"

He steps forward, into my personal space, and I blink up. Our height difference is much clearer up close. "It means you had family, you had education, you know how to read. You are not just some girl from the 'streets.' You are clearly more than that. So why are you pretending that this is all you know?"

My mood sours, frustration quickly turning to anger. I'm ready to lay into the obnoxious know-it-all, but nothing comes out.

Could he be . . . right?

But just as I'm about to kick him to the curb, I glance over his shoulder and spot two men entering the market. They are wearing dark sunglasses and look similar to Farouk's henchmen back in Cairo. They could be twins, except one is slightly taller than the other. Both built like giant stone statues that live inside the great pyramids.

The rubber band stretches, as if pulling back, preparing to snap me forward. I jerk, stomach twisting into a knot, and grab T'Challa's arm.

"What it is it?" he asks.

"Oh Goddess, they're here."

T'Challa stills, his jaw clenching. "Who? Where?"

The two men prowl through the souk, searching, pulling aside people, and asking vendors questions. I can't read their lips, but one motions to his head, as if describing hair.

My hair . . . Oh no!

The bike is parked by the banana trees at the top of the

market beyond them, too far away. We won't make it, even if we run past them.

The taller man scans the area, turns, then flips over a table. There's a loud crash, wooden figurines scattering everywhere.

"Eh, what are you doing!" the vendor cries out, jumping back.

The market dissolves into chaos. The village people start yelling, in an uproar at the disrespect as they gather closer to the scene of the crime. Then, in the taller henchman's hand, I spot something that makes my blood go cold.

It's my black-and-red scarf, the one Moche gave me the night of the plane crash. I'd know it anywhere.

"Damn it," I grumble. They must have found it on the roof with the rest of my things.

I whip around to see the exit of the market blocked by a tuk-tuk cart. Trapped. I grip T'Challa's arm.

"Get down," I breathe, ducking behind a mango stand. T'Challa crouches beside me, peering over the top ledge.

"Do you know them?" he whispers, but my tongue is frozen.

A crowd forms around the two men. One steps up to speak.

"We are looking for someone," the tall one bellows. "An American girl, from Cairo. She has long white ha—"

"Brother, what is the meaning of this?" the vendor snaps. "There are dozens of little girls that come through here every day. You expect us to stop for each—"

The man snatches the vendor by the throat, lifting him off the ground in one quick move. The vendor gags, dangling feet kicking frantically. The woman behind him screams. Two vendors run over to help him, only to be knocked down, their noses bleeding.

The vendor's face turns beet red as he chokes, fighting for air.

My hands fly up to my mouth, and I shudder.

"Stay here," T'Challa whispers in my ear.

"What? Where are you . . ."

But he is already gone, stealthily crawling behind the crates. I'm too scared to move or breathe.

"I was speaking," the short man bellows. "She is brown, with blue eyes, and has long white hair."

I grip both sides of my scarf.

"How do you expect us to see through a hijab?" another vendor cries.

"We don't know who you're talking about! Please let him go! You're killing him."

The taller one cocks his head back, sniffing the air. My eyes widen as his nostrils seem to expand unnaturally, but I seem to be the only one who notices. Everyone is too busy trying to save the vendor, whose eyes are rolling back into his head.

My whole body seizes in terror. They're going to kill me.

Something brushes against my leg, and it takes everything in me not to scream.

T'Challa.

He puts a finger to his lips, motioning for me to follow. We keep low, army-crawling to a back room filled with empty shipping containers. T'Challa softly clicks the door closed, grabs my hand, and yanks me over to a small window.

"This way," he breathes. I climb out the window and into a narrow slit between the buildings.

The moment I feel the walls touch both my shoulders, my body nearly combusts.

T'Challa peers inside, then grabs my hands, pulling me out of sight.

"We've been followed," I gasp, in full panic mode. It's too tight back here. I can't breathe.

"That is not possible," he says, staring out the gate, scanning the road.

I shake my head, throat closing. "I knew it! I told you we shouldn't have stopped."

"No one knows where we are." He turns to me. "If someone were using technology to track us, I would have picked it up on my kimoyo beads." He shakes his head. "Whoever is chasing you, they are miles away from here. I don't think these men are after us."

"No. You don't understand—he's out to get me!"

He scowls. "*Who* is out to get you?"

I groan, fist balling up. "What did we talk about? No nosy questions!"

"It is not nosy. It is information we can use to make sure we are safe! How am I supposed to protect you if I don't know who I am protecting you from?"

I nearly shove him away. "What are you talking about? I do *not* need saving."

"I did not say *saving*. I said *protecting*. There is a difference. You do not seem like the type who needs a hero. Just someone to be there." His voice softens. "That is why I followed you in the market that day. I do not care about your foolish pride or how it may make me look, as long as you are safe. Why is it so difficult for you to accept that someone wants to be there?"

My chest tightens and I shut my eyes, jerking my head. "Because it has a cost!" I say wildly, my voice reaching a higher pitch.

He shakes his head. "Not when someone truly cares."

I bite back a response, holding my breath to fight the threatening tears. But caring always has a cost, doesn't it? I think of Mommy and Daddy, their arms shielding me from the crash. My brothers standing around me, ready to face Farouk and his men. Moche, and the look in his eyes as he sent me away with cash and a prayer.

A tingling sensation trickles down my arms into my fingers. The pressure in my chest pushes against my lungs.

Oh no.

I close my eyes, wheezing as a tingle starts in my shoulders, working its way down my back.

"I, uh," I breathe, "I think I need another joke, T'Challa."

He spins around, tensing. "Really? Now?"

Hands trembling, my breath comes out in short, raspy bursts.

"Yes. I need . . . something good."

"Uh, okay. What did the buffalo say to his son when he dropped him off at school?"

I snort. "Bison."

"Oh. So you know that one? How about what is a cheetah's favorite food?"

"Fast food."

He frowns, pensively stroking his imaginary beard. "I think I am beginning to lose my touch."

I hiccup a giggle. "I think I'm laughing more at the fact that you're telling these trash jokes than them actually being funny."

T'Challa grins. "At least it is working."

"Do these terrible jokes work on girls?"

"They do. But then again, I don't meet many girls like you."

My heart does that fluttering thing. *Is he flirting with me? No way.*

I squeeze my hands into fists, my nails biting into my palms. *Get out your head, Ro. He's just being silly. There is no way he'd be interested in you.*

"So . . . ," I say casually. "You've dated a lot? Figures. You are a prince, after all."

T'Challa only smiles. "What about you? Is there a special someone you are trying to get back to in Cairo?"

"Ew. No."

He chuckles, and something inside me melts a little bit. His dimples are quite distracting. "I meant no disrespect."

"I don't have time for love," I mumble, and then wince. Foolish—I hadn't meant to say that out loud.

He looks down at me with those soft brown eyes and smiles.

"Everyone has time when they truly want to," he says lightly.

I freeze, biting my tongue to keep from making an even bigger fool of myself. My eyes drift toward that soft smile, and I swallow.

Stop it, Ro.

Shouts inside make us turn back to the window. My heart quickens again. How many countries will they do this in, just to find me?

"Well, now that you are a touch better," T'Challa starts. "We need to move before they come back here looking."

I sip in some air. "Okay, what's the plan?"

"I can tackle the first one. That'll give you time to make it to the bike."

I shake my head. "And watch the second one rip your head off? No."

I think of Moche, wonder what he would do in this mess. Well, for one, he probably would never be in this mess. But what would he do if he was?

Achmed always told us to hide, but Moche never liked those odds. You can't run fast enough through crowds of people. So, he'd probably find a way to climb upward and run across the roof, where no one could break his stride. *Hide or take to the sky,* he'd say with a laugh.

The roof.

I look up, measuring the distance, calculating each extended brick I could use to balance myself.

T'Challa follows my line of sight. "You want us to scale a building? Can you do that?"

"Watch me," I say before reaching for the first brick, hoisting myself up. T'Challa smirks, backing up to a running start. He leaps, using the window ledge to jump clean over me, and locks himself on the upstairs window.

"Tuh. Show-off," I mutter. He's pretty agile, climbing with the ease of a cat.

He hops up to the roof and swings upside down, extending his arm. "Grab hold."

I grasp his hand and he swings me up, catching air. He flips us onto the roof, and I slam into his chest with a thud. His hands grip my lower back, balancing me, his heart steady under mine.

We stay frozen in that position for less than five seconds, and then I quickly snake out of his arms, adjusting my hijab. I turn in time for him to wipe the smirk off his face, and he charges ahead.

We sprint across the roofs, jumping from one to the next, before reaching the end of the block and tucking low, out of sight.

"Is the coast clear?" I ask, my voice cracking.

He peers over the edge, at the ground. "Yes. There's a truck right below us. On the count of three, we jump down into the truck bed. The trees should give us cover." He shifts, poised for a jump. "Ready? One, two, three!"

"Wait, I . . ."

But T'Challa leaps faster than I expect, and I scramble to follow him. I miss the truck bed and land on the roof instead, rolling down the hood and plopping onto the dirt road.

"Oof!" I whimper, the wind knocked out of me. My head snaps up. I've landed right in front of the market door. I see the backs of the two men, who are still interrogating the people trying to escape their grasp. The shouts and screams are getting louder, people crying for help as the pair grab at whomever they can reach.

Guilt washes over me. *This is all my fault.*

I scramble up to my feet, teeth chattering, just as T'Challa rushes to my side.

"Ororo, are you all right?"

I nod, torn about what to do. Shouldn't we help the people? But what if the men catch us in the process? I open my mouth, but no words come out. T'Challa grabs my hand and takes off running.

We stay low, hiding behind trucks and carts before making a quick beeline for the bike, hidden behind the banana trees. As soon as he lets go of my hand, I immediately feel the loss of warmth and am hit with a strange wave of longing. . . .

Stop it, Ro.

He isn't a part of the plan. There is no time for boys in this plan. What would he want with me, anyway, when he's a prince of some magical country?

I'm realistic enough to know that he is completely out of my league. I mean, what do I expect—for him to fall in love with me? Swoop in and whisk me away to his kingdom? Turn me into a princess and save me from my impoverished life?

It's not reality. There is no glass slipper. That Cinderella fairy tale doesn't happen to girls like me. Besides, he may be built like a god, but he's too green. I'd just about have to teach him everything. I need to focus on making it to Kenya, finding my people, ridding myself of this stupid curse, and getting back to Cairo as soon as possible—without being caught by the Shadow King's henchmen in the process.

So I numb my scattered nerves and jump on the back of his bike, clinging to his stomach, ignoring the firm muscles underneath and pretending it's Moche I'm holding onto instead. He stiffens for a moment, I suppose surprised by the sudden closeness, and peeks over his shoulder at me before pushing off.

Just a few more days of this. Then we'll be out of each other's hair.

X

I wanted to ride through the night, but T'Challa insists the roads are too dark and dangerous, so we make camp not long after darkness falls. I throw my bag on the ground. I've been on edge since we left that last village, but I swear this boy is so nonchalant about everything. Never in a rush, unfazed by the danger. It's driving me crazy.

There is a strong breeze that adds a chill to the air, so we agree to light a small fire. The dancing light of the flames is a welcome distraction from my racing thoughts.

Come home, Ororo.

I turn my face to the east, feeling the cord in my gut tug me in what I hope is the right direction. I still have no idea what I'm going to do when I finally make it to Kenya. I don't even know who or what I should ask for once I'm there. It'll be a needle-in-a-haystack type search.

But somehow, it all feels right. Even while we're stopped off the main road, something inside me confirms it. The constant unease I felt in Cairo, always scratching at the bottom of my feet, isn't there.

I was meant for this journey.

"What happened to your parents?"

I don't know that I was meant for nosy princes, though. I snap in T'Challa's direction across the fire, just a few feet away from my mat, "Leave my parents out of this."

T'Challa stares without blinking, his hands held up.

"I am sorry. I only asked so that—"

"They're dead. And that's all there is to it."

He nods, looking wounded. I huff and turn over on my mat.

"You were somewhat right the other day," he says quietly. "My walkabout is to prove myself. But not to my father. He was . . . murdered."

I lean up on my arms quick, my annoyance evaporating. That recognizable pain in his voice . . . my heart stretches out to him in an instant. "I'm . . . sorry."

T'Challa stares into the fire. "It happened right in front of me. Just over a year ago." His eyes flick up to mine. "Does it . . . get any easier?"

I sit up, wrapping my arms around my knees, wishing I didn't have so much experience with this.

"I've been an orphan since I was six. And the one thing I can tell you for sure is that it doesn't. It rearranges your heart, and it becomes like a shadow you can't feel all the time but you know is there. So you just learn to live with the pain."

T'Challa takes me in and frowns. "You have been on your own since you were that young?"

"Well, yes, but I wasn't alone. I had my brothers. They saved me."

"Yes. But at what cost?"

I start to glare at him when something hits me.

"Wait, with your father gone . . . doesn't that mean you are the king already? Doesn't that stuff gets passed down?" I sit up, my back straight. "Am I sitting here talking to a *king*?"

He shakes his head. "No. I'll have to challenge my uncle for my rightful place. But sometimes I wonder if I should, or if I will make a good king."

"You will. You're very . . ." I eye him in the moonlight, searching. ". . . practical."

He chuckles. "I will take that as a compliment."

"I mean, I don't really know you well, but you seem even-keeled, cool under pressure. Nothing ruffles you much. Sounds like all the things a good leader needs."

"Yeah. But I wonder if maybe Wakanda needs more."

He stares up at the stars, and I take a moment to appreciate the sharp line of his jaw, his perfectly smooth cocoa skin, his long black lashes.

My chest floods with warmth the longer I stare. Any girl would be lucky to have him.

Not a girl like me. I'm not that lucky.

"My last allowed question of the evening," T'Challa says without looking at me.

Caught up in the conversation, I didn't realize he'd been keeping count. I nearly chortle. Of course the perfect prince would keep count.

"Okay," I say, holding in a groan.

He smiles. "Today, before I told you my brilliant jokes, did you feel something as the weather shifted?"

I debate telling him a lie, but just shrug. "Yes."

This seems to excite him. His eyes light up as he leans toward me, just a little. "So, if you can sense it, then maybe you can control it in different ways."

I pause, not really sure what to make of this. Why is he so obsessed with me having these "powers" anyway? What good are powers for someone who doesn't know how to use them and doesn't want them to begin with?

But he'll probably never understand that. He grew up with power, he's used to its appeal.

I sigh, rolling back on my side. "Good night, T'Challa."

"Good night, Ororo," he quips.

TEN

T'Challa careens down a dirt road splitting through a dense forest, his lone headlight not giving us much to go by in the pitch-black night. We've been riding like this for most of the day, and my butt is starting to hurt. I've become used to bumpy potholes, sharp turns, and bugs slapping my face while holding my scarf to my head for dear life. But I don't complain. The longer he drives, the faster we'll be in Kenya, and the faster this whole nightmare will be over.

Orange streetlights glow up ahead, and we enter what seems to be a small town in the middle of nowhere, the paved streets practically empty in the late hour.

T'Challa slowly winds down the empty main road, toward a cluster of yellow brick buildings, passing carts, roaming cows, shanties, and political billboards. The humid air smells faintly of burning compost. He pulls in front of a garage next to various tut tut carts, the lights still on inside. Across the street, men dressed in baggy T-shirts and dusty jeans load a pickup truck with tires and scrap metal. They don't even look up at us, focused on their work, as if there's some ticking clock about to go off.

"Why are we stopping here?" I ask, nodding up the road. "We need to go in that direction, right?"

T'Challa takes a large gulp of water. "We need petrol. The next town is miles from here, and it's not safe for us to camp anytime soon."

"Why?" I ask. It's not like him to not want to take a break.

T'Challa glances around the empty road before looking over his shoulder at me. "These roads are known for kidnappings," he whispers, his voice calm but serious. "We should ride through the night this time."

I nod in silent understanding, and I climb off the bike, an immediate relief to my thighs.

"Where are we, exactly?" I lost track hours ago of where we could possibly be.

He checks his watch thingy. "We're far south of the capital. I'm trying to keep us off the main roads, as promised."

I rub my sore bum. "Thanks."

He nods toward the garage. "I'm going to see if they have any petrol or know where we can find some. Stay here. Scream if you need help."

I bow. "Yes, Your Highness."

He gives me a look but can't keep the smile off his face. I watch him walk over to the men and exchange a few words before they step inside.

Alone on the street, I survey the abandoned town, my knee bouncing. I adjust my headscarf before wiping my clammy hands on my pants. The rubber band quivers, as if someone came along and plucked at it, calling my attention. We should have at least done a loop before stopping. This place feels haunted, and I can't shake the feeling that someone is watching me. Waiting.

Could the Shadow King know I'm here, somehow? We've been careful, but what if he looked up different routes and is waiting inside the body of someone new? How would I even know it's him before it's too late?

I'm about to run inside after T'Challa when there's a soft, childlike sob.

What was that? I flinch, whipping my head around at the sound echoing from a narrow alley on the opposite side of the garage.

"Hello?" I call out. Maybe there's a kid in trouble—no kid should be out this late. I glance at the garage again.

Stay on the bike. Wait for T'Challa.

Somewhere outside, a car door slams shut. No, more like a truck door. Grown men shouting, drowning out whatever child I heard.

What's going on?

More angry shouts. I take one last look at the garage before I creep away from the bike, turn down the alley. My senses are screaming that this is a bad idea, but I can't just ignore a crying kid.

Keeping my steps light around the broken cement and glass, I maneuver farther down the dim, narrow alley. A dark green tented truck takes up most of the crumbling alley, its bright headlights shining into a dead end, where there are five men arguing in Arabic. Armed men in green uniforms, guns strapped over their shoulders. No kids.

But I could've sworn I heard cries. Am I imagining things? This is not the time to lose my senses.

I creep closer, keeping hidden behind the truck, and try to decipher their conversation. I pick up snippets. . . . Something about their next shipment, but of what?

A small brown hand reaches out of the truck bed and touches my shoulder. I jolt and it takes everything in me to keep from screaming.

What the hell?

Slowly, I pull the tarp back half an inch and freeze.

In the back of the truck are kiddies. Little boys. A dozen

chocolate faces with bright glassy eyes stare back at me through the bars of a tight metal cage better fitted for animals.

I gasp, hand flying to my mouth.

One boy lunges forward, gripping a bar, his face so close to mine, I can smell his soiled clothes. He mumbles desperate pleas in a language I don't speak.

"I'm sorry, I don't understand," I whisper, tears prickling my eyes as I test the cage door. Locked. I grip the giant padlock.

"Oh! Sista! Please help us," the boy says in stuttering English. "They are taking us away to be soldiers."

"They took us from home," another little boy cries softly beside him.

"Please, sista. Please," he begs, tears in his eyes. "I do not want to die."

My feet root me to the ground. I don't know what to do first—ask more questions or burst into tears. Soldiers? But they're babies. Some don't look older than five. Who would kidnap children?

I glance over my shoulder, wondering if I should run back and tell T'Challa. How would we go about freeing them?

Up front, the soldiers' argument becomes louder. One breaks from the circle, walking toward the truck.

Damn!

I put a finger up to my lips and slip away, then duck behind the large tire on the opposite side of the truck and sneak a glance.

A dark-skinned soldier strolls over to the cage, smacking his lips on a red apple. I duck lower as the boys scramble away from the cage door, eyes wide in horror.

"Hungry, eh?" he says in English, waving the half-eaten fruit in front of them. He snickers and tosses the core into the cage, like throwing scraps to scavengers. One boy picks it up cautiously, gripping it in his little hands.

"Disgusting little street rats," the man mutters, and I nearly break my nails on the tire.

I want to scream. I want to ram a foot into his thick neck. But I don't have the chance.

The truck's engine spurs to life, rattling the cage. The boys gasp, huddling tighter together. The soldier turns, yelling at the others as he walks back, leaving the boys alone.

If I'm going to save them, now is the time.

I hop on the back of the truck, letting the tarp fall around me, hiding us from the world.

"When I open this door, you need to run as fast as you can and hide," I whisper, slipping a needle out of my hijab. "Do not come out until dawn. Understand?"

The little boy explains to the others, and they nod in agreement.

I grip the padlock hanging on the cage door and dig my needle into the keyhole, feeling around for the latch in the low light. Sweat drips down my forehead as my stomach tightens.

"Focus," I scold myself. This is life or death.

A few quick twists and it clicks open. I take a deep breath, listening to the men argue, making sure they're distracted. We only have one shot at this.

I grip the cage door, planting my feet on the ground, keeping out of sight. Hot truck exhaust hits my legs, the cage shaking.

"Ready?"

The boys scurry to their feet, gathering closer to the door. It's a clear path back to the main street. If they run fast, under the cover of darkness, they may have a chance.

"Okay . . . ," I whisper. "Now!"

I swing the squeaky cage door open and the boys hop out of the truck and take off down the alley, toward the street, their little bare feet pattering away as I hang back.

"Hey!" one of the men shouts, then yells for the others.

Boots stomp in our direction. Hiding behind the truck, I put my foot out, tripping the first soldier, and a few go down like dominoes. I race for the street, praying T'Challa is ready to jump on the bike and book it. The boys have scattered, spreading out like water, running as hard as their feet can carry them toward different cross streets.

One trips, skidding face-first with a cry. I sprint, lifting him up just as a soldier makes it around the corner, his rifle up, pointed right at us.

"No!" I shout, throwing my body in front of the boy, my hands held out. Suddenly, my body jerks and a wave of . . . something rolls from my toes, up my legs, into my arms and into my palms.

A burst of wind explodes from my hands like a cannon, the air rippling, lifting the man off his feet, knocking him into the others like a bowling ball hitting pins. The gust twirls into itself, dust and leaves flying in a tiny tornado. My mouth drops.

Did I just . . .

Heart thumping against my chest, I spin around. The kid is still standing behind me, mouth ajar, staring at the tornado as it evaporates. He saw *everything.*

"Keep going!" I shout.

My voice jolts him out of a trance. He takes off, rounding a corner down another side street, and disappears along with the rest of the boys.

The men shout as they jump back onto their feet. I charge into one, scratching his face, swinging around to kick another. The boys just need more time to run.

Maybe I can use my hands again.

As the third soldier approaches, I thrust my hands out. Nothing. The man reaches me in three quick steps and slaps me across the face. My head snaps back and I grunt, bracing myself before I lunge at him again. He easily shoves me to the ground, his gun drawn.

My heart is a battering ram against my chest as I lift my hands, staring at the gun.

"Wait, I—"

T'Challa suddenly appears from my left and fly-kicks into the man's face, disarming him before charging at the next soldier. He takes out three men within seconds before he glances at me and comes to a stuttering stop.

A gun cocks next to my ear and my breath hitches.

"Stop or I'll kill her," a man hisses behind me in a thick accent.

T'Challa nods, not taking his eyes off me.

"Hands up! Don't move."

T'Challa does what he is told, giving me a hard stare. Slowly, he looks to my outstretched palms. A silent conversation passes between us.

He wants me to do that thing with my hands again. But I don't know how. Even as I fall to my knees and lace my fingers behind my head, I'm hoping that the light will just appear on its own like it did in Luxor.

But nothing happens.

The man grabs me by the hair, through my scarf. In an instant, I'm back in the great hall, with the Shadow King and the boys surrounding me, staring at my exposed hair. Panic surges and takes over as I let out a guttural cry.

"NO!" I scream. This time, I won't let him unmask me, I won't let him take my scarf.

"Get off me!" I flail, kicking and screaming, fighting an invisible monster. I can feel the blood tingling in my toes. All I need is a gust of wind, lightning, *anything*.

The butt of the gun hits the back of my skull, and I take one last look at T'Challa's distressed face before everything goes black.

X

My head is in T'Challa's lap as I come to.

"Are you okay?" T'Challa asks, staring down at me, his fingers grazing my cheek.

"Uhhh," I moan. I sit up and the bumpy world spins, my hands pinned in front of me. We're inside the cage on the truck bed. I peer out the flapping tarp into the night sky as we speed down a dirt road, thick trees on either side of us, the smell of the truck's exhaust nauseating.

"Why haven't they killed us yet?" I ask, my mouth dry.

"They are taking us to their camp," T'Challa says, his tone clipped.

We hit a hard bump and I knock into him, causing him to grunt. That's when I notice both his hands and feet are handcuffed. Faces inches apart, we lock eyes. He doesn't look away, doesn't blink, and my breath hitches.

We're in deep trouble.

I straighten, taking in our surroundings as the whipping air slides through the cage bars, tugging at my scarf.

"Who are they? Do they work for the government?"

He shakes his head. "No. Must be some sort of rogue group. The town is just a pickup point before their final destination."

My heart races as I gulp. "Do they know who you are? Who I am?"

He shakes his head. "I don't think so. But once we get there, they will learn. And then . . . who knows. They might try brokering a trade. But they know you're American. That might weigh more than the children you saved."

If they know who T'Challa is, it won't take long for them to figure out who I am. I pull at my restraints, shutting my eyes as I try to calm myself down. Just how far is the Shadow King's reach?

I roll my neck, head aching, and glance down at my handcuffs.

Handcuffs. Perfect.

I lean my head down toward T'Challa's lap. "Take the pin out of my hijab and give it to me."

Startled at first, T'Challa nods, fingering through my hair. The scarf falls around my shoulders and he gasps, eyes wide.

"Your hair," he mutters in shock.

"No time to explain," I say, grabbing the needle and bending my wrist to work on the handcuffs. I'm too focused on escaping to worry about his reaction. I flex and fish around the lock until I hear the light click of freedom.

"Where did you learn that?" he asks as I pocket the cuffs and begin working on the ones around his ankles.

Click.

I suck my teeth, grabbing his hands. "You ask way too many questions in times of crisis."

Click.

Rubbing his wrists, T'Challa rolls into a crouch, examining the truck bed. He yanks at a rope tying the tarp over the cage.

"Can you open that lock, too?" he asks, jutting his chin at the cage door.

I grab the lock and frown. "It's already open. These geniuses."

T'Challa winds the rope around his hand twice and tugs.

"We jump on three," he says, peering out into the dark.

Jump? From a moving truck?

Wind whistles around us, the truck careening deeper into the jungle.

T'Challa quickly wraps an arm around my waist, pulling me to his side. "Hold on."

"We're really doing this," I mumble, grabbing hold of his neck. He kicks the cage open and steps on the bumper, and we jump, swinging out and then around. T'Challa plants his feet and runs along the truck's side, yanking the tarp free and throwing it so it goes flying into the windshield, blinding the soldiers' view.

The driver lets out a cry and the truck swerves. And in that exact moment, my hold slips as I fall, screaming.

"Ororo!" T'Challa yells, riding the truck as if manning a sailboat on the Nile.

I tuck and hit the ground with a thud, rolling once, twice, before slamming something hard and coming to a stop. My head pops up just in time to see the truck crash head-on into a giant tree a few feet away. Dust and smoke plumes, the truck's lone working headlight breaking through the smog.

Silence. Stillness.

Oh Goddess . . . is anyone alive?

"T'Challa?" I utter as a slice of panic courses through me. What if he got caught on the rope? What if he's hurt?

I try to stand, but a shooting pain rips up my leg and I let out a whimper, feeling something wet on my pants. Blood?

The passenger door creaks open, thudding against the tree, leaves rustling. A man falls out with his rifle, hacking and coughing. He stumbles a few steps, crying for his friends, before he spots me on the ground. My heart stops. Mouth falling open, I watch the blood drip down his face from the gash above his eyes. His arm dangles out of its socket.

Run, my instincts scream. But I can't move.

Just as the man raises his gun, T'Challa sprints across the road, scoops me up off the ground, and slices into the tall reeds, running at breakneck speed, faster than any man I've ever seen, through the forest. Faster than the bullets flying after us as the soldier shouts curses at our backs, aimlessly firing into the dark. T'Challa keeps running, not stopping until we're deep in the forest, and hides us behind a thick tree trunk. He squeezes me so hard to his chest, I can feel his heart racing.

"Shh," he whispers, his muscles stiffening, standing so still he could blend into the woods like a chameleon. I slap a hand over my mouth, trying to stifle my ragged breathing.

The voices and gunfire seem so distant, snuffed out by the screaming insects and hooting birds around us. We wait for what feels like an eternity, barely breathing, frozen still, until there's nothing but the sounds of animals around us.

T'Challa peers out from behind the tree. With the coast clear, he slowly makes his way through the forest, keeping his eyes locked toward the way we came.

"Are you okay?" he asks, his voice steady, still cradling me in his arms as if I weighed nothing.

"Yes, I think so."

His grip tightens as he trudges through the forest, stepping over fallen branches and giant vines, and through thick bushes. He walks like this for a while, holding me, and I'm not sure why he hasn't put me down yet. Honestly, I don't want him to. The way he holds me makes my whole body tingle, his warmth intoxicating. Besides, why should I have a problem with a prince sweeping me off my feet?

But his face is stern, his brows furrowed, and he won't meet my eye.

"You're mad at me." I say it more as a statement than a question.

His lips purse. "What possessed you to do something so foolish? Throwing yourself in front of a gun. You could have been killed."

Typically, I would argue, tell him to watch his tone, but even I can be fair sometimes.

"I wasn't thinking," I admit, chin tucked to my chest. "I'm sorry."

He keeps walking as if I said nothing. Maybe he's not looking for an apology. Maybe he's looking for an explanation.

"They were making fun of those children. Starving them," I mumble. "I was once recruited like those kids. It saved my life.

But . . . things could have been different for me if I had gone another direction."

His expression softens. "Do you ever think of stopping? Starting over. Doing something more meaningful."

"And leave my family? The very ones who saved me?" I shake my head. "It just seems so . . . ungrateful." Ordinarily I would stop there, but after everything we've been through tonight, my guard feels slippery. "But . . . it doesn't mean I don't feel some guilt about what I do. I know it's not right."

He nods, eyes scanning the woods. "You have a good heart. You are a most loyal friend."

A compliment? Even after I almost got us killed?

"Uh, thanks."

"But it would be nice to have some sort of warning next time you decide to take on a group of soldiers on your own."

I let out a chuckle. "I'll do my best."

His lips curve into a smirk. He stops and finally looks down at me, brown eyes almost glowing, stars twinkling above him. My breath hitches, and I'm sure I still have a concussion from earlier, because I feel my resolve waning. He swallows, then glances up at a nearby tree.

"Um, do you think you can climb?"

I step onto the ground, my leg stinging but stable. Slowly, we maneuver up an acacia tree that has plenty of low limbs to scale. We sit on a branch high enough that the leaves and dangling vines, give us plenty of cover not to be spotted by anyone below.

"We will stay here until morning, when the coast is clear," T'Challa says. "Then we will walk back to town. It should only be a few kilometers."

Across from us, a monkey stares, unblinking. I don't blame him, since we're pretty much invading his home.

T'Challa balances himself, then reaches up to take off his

shirt and . . . whoa. Muscles. I felt them under his shirt, but seeing them again, this close, is a whole different story. I pick up my chin and somehow manage to find my tongue.

"Um, what are you doing?"

He spins around, straddling the thick branch to face me, and then tears off a piece of shirt.

"Let me see," he says, tapping my thigh.

I must have hit my head harder than I realized. Because my heart feels like it's lodged in my throat, and I suddenly have this wild worry that if he touches me, what little sense I have left will go out the window.

"Are you a doctor now, too?" I let out a nervous chuckle. "It's fine! I'll look at it later."

He huffs. "Do you want to risk infection and lose your leg?"

I blink, considering the options. "Well, when you put it that way."

I lift my leg with a wince, and he grabs my ankle, placing my foot in his lap.

"Hold still or we will fall."

I roll my eyes. "No pressure or anything."

I stiffen my grip on the branch bark. All businesslike, he rolls up my pant leg, his expression stern, as if he is about to perform surgery. I want to laugh, but any humor I feel dies down as his fingers slide up my calf. A shiver runs down my back, my arms shaking.

He meets my eyes. "Are you all right?"

Mortified by the way my skin is probably turning bright red, I nod wordlessly, and he continues.

T'Challa presses on the wound, and I hiss through my teeth.

"I do not believe you will need stitches," he says, focusing on the cut. "But we should wash this off as soon as possible."

I swallow, trying to distract myself, and glance up. The stars never looked this bright in Cairo, except maybe deep in the desert. We're so high, they seem so much closer now, like a dark blanket we could reach up and grab.

I've never really been in the forest like this before. It's unnerving—but, strangely, it's also somewhat comforting. Like I could live in this world. Like I belong here.

I glance back at the monkey, now gone. Where did he go? Does he know something we don't?

"Um, are we safe up here?"

"Yes," T'Challa says, tying the ripped piece of shirt around my wound.

"You sure no . . . giant cats, snakes, or spiders are going to eat us?"

He smirks. "Spiders do not eat people."

No comment on the other predators. I glance down and immediately regret it. We're at least ten stories up.

"What if I fall?" I cry, no longer feigning bravery. I am fully terrified now.

He hops up on his feet, stealthy and agile, then climbs over me, sitting with his back against the trunk as if plopping down on a comfy sofa.

"Come," he says, waving me over.

I scoot, leaning against his chest. He takes a nearby vine, ties it around our legs, and wraps his arms around my stomach like a seat belt.

"Just like on the bike," he says cheerfully. "Except now I hold on to you."

I gulp, fighting to ignore my thumping heart.

Calm down. He's only doing this to keep us from falling.

"Are you always this comfortable in the jungle?" I ask. His chest is warm against my back, and I try not to think about the fact that the only thing between me and his bare chest is my flimsy T-shirt.

I feel him shrug. "It is second nature to me. It is in my blood."

That I can understand. "I guess that's me in cities."

He grips me tighter. "I think it is time for my questions."

I snort. He can't possibly be serious. After the night we had, he still wants to dig into my personal business?

"I'm pretty positive you've exceeded your limit," I say. Then I sigh. "But since I'm alive because of you, I'll allow it."

I can feel his hand hovering behind my head, as if he wants to glide his fingers through my hair.

"Your hair is . . . white," he says, voice hushed in awe. "Why did you not tell me?"

The question doesn't seem investigatory. He sounds more hurt by my secret than anything else. In fact, until he asked, I almost forgot I didn't have a scarf on. Maybe because there's no one else around to stare at me like I'm some sort of circus act.

Thoughts of the boys' expressions run through my head, and I sigh. "It's . . . embarrassing."

T'Challa stays silent, as if considering this. He tightens his hold on me, fingers drumming against his knuckles, sending tiny shock waves down my belly. "Did something happen to you?"

I jerk back. "Huh?"

"Usually when one's hair is white, it means they are either old or something very traumatic happened."

I want to laugh. So much has happened in my life, that would almost make sense, but I shake my head. "I was born with it."

"So, you were born with your power as well, then?"

"*Power?* Ha! No, it's not power. I'm no superhero. It's just a silly curse. I'll be rid of it soon."

He is quiet for a moment. "Is that why you want to reach Kenya? You think the cure is there?"

My thoughts drift back to my dreams. To the strange old woman, her hair like mine, her voice in my ear. Her white eyes.

"*Something . . . is there.*"

Leaves rustle above us. Two more monkeys. T'Challa tightens his hold, breath tickling my neck.

"Well, I think it is beautiful," he says, delicately swiping my braid over my shoulder, fingers lingering on my collarbone. "But I can see why you would want to keep it covered. You would certainly give people something to talk about."

"It's distracting. Makes me the center of attention."

"And what is wrong with that?"

I roll my eyes. "Maybe you're used to that, my king. But that doesn't fly in my line of work."

"Your line of work, eh?"

I lightly elbow him in the gut, and he flinches.

"Eh, eh! Are you trying to kill us? Again?"

I stifle a laugh. "Sorry."

He sets himself right, mumbling under his breath.

"My hair runs in my family," I admit, finding it easier to talk to him without seeing his face. Something in my chest feels tender. I haven't talked about the origins of my hair with anyone in so long. Not even with Moche.

His next words come slowly. "So it is possible that . . . other things run in your family as well? What do you know about your people?"

A bird hoots above us, disturbed by our chatter. I lower my voice. "My mother didn't have a chance to tell me all I needed to know. But I remember some things."

"Like?"

I close my eyes, thinking back to that last day, in our living room, and can almost smell the incense burning on the bookshelf. "She told me that many of the women in our family had blue eyes and white hair. That they were a tribe of powerful women before they disappeared." As I say it out loud, I realize this almost sounds like a dream. My memories of Mommy are

141

the only things I have left of her. "I wish she'd told me their names, so I would at least have something to go by."

I can feel him nod. "Powerful women are not easily forgotten. They often stand out. I am sure someone knows."

I think of Daddy, how he always used to say he saw my mother from across the room as if a spotlight were on her. Even without white hair, she stood out in the crowd.

Stood out . . .

"That's it! That's how I'll find my people. I'll just go to the city and be myself. If anyone takes one look at me and my hair . . . I'll have to dust up a memory or something, right?" And if the Shadow King has men in Kenya, I'll deal with that problem then.

T'Challa grips my side, steadying me. "Yes. We should start by asking some of the elders. Maybe they can recall something or someone mentioned in passing."

"We?" I cough out.

"Well, yes. Unless you don't want me to help you on your search?"

My heart flutters at the thought of him wanting to stay with me, despite all he's seen.

"Uh, no. I mean, yeah, that would be cool. Thanks."

A comfortable silence settles between us as the insects take over the night. His chest rises and falls on my back, warm arms firm around me. I wonder if he can feel my heart pounding. It's almost deafening in my ears.

T'Challa takes a deep breath, arms squeezing a touch tighter. "It was good, what you did back there," he says softly. "For those children." He shifts closer, lips right by my ear as he murmurs, "You are a good person."

My throat closes. I think of that backpacker whose wallet I stole. I think of Moche and the boys at Farouk's mercy back home. All the people I've hurt—that henchman lying dead in that alley.

I can't believe someone like T'Challa could see any good in me. After all I have done.

It's because he hasn't really seen that side of you. Yet.

I lean my head back, letting the tension ease out of my shoulders.

"Good night, T'Challa."

He rests his cheek on top of my head, grinning. "Good night, Ororo."

ELEVEN

I wake up to a peach-pink sky, T'Challa dozing softly behind me, birds chirping their songs around us. It's peaceful up here, and in the morning light, not exactly the dangerous jungle it looked like at night. Cocooned in the warmth of T'Challa's arms, I snuggle into him and find myself wondering why it can't be this way all the time. Why I can't wake up every morning in his arms.

Because he's a prince. And you're nothing.

Something inside me aches a little. But it still doesn't stop me from enjoying these stolen moments. I can't even remember the last time I was hugged, truly, by anyone. Moche?

Maybe that day . . . with Mommy.

My vision blurs, the trees creep in like dark clouds, and I'm back under the rubble with bloody fingers. The plane's roar silences the birds.

Stop it!

I jolt up, quickly untying our vines. T'Challa stirs.

"What are you doing?" he moans, voice hoarse with sleep as I crawl away from him.

I just need space. I just need to . . .

It happens so fast. My hand slips on a patch of moss and I tumble off the branch, screaming.

"Ororo!" T'Challa shouts, his fingers just reaching my foot. But it's too late. Air whistles through my ears as I plummet, grasping for anything to hold on to, anything to stop my fall.

A burst of cold slips under my skin, my legs weightless, almost numb. The ground races toward me, and I wrap my arms around my head and squeeze my eyes shut, bracing for impact, bracing for my death.

But then suddenly . . . I stop.

Slowly, I unwrap myself and find that I'm merely a few feet from the ground, swaying the rest of the way like a drifting feather.

What the hell?

I twirl, arms flapping like a bird that just learned to fly. Soft wind whips under me, and I land in a bed of leaves. I stare up at the sky, stunned.

"Ororo!" T'Challa calls from somewhere above, the large branches and foliage blocking my view.

I'm alive. But how?

I scramble to my feet, look up at the tree with a shudder. The fall should have broken my neck. Yet it felt as if I fell into an invisible cloud and floated down.

Floated? That's impossible. The wind must have slowed my fall. But there *is* no wind.

Unless . . . unless. . . .

Branches shake above me as T'Challa slides down the vines. I yank leaves and snap twigs out of my hair, trying to collect myself as he rushes toward me.

"You okay?" he gasps, panting, eyes raking over me in search of the damage. He must not have seen me float.

Act normal.

"I'm fine!" I croak out, dusting myself off.

"Fine?" He looks at the tree, craning his neck up toward the high branch we were on, and then turns back to me.

No way can I tell him what really happened. It'll only make him more interested, when he should be focused on helping me rid myself of this thing.

"Yeah. The leaves broke my fall." I let out a weak laugh. "What a wake-up call, right?"

He glances up at our spot in the tree again, then back to the ground, doing his own calculations.

"The vines," I offer, sensing his doubt. "I got caught in them. They slowed me down."

He straightens with a raised eyebrow, not buying what I'm selling.

"Um, we should get going," I insist.

He nods, and I can tell this is not the end of the conversation. "We need to get back to the bike."

In all the commotion of my fall, I almost forgot we were being hunted. I spin around, scanning the trees.

"You sure that's such a good idea? What if they come looking for us there?"

"They won't come back to the town. Not after those children have escaped. They have probably moved camp."

I take another look around, not sold on the idea that the soldiers would give up so easily.

T'Challa offers his rolled-up, torn T-shirt. "For your hair."

I frown, trying not to stare at his bare chest. "What about you?"

"I will be fine," he says with a knowing chuckle, and places the shirt in my hands.

It smells like him, and I want to bury my face in the scent. I scold myself at the instinct.

You're being ridiculous. Get it together!

I manage to wrap my hair up in a bun and stuff it under the shirt. At the next village, I need to find a new scarf as soon as I can.

We trek through the forest with T'Challa leading the way,

giving me a perfect view of his back, muscles rippling as he pushes through vines and thick foliage.

"How is your leg?" he asks.

"Fine. Stings a little."

He nods with a yawn and glances back, giving me a tired smile.

"Didn't you get some sleep?" I ask.

He shrugs. "Not really. I only maybe dozed right before you untied us. I was keeping watch. It was kind of interesting."

"What do you mean, interesting?"

"A few animals came by. I did not want to wake and startle you. But they only looked . . . curious." He gives me a questioning look, a smile pulling at his lips. "Curious about you."

I think about the dogs following me around in Garbage City. The camels that bowed in Giza. Did they sense something . . . more about me? Even when I was younger?

For the first time, doubt nags at the back of my mind. What if this curse isn't new? What if this has been with me all along?

T'Challa walks backward to check my reaction, and I keep a straight face, despite my stomach dropping. I can't even begin considering it—that this could be my new reality, rather than temporary. That after trying to blend in my entire life, I'm more different than I could've ever imagined. A freak after all.

"What can I say?" I quip. "Animals love me."

"Hmm," he notes, turning back. "So it seems." He pauses, and when he speaks again, I can hear the smile in his voice. "You slept well."

I'm glad I'm behind him so he can't see me flush at the memory of his arms around me. I did sleep well. Better than I have in years. Didn't even have nightmares.

"But when we get back to town, we need to get you something to eat," T'Challa muses. "You are very light."

"What? No, I'm not!"

He laughs. "Tall, thin, and weightless. You are like an angry praying mantis with wild white hair."

My stomach drops to the ground, and I raise a hand automatically, protectively, to my hair as that childhood taunt creeps back in.

White jungle monkey.

"What did you just say?" I snarl, anger spiking.

T'Challa freezes, hearing the edge in my deepening voice.

"I . . . I mean . . . I didn't mean . . ." He backpedals. But it's too late.

He's making fun of me. Making fun of my hair.

But he said it was beautiful, another part of me whispers before my fury quickly shoves it aside, my blood boiling.

I'm just a joke to him . . . like I was to all the other kids.

"Did you just compare me to a damn *insect*?"

A bolt of lightning hits a nearby tree, and I shriek. We both jump back from the flying sparks that dig deep into the trunk, the bark splintering. The crack travels down the base of the tree, stopping at its roots.

We stand, gaping at the giant charred mark, waiting for the entire tree to fall. T'Challa slowly turns to me, and I've lost my tongue.

"I . . . I . . ."

His blank expression breaks and he roars with laughter. I mean, hands on his knees, buckled over. Has he gone mad?

I cross my arms, glaring. "I see nothing funny about this at all."

"I am sorry." He cackles, holding his abs. "But where was all that when we needed it yesterday?"

Shame creeps in. I wanted to help T'Challa, I wanted that weird light to pop out of my hands. But I couldn't do anything. And we almost died.

But the boy keeps laughing, holding his stomach, and I can't help it—I crack a smile. It feels like it's been so long since I've just laughed with someone else.

"Seems like you didn't really need me," I say, patting my eyes dry. "You handled those men all on your own."

He shoves through a thicket of bushes, leading the way. "I have trained in hand-to-hand combat since I was a child. You have good reflexes. With the proper training, you could really learn to defend yourself."

"Tuh. I did pretty well. Saved you back in Luxor."

"Yes. And you are still not sure how."

I wave him off. "I don't need all of that. I know how to fight, too."

He raises an eyebrow. "Really? You call what you did yesterday fighting?"

"Hey! I've taken down my brothers several times."

He stops to face me with a skeptical eye, a laugh on his lips. "What? What is it?"

"Attack me," he says, his arms crossed, chest puffed out.

I frown. "What? Now?"

"Yes. Right now. Give it your best shot. If you can."

Tuh. The boy doesn't know me well. I'm not one to skip out on a challenge. I roll my neck.

"Okay. Fine."

I've practiced sparring with Moche and the boys plenty, but never with a stranger. Unsure of how to start, I throw a fist and he dodges to the right.

I throw another and he dodges to the left, almost politely, but there's a small smirk on his face. Frustrated, I charge at him, but somehow he spins me around.

"Ugh!" I step back, trying to trip him, but he rounds me until my legs are in the air. I nearly land on my ass with a yelp before he catches me by the waist.

I stare at the prince, a grin on his face, fire in his eyes, and I promptly lose my breath.

"Go for the throat next time," he says, his voice low, before standing me upright. "You are tall and have a height advantage."

He raises my hand and curls my fingers into my palm. "Always wrap your thumb over your knuckle. Hold your fist tight and strong."

He places his hands on my hips again and corrects my posture.

"And you need to shift from your core, so as not to lose your balance . . ."

I'm no longer paying attention. Too distracted by his hands seamlessly moving over my body, the sweat dripping down his shoulders, the tingle in my chest whenever we connect.

"Everyone should know their own strengths," he continues. "If you were to use your powers . . ."

"I don't have powers!" I snap.

He holds his arms up in surrender.

"Okay, well, *if* you had powers, you would use them to strike first, to unnerve your opponent, aim to disarm their senses." He raises my hand again and pulls me closer until we're inches apart. "But if your opponent becomes too close . . . that is when you must strike."

Chin raised, I stare up into his eyes, my heart pounding. His smile slowly fades, body softening, but he doesn't look away, doesn't loosen his grip. And it almost feels as if he were about to tip forward into me. Right into my lips.

Or that's what I imagined would happen.

"Um, I can teach you more," he breathes. "If you would like."

I would like. Very much. But as I inhale his scent and come to my senses, I step back, clearing my throat.

What in the world am I doing? He and I are *not* going to happen. No need for favors outside of our arrangement. I need to stay focused on the task at hand, which is making it back to the bike before those soldiers find us.

"I'm good on my own, thanks," I mumble, fidgeting with my makeshift scarf. I turn away and nod in the opposite direction. "Um, it's this way."

He smirks. "How do you know?"

"I don't know," I groan, marching away. "I just . . . *know*."

"Just like you know the weather," he says, following. "You just happen to know which direction we should go. Have you been feeling this all along?"

I blink, stuttering to a stop.

He steps closer. "You have not looked at a map this entire journey. Yet somehow you always know exactly where we should be and have not been wrong once."

My mouth opens, but nothing comes out.

Because in truth, I somehow know we're on the right path, even while we trek through the jungle. The curse feels stronger, coursing and speeding through my body. Always humming in the background of my mind. A song only I can hear on repeat, driving me crazy.

And I can't wait to be rid it. Whatever it is.

X

Covered in sweat and dirt, we reach the outskirts of the town by early afternoon stopping at the first small market we see for water.

"Do you think the bike is still there?" I ask, breath ragged. I wash off my bloody leg, wincing through the stinging pain, and tear a fresh piece of T-shirt to wrap it. "What if someone stole it?"

T'Challa chugs down a bottle of water, sweat glistening off

his chest, and checks his bracelet. His eyes narrow as he studies the hologram that rises up.

"It is in the same spot . . . but there is someone with it."

Dread fills me. "The soldiers?"

T'Challa looks up at me, rubbing the back of his neck. "I am not sure."

We must get out of this town before the soldiers come back looking for us. And there's no way we can make it anywhere on foot and expect to live. We need the bike.

I roll my shoulders back and nod. "Well, we'll go together and see."

T'Challa opens his mouth to argue but seems to think better of it. "Okay."

The town is busier than last night, people going about their daily routines. But that still doesn't stop anyone from staring at the bare-chested boy and the girl with a T-shirt on her head walking through the streets. T'Challa's jaw clenches, his fists ready, bracing himself for a fight. Meanwhile, I'm tenser than I've ever been, checking the face of each person we pass. We're too exposed.

Anxiety pushes through each step we take, and my mind runs wildly through the possibilities of who might be waiting for us at the bike. Maybe it's not the soldiers. Maybe it's the Shadow King's men. That soldier who survived saw my hair. If he made it back to camp, he could have told someone. It wouldn't take long for word to spread. If it's them . . . it would all be over.

I glance up at the sky, then down at my sweaty palms.

Now would be a really good time for some of that lightning.

We take a side street, running behind the garage to keep the element of surprise. Then we peer around the corner, searching for the bike, and find it still parked in its same spot.

But no one is there.

T'Challa checks his beads as I scan the road, surrounding buildings, and passing tut tuts. Nothing seems out of the ordinary. But when dealing with the Shadow King, anything is possible.

"I don't understand," T'Challa mumbles. "Wait here."

I grip his wrist. "No! You could be walking into a trap."

"Just wait," he says, leaving no room for argument. "Watch my back."

I hold my breath as he creeps over to the bike. He circles it once, stops short, staring at something on the other side of it that I can't see. He looks up and calls me over.

A little boy sits beside the bike, staring up with frightened eyes and dry lips.

The boy from the cage.

I gasp, dropping to the ground, offering him water. "What are you doing here? In broad daylight!"

His eyes fill with tears. "I did not know where to go. I watched them take you and was scared."

"Why didn't you go home like I told you?"

The boy hesitates, wiping his face clean. "I do not think they want me there."

I glance up at T'Challa, his eyebrows pinched with determination.

"Don't want you," T'Challa echoes, his voice low. "What is your name?"

"Ameen," the boy mumbles.

"And where is home, Ameen?"

He hesitates, then tells us about a small village several kilometers outside of the town. I glance at the sun. Time is slipping through my fingers. We've lost over a day's travel time, but we can't just abandon the boy.

Once I buy a new hijab and T'Challa buys a black tunic, we clean my wound again and set off. Ameen rides between us on the bike as we head east, away from the setting sun. T'Challa remains stoic on the journey while I'm busy wondering about the tiny boy between us. What happened to this poor child that he feels his own people don't want him? His eyes are closed as he nuzzles into T'Challa's back.

He reminds me so much of the kiddies back in Cairo.

My stomach churns at the thought of everyone back home. What if no one is helping them find food? What if the Shadow King hurts the young ones to get to me? Would he be so cruel?

Ameen's desert village is small. So small that almost everyone steps out of their tiny homes that form a small U-shape when they hear our bike pull up in front of a white stone house. I adjust my new hijab, the curious stares making me fidget.

A thin woman in a deep-blue chador steps outside, carrying a basket, her wheat-brown skin glowing. But when she sees Ameen, she almost goes white, her body turning to stone.

It's clear all the villagers recognize Ameen, but this isn't the homecoming I'd expect it to be. They seem almost wary of him. I clench my jaw.

Is this how it's going to be for me when I go back to Cairo?

T'Challa scans the crowd with a raised eyebrow. "Wait here," he whispers to me.

Ameen hops off the bike, biting his thumbnail. He glances up at me.

"Thank you," he says. "For saving me."

In that moment, all I want to do is hug him. To press him into my stomach and never let him go. To tell him it's going to be okay. But with so many eyes on us, I grip the bike and give him a nod as T'Challa walks him over to the woman.

They talk in hushed voices, their conversation escalating. She doesn't speak English, like Ameen does, but she manages to keep saying *no*. A universal language.

The woman shakes her head with a stone-cold expression. Denying her son.

Ameen looks stricken. It's too gut-wrenching to bear.

I jump off the bike and stalk toward the family, skin on fire.

"What's going on?" I snap.

T'Challa hesitates. "Apparently, there was an arrangement with the soldiers. She is saying that we should not have brought him back."

Immediately, I see red. Of all the terrible things I've witnessed, this by far tops them all. She sold her son, a kid, to those disgusting madmen.

"*What did you do?*" I shout at the woman, blood sizzling. "How could you just give your son away? How? Do you know what they do to children?"

"Ororo, calm down," T'Challa warns.

"Don't tell me to calm down!" I hiss. "She's a monster!"

"She didn't have a choice!"

I glance down at Ameen, choking back a sob. So this is what he meant by not being wanted.

A sharp breeze threads around us, so quick I almost lose my footing. The woman shakes her head, tears in her eyes.

"He was all alone," I bark, not caring if she doesn't understand. "In the streets. Scared. He could have been killed. Starved! Abused! Do you have any idea what that's like? To be all alone!"

Shadows dance across the sand. The sky grows darker, but I can only see the woman in front of me, Ameen cowering from his own family. The woman looks up, horror in her eyes.

"Ororo, please," T'Challa begs, a hand on my shoulder, pulling me back.

"Don't touch me!" I snap, slapping him away.

T'Challa's eyes widen. He takes a staggering step back. "Ororo, your eyes!"

"What?"

"Your eyes!"

I whip around to the crowd. The woman takes one look at my face and lets out a guttural scream. The rest of the villagers back away and scatter, shouting.

I freeze, immediately transported back to my own scream. Back in the bathroom at the Villa. When I stared into the mirror to see that my blue eyes were gone.

This time, others can see the white fog.

I snap my eyes shut, grabbing hold of my hijab.

"T'Challa," I whimper, waving a hand about. He grabs hold and pulls me back to the bike, helping me on.

"You have to calm down," he says as I feel the first drop. Then another. Rain comes down slow, a soft trickle of mist.

The once-hectic voices surrounding us grow quiet, almost silent.

"It isn't real, it isn't real," I cry out, shaking my head.

"It is real, Ororo," T'Challa says, his voice hard. "And you are doing this."

"I'm not," I sob, trying to deny it. But the water feels so pure against my skin. So cool and healing. I almost want to drown in it.

T'Challa jumps on the bike, and I press my face into his back, squeezing hold of his stomach.

"Wait, Ororo. Look!"

I open one eye to peek. Rain pours down from the sky . . . but only in the spot above us, around the bike. I raise my head to get a better look and see the sun shining in the distance. The rest of the desert remains bone-dry.

And the villagers are scrambling, grabbing buckets, bowls . . . all smiling as they collect the water. A small chant rings out, people singing and dancing.

Some of them reach out to me, saying words I don't understand, but their gratitude is clear.

Ameen's mother stares at me with new eyes, her expression unreadable. Then, slowly, she looks at her son, still cowering from her. She bends toward him, arms outstretched.

A moment passes before Ameen runs to her, sobbing.

I blink slowly, stunned, my body going limp.

T'Challa revs the bike and pulls off, leaving the rain cloud behind.

X

There is a dull pain in my chest. The longer we ride, the heavier it weighs on me. T'Challa speeds down the road, his back tense, not turning once to check on me. We haven't uttered a word to each other since leaving Ameen's town.

Just after sunset, T'Challa pulls off the road, stopping in a small clearing surrounded by a scattering of desert gum trees and prickly bushes, mountains far in the distance. As night falls, we set up camp in silence. No food tonight—we didn't have a chance to stop at any local villages.

T'Challa pokes at the small fire. My mind races as the quiet between us becomes deafening. He hasn't looked at me once. I fear his reaction and curiosity in equal measure.

The white hair, the strange eyes, the sudden manic clouds . . . this *has* to be too much for him now. He would be mad to stay with me. I wouldn't, if I were him. He'll probably be gone by the time I wake up. And by morning, word of a miraculous rainstorm will make its way to the Shadow King.

I'm doing a horrible job of keeping a low profile. I'm practically leaving a road map for him to follow.

I sit opposite T'Challa, combing through the tangles of my

hair with my fingers. I've only ever done this freely in front of Moche. That's how comfortable I've become with T'Challa. And the thought of him leaving me alone makes my heart ache.

I never asked for a companion, but now that he's been with me so long, it's hard for me to imagine traveling without him. The loneliness will devour me.

"I'm sorry I yelled at you," I whisper to the fire. "You were only trying to help."

He takes a deep breath, rubbing his face. "We need to talk about the rain."

I wince. "Can we please talk about anything but that?"

"There is no denying it," he says. He looks up, and his face is almost stern, but his eyes burn bright. "You can control the weather! Do you know how miraculous that is?"

I puff out air and braid my hair into a long ponytail. "It's . . . something."

"If I could just get you back to our labs in Wakanda to do testing, to further understand your genetic makeup. . . ."

"I'm not a science experiment!" I snap.

T'Challa leans back, his face going slack. "That is not what I am implying at all."

"But that's what you want to do, right? Poke at me like I'm some kind of freak."

He shifts his jaw, eyes narrowing.

"So that is it? It is not this power that frightens you. You are worried about what others may think of you."

He snatches the words out of my head so fast it gives me an instant headache. He jumps up and stands over me.

"Do you have any idea how extraordinary you are? The things you can do . . . You cannot just ignore this!"

"Tuh! Watch me," I grumble, turning over on my mat. "Good night, T'Challa."

T'Challa throws up his hands.

"Fine," he grunts, stomping back to his mat. "Good night, Ororo."

The crackle of the fire sizzles between us. Everything is spinning out of control. The whole point of this trip was to find a cure so I can go back home. Not to fight kidnappers or be shot at. Not to make it rain in the middle of the desert.

I made it rain. . . .

"Ugh," I grumble, slipping my shoes back on.

"Where are you going?" he asks, annoyed. As if he has the right to be.

"To the bathroom. Are you going to watch?"

He purses his lips as I stomp off, my skin prickling. I don't want to admit it, but I'm unnerved by our fight. Even if it isn't really a fight—I know I'm just denying what's right in front of me. But I can't help it.

I just need some space. Away from him and his annoying insistence.

Why can't he just leave this alone? Isn't it obvious this is the last thing that I want? I'm already so different from my brothers—a girl, an American with white hair—I don't need to add anything else to the list.

I'm just a few yards away from the orange light of the campfire when that pressure starts to build again, a breeze kicking my hair off my shoulders.

"No! Stop it!" I tell the wind, as if it will listen to me.

Wait. . . . Is that even possible?

My thoughts churn. Slowly, I extend my hand toward the lingering breeze and stare. Just stare. Because I don't know what else to do. All these things keep happening when I least expect them, until there's that tightness in my chest, that aching of the rubber band around my belly.

I shift, finding that the tightness is strongest when I am facing south. I close my eyes for a moment, sinking into that feeling. Pressure lumps in my throat, and I let out a gasp.

A puff of breeze blows through the trees, short but precise. *No way . . .*

I lower my hand, letting the dark and heat swallow me. Tears threaten to bubble over, and my vision blurs. What can I do? How can I turn back time? Back to when I was in full control of myself, when I was safe?

Were you ever really safe in Garbage City, though?

Deep down, I've always known the way we lived wasn't legit. But it's hard to dig yourself out of a hole once you're in it. You only end up burying yourself further. Always walking on eggshells, living life on the edge of a sharp knife waiting to cut me open. Every score a risk, every building a potential tomb.

When have I ever felt safe?

I glance back at camp, thinking of T'Challa's arms. And I walk back.

"T'Challa?" I whisper as I approach.

"Yes," he answers dryly, keeping his back to me.

"Um," I say as my voice dies in my throat. *He's still here,* I tell myself. Even after everything we've been through. *He isn't gone yet.* I try to slow the beating of my heart. "Can you show me those fight moves you were talking about again?"

He glances over his shoulder, shock apparent. "Yes. Of course, yes."

He scrambles up to face me as I shrug out of Moche's jacket. He stares at my face for a long moment, but I refuse to meet his gaze. I swallow, rubbing at my eyes with my palms.

"You were clearly taught tactics to escape," he starts. "But you should also know how to defend yourself. You may not always have the space, or know where to run. You may have to stand your ground."

He steps closer and holds my hand up.

"Strike with the heel of your palm," he says, pointing. "Don't give them a chance to break your fingers. Try an elbow strike. You want to get your attacker away from you. You need distance, the upper hand to use your powers. . . ."

"T'Challa," I warn.

"Too close and they can take advantage of you," he continues as if I said nothing. "Avoid the chest, that won't give you the maximum impact you need. Stabilize your center."

He stands firm, knees bent, and I mirror his position. "Root your feet. And hit."

I throw a quick jab toward his jaw, and he blocks it easily.

"Good. Again."

TWELVE

T'Challa doesn't leave, after all, and he doesn't ask about my "powers" again. We cross into Ethiopia, continuing to make our way, staying off main roads, stopping each night to camp and practice fighting techniques.

"Now go for the neck!"

Adrenaline surging, I swing my leg at T'Challa's head, and he ducks with a grin.

"Right. Now left elbow," he orders.

I spin, jabbing my left elbow toward his nose, and he blocks me. I try the other elbow but pitch forward and fall into him.

"AH!"

T'Challa catches me and lets out a joyful laugh. "Good! That is good. You are getting the hang of it!"

I grumble. "If you think falling on your butt is a good sign, then I have a variety of pyramids to sell you back in Cairo."

When we're not training, each night we trade childhood stories. My childhood and his are polar opposites. He tells me all about the history of Wakanda, showing me videos and pictures on his bracelet thingy, all holograms of sleek buildings, cutting-edge technology I couldn't even dream of. It feels like I have to pick my jaw up off the floor each time he shows me something new. Hard to believe such a magical place even exists.

"How do you keep all of this secret from the rest of the world?" I asked him one night, but he just gave a mysterious smile.

"We have our ways," he said teasingly.

It is exactly what I need. A distraction from what is happening to me. If I don't pay attention to it, it all just goes away.

But the farther we travel, the more the rubber band pulls at me. And with each night, it feels stronger than it did before.

X

Somewhere past Addis Ababa, T'Challa pulls over on the side of the highway, and checks his map.

"Why are you stopping?" I ask.

"There's a lake not too far from here," he says, and looks over his shoulder. "Let us camp there tonight."

I'm used to T'Challa suggesting spots off the road, hidden deep where no one can see us. A lake seems like we'd be too exposed. But then he pulls up and the sight of it takes my breath away. Crisp, dark blue waters lap at the sandy bank, circled by tall grass and boulders. The sunset is just turning the sky a dusky pink, and the clouds cast purple shadows over a beautiful view of the surrounding mountain peaks in the distance.

"It's beautiful," I breathe. "Do you think other kings who did walkabouts came to this very lake as well? Are you following in their exact footsteps?"

"I do not know," he mumbles, taking our packs off the back of the bike. "I will not know what others did until I become king."

As the sun heads home for the evening, we set up camp and practice near the edge of the lake. It is a different type of hot out here. Egypt can blaze, but the humidity in this part of Ethiopia makes it feel like the heat is frying every organ I have. Even in the pitch-black night, my clothes stick to me like a second skin.

"So, let me get this straight," I say after we finish our dinner of fresh catfish plucked right out of the water. "Once you take this special herb after you win the challenge day, you'll officially be the Black Panther and you'll be superhuman . . . like me?"

"Well," he says slowly, "not exactly like you." He gazes into my eyes. "There is . . . no one like you, Ororo."

Heat rushes to my face. He glances down at my lips, and I feel them part. In this moment, all I want is to lean into him and—

Stop it, Ro!

I blink, reeling back, wrenching away from T'Challa's eyes. "Oh! Wow! Look at that moon," I cough out, needing a distraction. "Isn't it something?"

He follows my gaze to the half-moon blazing bright in the sky. Only a couple weeks left before the worm moon, whatever that is.

He smiles. "We have a space program in Wakanda. I'd like to take you to the moon. Someday."

Me on the moon. I know he is serious, but even the idea sounds impossible. "Ha! What don't you have in Wakanda?"

He thinks for a moment and snaps his fingers. "White people."

I cackle. "Sounds amazing!"

His eyes rake over mine and I gulp, aimlessly playing with the rocky sand. There's an electric charge in the air tonight, and it takes everything in me to dodge it like the plague.

"Hey, why is Wakanda so secretive?"

T'Challa reels back. "What do you mean?"

"I mean, you have, literally, everything. But you just keep it all for yourselves. You don't share your knowledge and fancy toys with the rest of the world."

He frowns. "It is . . . complicated."

I raise an eyebrow. "You know what else is complicated?

Starvation. Homelessness. Dealing with white people. All very complicated."

His eyes shift away, staring out at the water.

"Would you care to go for a swim?" he asks.

The word *swim* makes my thoughts cloud with fantasies of us twirling in the water together like mermaids. I steel my nerves and put on my game face.

No big deal. It's just water. I can handle that.

But my skin feels like it is on fire.

"Yes! Yes, I would." I jump up and run down to the water.

"Ororo, wait!" he calls behind me.

No. I can't wait. I need to put some distance between us.

I shed my flats and pants, and cannonball into the lake in my T-shirt with a giant splash. The water is heaven on my skin and scalp, hair flowing freely, but as I come up for air . . .

"Ugh!" I cough, cringing at the net of slimy moss and reeds covering me like a prickly blanket. Little gray fish swim by my legs, angered by the disturbance.

T'Challa strolls down to the shore, hands in his pockets, a smirk on his lips as I pluck leaves that are tangled in my hair like a silly crown.

"This is the first body of water we've seen since the ferry," I say as an excuse, wiping my face clean. "I needed a refreshing dip."

He shrugs. "I am just surprised that you would jump into a lake with crocodiles."

My jaw hits the water. "What? Where?"

I spin around, searching the dark, unsure of how or where to move.

"Do not worry. They will not bother us if we do not bother them."

"Right, don't worry about hungry crocodiles waiting to make me their dinner." I turn to him. "Does *anything* scare you?"

He pretends to think. "Hmm . . . not really."

"That's a lie."

"We shall see," he says. He locks eyes with me, then proceeds to take off his shirt.

And . . . there are his muscles again. I turn my back to keep him from seeing my reaction. This is ridiculous. I have no time to be caught up in silly fantasies about a prince. It's not like anything could ever happen between us.

Suddenly, he calls out something, then jumps into the water, letting a giant wave splash me.

"Ah!" I scream.

"I was just following your lead," he says, a laugh on his lips.

I shove water in his direction and can't help laughing. "I bet!"

Our laughter dies down to a silence, the water smoothing out like a pane of glass. We wade around each other slowly, two passing ships, as if we instinctively know if we drift too close, we'd light the lake on fire. But the sight of T'Challa's wet muscles as he dives under . . . whatever I feel stirring up, I have to fight hard to push back down.

He floats closer, long wet lashes glistening, determination in his eyes, and my heart beats faster. My toes grip hold of the rocks on the lake floor and I swim away, too afraid of what I may do with him too close.

X

Back on the beach, T'Challa enjoys a marula plum while I go toe to toe with my hair. I should have known jumping into a murky lake would be my end. Not only is my hair drying into a tangled heap, but it is also filled with random elements from the lake. I would rather the crocodiles have their way with me.

"Ugh," I groan, untangling another blade of grass that's tried to braid itself into my hair.

T'Challa chuckles, wringing his pants dry. "You wanted to swim."

I shoot him a murderous look. "Well, don't just sit there. Help me!"

T'Challa's face falls for a moment. But he clears his throat, collects himself, and jumps up to sit behind me. "What do you need me to do?"

"Take anything out of my hair that doesn't belong there. It shouldn't be hard to find."

His jittery hands touch the ends of my strands, and I feel a small yank.

"Ouch. Gentle!"

"Sorry," he mumbles, a nervous quiver in his voice. Then, slowly, he combs through my hair with deft fingers.

We're quiet as we work, enjoying the balmy night air and the soothing sounds of the lapping lake. Sitting this way reminds me of the tree in Sudan. He played with my hair then, too.

He gently grazes my scalp and I still, breath hitching. I close my eyes and lean into him.

T'Challa pulls out a piece of trapped bark and chuckles.

"Girls and their hair," he muses with a tongue click. "My sister hates having her hair done, too. I wonder what she would say about yours."

I freeze. "You have a sister?"

"Yes. Shuri. I have witnessed her with a braider. It is like watching someone suffer through surgery wide awake."

I cackle. "What is she like?"

"Ah, Shuri is the smartest person I know. She is also very stubborn and annoying." He is silent for a moment, fingers combing gently through my hair. "I felt bad for leaving her. The last few years have been hard. She misses Baba as much as I do. We are just grieving in different ways."

The sadness in his voice makes me turn to face him. This

closeness feels different from the bike. That is more perfunctory. This way, I can really see the depths of his eyes, the emotions swimming behind them.

"And how are you grieving?"

He fakes a smile. "I am . . . riding around Africa on an old bike."

The moon shines down on his rich skin, and I can't resist asking something I would never in a million years want someone to ask me.

"What happened to your father?"

T'Challa's shoulders slump, as if he was waiting for this moment.

"Baba was considering making our existence known to the world," he starts. "But some dignitaries came to Wakanda, wanting access to our vibranium, which is the most powerful energy-absorbing metal on this planet, for their own weapons." His eyes shift away, as if he can't bear looking at me when he says what's next. "When Baba refused, a man named Klaw opened fire on us. Baba did as best he could in the fight. I tried to help, but Klaw turned on me, and Baba jumped between us. He died saving me."

I move closer to him. "T'Challa. I'm so sorry."

He nods, but still can't meet my eyes. "I managed to use their weapons against them," he continues. "But I was only able to shoot off Klaw's arm before they escaped. We searched everywhere, but they had disappeared." His voice hardens. "I wanted to kill him. I wanted revenge. So I have been hoping . . . that on my journey . . ."

"That you happen to bump into the man who murdered your father."

He sighs. "Yes. The thought of finding him consumes me every day." His hands roll into fists, digging hard into the sand.

I pull my legs up to my chest, wrapping my arms around myself tight. I can't picture T'Challa having a violent bone in his body. But if I had someone to blame for my parents' death, we would be one and the same.

"But I still haven't found him," he utters. "So if I could not save Baba or avenge him, do I even deserve to be king?"

My head pops up. "Are you kidding? T'Challa, I see you every morning training for the challenge. And the way you talk about Wakanda . . . no one could question your love and loyalty. You deserve to be king! And you'll be so good at it." I put a hand on his arm. "What happened to your father, it wasn't your fault."

He gazes at the water over my shoulder.

"I thought I would have more time with him," he mumbles. "There is so much I have left to learn. I know I will see him again, in the Ancestral Plane. But I worry about what he will say about how I have led his people." His eyes shine; he is no longer even speaking to me. "What if I mess this all up? How will I ever live up to his legacy?"

I touch his knee. "You won't. You'll make your own legacy. That's what kings do. Do you know how many pharaohs ruled Egypt and completely changed the ways of their predecessors? King Akhenaten, who married Nefertiti, literally changed their art and religion. You can do things *your* way. Think of all the amazing changes you can make!"

He twists his lips. "We considered opening the doors once before. And then we lost Baba. But after all that I have seen in so many countries, it is hard to imagine us staying the same. I wonder what is best for Wakanda." He looks at me, but it's almost as if he's looking past me, to something beyond. "Should we continue to live in secret or . . . help the world?"

I cock my head to the side. "I thought you weren't scared of anything?"

T'Challa opens his mouth to reply and lets out a laugh instead. "Has anyone ever told you that you are quite wise?"

"It's often implied." I beam. "T'Challa, your father wanted the best for you and your people. So I have no doubt he would be proud of you, regardless. He probably believed in you before you were born."

He sighs. "Baba saw so much more in me than I saw in myself."

"Parents tend to do that," I quip.

"Is that what your parents did?"

The wind knocks right out of me, and I shift away from him.

He blinks in shock, leaning forward, as if to catch me, arms resting on my knees. "Oh. I am sorry. I did not mean to . . ."

"It's okay," I mumble.

We grow silent, letting the bugs and night noises do the talking, but his arms don't move away from me. I don't know why I can't talk about my family. It's like a block within me. Like the mention of their names and what happened to me would steal the memories, which is all I have left of them.

"I will say . . . ," T'Challa starts, his voice low, and I suddenly realize how close we've moved toward each other's faces. "Instead of running into Klaw . . . I ran into you. And I have not thought about revenge as much." He bumps his arm into mine, a small smile on his face. "It is very easy to talk to you, Ororo."

I smile up at him, trying to ignore the butterflies in my tummy, looking down at our intertwined legs. I scramble to free myself. How on earth did that happen?

"Um," I say, backing away. "Good night, T'Challa."

T'Challa hesitates, then says, "Good night, Ororo."

I plop down on my mat and roll into a ball, trying not to feel guilty for holding back when he has told me so much.

X

170

We next stop for petrol at a settlement in a valley just a few kilometers outside of Hawassa. There's a scattering of circular homes made of stone with thatched roofs, and one red dirt road dividing the little town in two. We're surrounded by lush mountains—twin peaks in the distance—and flat farmland.

T'Challa argues in Amharic with a group of men as I sip some water under a plastic tarp held up by sticks, hiding us from the violent sun. Little children ride by on rusty red bicycles, others playing hand games, while their mothers, heads covered with white netela cloth, work in the market and watch on. I'm mesmerized by their smooth dark skin and joyful laughs. I never learned how to ride a bike or play such games. I almost start to feel sorry for myself until I think about all the fun I've had competing with the Moche and the boys. Even if it was for my survival.

But Moche would have loved to try riding one of those things. I'd even ride behind him.

T'Challa scowls while walking away from the other villagers, cracking his knuckles into his palm.

"Bad news?" I ask as he approaches, offering him water.

He stands in front of me, releasing a frustrated breath, and I almost want to laugh at his pouting. Poor prince can't get what he wants when he wants it.

"The nearest petrol station is eighty kilometers out," he states, sweeping his arm down the road. "We'll never make it. They are waiting for 'someone' to bring back a can of gas from the next town over."

I click my tongue. "So. We wait?"

"Either that or we hitch a ride to the nearest city."

I shake my head. "No cities. Not until we reach Nairobi."

He scans the market, considering. "I agree. But I am not sure how long we will have to wait."

T'Challa plops on the ground beside me. We watch the

villagers and merchants trade goods and bicker over prices. It almost feels like the souks back home. I tap my thigh out of habit, making sure my wallet is still nearby.

"I'm running out of money," I mumble, really to myself. Without scoring another wallet, I'm not sure how long I'll make it in Kenya.

T'Challa takes a long chug of water, gasping. "So am I."

I glare at him with pursed lips. "How is that possible . . . my *king?*"

T'Challa rolls his eyes. "As I have said, I wanted my walk-about to be authentic. We could always stay here for a while and find work."

"Work?" I say in mock astonishment, hand to my throat.

"I found work along the way," he says, his chin tipped upward. "Cleaning floors, planting seeds, cutting timber. In Nigeria, I was a waiter at a hotel restaurant. I did not last very long."

I chuckle, crossing my legs. "Bet those people would piss themselves knowing they were being served by a prince."

He smiles proudly to himself.

"I even worked on a boat, as a fisherman, like my father once did. They let me off at the nearest docks after I became seasick. I told myself that I must remember to ask Baba in the Ancestral Plane why he agreed to such madness." T'Challa's warm chocolate eyes crinkle as he looks off in the distance.

I wonder if the girls in Wakanda notice the specks of amber that glint in them when he smiles. Or the way the muscles in his shoulders soften when he talks about his Baba.

Something nags at my memory, and it occurs to me that I've heard of that place before. Astral Plane. It was what the professor said right before he . . .

My body jolts and I whip around to T'Challa. "What is the Astral Plane?"

Startled, he turns to me before letting out a light laugh. "What?"

"The Astral Plane," I spit out, my thoughts moving faster than my words will allow. "You said you will 'go' there. What is it? Where is it?"

T'Challa waves a hand, correcting me.

"No, no. I said the *Ancestral* Plane. But it is a part of the Astral Plane. How do you know—"

"But what *is* it?"

Confused, he fumbles through an answer. "The Ancestral Plane is where our ancestors' souls are at rest."

"And it's a part of the Astral Plane. What do you know about it?"

T'Challa stares at the ground, hesitating.

"The Astral Plane is an alternate mirror dimension," he says slowly, and I can tell he's trying his best to articulate it in layman's terms. "It's accessible by sorcerers or powerful psychic beings, where it is said their souls can take different shapes. The world is fluid, boundless, even."

Psychic beings. Is that what the professor is? He was able to read my thoughts, talk to me without moving his mouth. But the Shadow King could, as well. I roll onto my knees, eager to know more.

"And you can go there?"

T'Challa shakes his head. "Only one who takes the herb and performs the ritual can visit the Ancestral Plane. Sorcerers can use their powers to gain access to the entire dimension."

"But how does it all work?"

He thinks for a moment before picking up a stick and drawing a sketch in the red dirt.

"You see, your soul is separated from your earthly physical form and transported there." He pauses to regard my face. "Ororo, where is this all coming from?"

Do I tell him about the Shadow King? What would he do?

Knowing T'Challa, he might try to face him. He could be hurt. Or worse, he might succeed, and I'd abandon my mission to rid myself of this curse. No, it's better to keep him in the dark. I'm not even sure what *I'm* dealing with. No way am I going to let T'Challa get involved with the Shadow King.

I roll back my shoulders. "I'm just . . . interested. I read something about it in a book. It's . . . fascinating, no?" It sounds unconvincing even to my ears, but I meet his gaze coolly.

T'Challa stares as if he can see right through me, and I have to force myself not to fidget. But, as always, he doesn't pry or poke further.

A donkey dragging a cart of palms stops in front of us and lets out an eager *hee-haw* in my ear. I reel back as T'Challa giggles.

"I agree, my good man," he says, patting the donkey on its side. "She is being too serious."

The roar of a beaten truck dusts up the red dirt road, pulling up to the bike. The men on the other side of the road start shouting, waving at T'Challa and pointing at the truck. The petrol ended up taking no time at all.

T'Challa jumps to his feet and I follow, grabbing his arm to hold him still. If he knows things about the Astral Plane, I need to learn as much as I can so I'll know how to fight the Shadow King if it comes to that.

"Can your ancestors leave the plane and come back to Earth?"

He shrugs. "It is improbable. But not impossible."

"Say more."

T'Challa crosses his arms, staring down at me. But he relents.

"Once they are of the plane, they are merely spirits. If they were to come back to Earth, they would need a body to inhabit. But in order for that to happen, one first would have to find an opening, a portal, which is like finding a very small needle in a vast universe. Then that opening would only last for a brief stretch of time. Minutes, a couple of days, maybe weeks, depending on the moon it serves."

It must be the worm moon! That's why Farouk kept mentioning it. The portal will close next month. But there's still the matter of why he wants *me* on his side by then. He can move through dimensions; how can I compete with that?

"What happens when the portal closes?" I ask, failing to keep the eagerness out of my voice.

"Well, if the spirit does not find a body to inhabit before the portal closes, it will cease to exist entirely."

I gulp. "And if someone were to . . . die there, in the plane . . ."

"No one can truly die there. They are merely stranded for the rest of eternity."

A chill runs down my arms.

So that's it. The Shadow King came back through a portal and has the power of possession. But his reach is long; he can live inside anyone.

"How do you know all this?" I ask, breathless.

T'Challa's eyes shift, avoiding mine. "In Wakanda, we make it our business to know all there is to know about the world outside of our own," he says, his voice hard. "Come. We should head back to the bike."

T'Challa finishes his exchange for the petrol as I buy a few slices of fermented bread, beans, two mangoes, and another bottle of water from the market, my mind still spinning. It's all coming together. The Shadow King must have somehow found a portal and taken the body of Farouk. He found a way back. But after surviving all he's been through and beating the odds, what would possess him to come after me? What do *I* have to give him?

T'Challa avoids my eyes as I approach the bike, his expression heavy, and for a change, I know what he's thinking. I assume my position on the seat, scooching forward, hugging T'Challa's back.

"You've considered it for yourself, haven't you?" I ask. "The plane, the portal."

T'Challa's body goes rigid. He grips the bike handles, knuckles turning white.

"Yes," he hisses, without looking at me. "I, too, have researched. Because I would have given anything to bring Baba back."

Then he doesn't say another word as we take off down the road, and I get it. If I had the chance, I would give anything to bring back Mommy and Daddy, too.

X

We reach the city of Moyale, a market town at the border between Ethiopia and Kenya. The pull in my stomach is stronger than ever, and somehow, I know we are close.

T'Challa confirms this when he says it will take us another day to make it to Nairobi. My stomach twists at the thought of our trip together coming to an end. I've grown accustomed to his laugh, his terrible jokes, and his blinding smile. A part of me wouldn't mind giving up my old life and just staying on this bike forever. But why would he ever want me? A prince with a street urchin on the run from . . . who even knows what. I have nothing to offer him.

And then, when I think of Moche, my brothers, the kiddies . . . I can't abandon them. I have to keep going.

We speed on, and somewhere past Moyale, the skies open up. Sheets of rain pour down like I've never seen. T'Challa tries to take it slow, but the bike swerves on the muddy road, and I let out a yelp.

"We need to pull over!" T'Challa shouts above the roaring water. "We will not make it far in this."

He veers off into a cluster of trees and turns off the engine. I run into the forest for the cover of the baobab trees as T'Challa pushes the bike over.

"The rain won't last long," I say, taking off my scarf to wring it out. "It's just a passing storm."

"How do you know?"

I stop short. "Just a . . . feeling."

He grunts. "Your feelings are often very accurate."

I rub my temples. Not this again. "Let's . . . make a fire to keep warm."

We each scan the ground, looking for dry leaves and broken bark. I pick up a few rocks to make a small circle, thinking distantly on my initial feeling of loss upon leaving Cairo. I've become accustomed to camping life in such a short amount of time.

"You know," T'Challa begins, "if you can make it rain, can you not stop it, as well?"

I pause to look up at him. "Is that a serious question?"

He shrugs, his face genuinely curious. "More of a suggestion."

I sigh and wave him off. If I am honest with myself, I guess I can understand his curiosity about everything that's happened with me. But with the Shadow King looking for me, his men watching my brothers back home, I just . . . can't. I can't let anything distract me from the one thing that will get the Shadow King off my back, once and for all.

We work quickly to build a small shelter with fallen palm leaves and branches, then lay out our mats. There isn't much dry wood, but T'Challa is still able to make a small fire. I hold my hand out to the flames, warmth seeping into the chill in my bones. My hair is drenched, and I unravel my braid to comb out the tangles.

"Well . . . ," he says, looking up at the trees. "We are almost to your family's homeland."

"Yeah," I say quietly, laying my scarf out to dry. "Almost."

All the adrenaline that has been coursing through my veins to make it to Kenya has been replaced by nervous prickles. With so many unanswered questions, what am I expected to do when I finally find my people? Do they even know about me? If so, why haven't they come and looked for me? I'm sure they must have heard about Mommy's death all those years ago.

Maybe they did come and search, and I was too busy stealing wallets and jewelry to be found. Or maybe they didn't. I'm not like T'Challa, I'm not someone to be missed.

I glance over and find T'Challa watching me.

"What?"

His eyes flicker to the fire before he clears his throat. "You should wear your hair out more often. It is very beautiful."

"Oh. Thanks," I mumble, trying not to let his pretty words sink too deep. But I can't ignore the thrumming tension racing through my veins.

"I'm tired," I lie, trying to find a way out of the awkwardness. "All this rain, I guess. Think I'll take a quick nap?"

T'Challa nods. "Okay."

I turn and lie on the mat. But I can feel his eyes on me, burning through my back. Though I don't feel tired, the sound of the rain and the soft warmth of Moche's jacket lull me to a light sleep. It feels like I've barely blinked my eyes closed before I hear T'Challa's frantic voice.

"Ororo, wake up!"

T'Challa is leaning over me, face marred with fright, hand gripping my shoulder.

I steel myself, stomach filled with dread. "What's wrong? What happened?"

His eyes soften. "You were having another nightmare."

I sit up, rubbing the sleep away, noticing that the rain has stopped. The sun has set, and night has erased all traces of the road ahead. The trees are thick with darkness—we must be deep in the forest.

I raise an eyebrow at T'Challa. "Another?"

He nods sheepishly. "You . . . do not really sleep. Your eyes close, but you toss and fight the air. Tonight, it seemed exceptionally violent. I couldn't let you suffer."

Heat rises to my cheeks. I didn't know my nightmares were so visible.

"Why are you watching me sleep?" I ask with a nervous laugh.

He crouches in front of me. "I . . . worry about you."

"Oh," I mutter, wincing, and quickly look away from him. My voice is small when I speak again. "Are you worried I might . . . hurt you?"

I wouldn't blame him. He's practically traveling with a ticking time bomb.

"What? No! Why would you think that of me?"

"Because I don't have control over"—I wave my hands—"whatever this is that's going on with me." I sigh, hating myself a little as I say it out loud. "I'd understand if I scare you."

He shakes his head, as if I'm such a disappointment. "I told you, I do not scare easily," he says sharply, and stands to walk back to his mat.

My heart surges at the thought of being away from him. "Hey!" I blurt out before I can stop it, then lower my voice, sheepish. "Can you . . . stay close?"

He blinks at me for a moment, mouth gaping. "Yes. Of course."

T'Challa comes back to me slowly, and I scoot over to make

room. We sit with our backs against the tree, side by side, looking out on the blackness of the savanna.

I lean my head on his shoulder, just to ground myself to something real, to feel his comfort again, like the way we were up in the tree. His muscles twitch, skin warm. He turns, lips almost pressing into my hair.

"What are your nightmares about?" he asks.

I squeeze my eyes shut at the pain. I don't want to talk about them, not with anyone. But I know I have to. Once we arrive in Kenya, I'll have to talk about them a lot to find my family.

This feels like a good start. A safe start.

"My parents," I admit, my voice scratchy.

He stiffens. "Oh. Do you want to talk about it?"

Normally, I would have said no. But there's something about tonight, less than a day out from Nairobi. The last night, maybe, before I find my mother's family.

And maybe our last night together.

I look up at him, and his eyes are gentler than I expected. It feels like there is so much riding on being honest.

I glance down at my feet.

"A plane crashed into our home. I remember my mom wrapping her whole body around me, and my dad trying to wrap his body around the both of us as the building fell. So, you could say my parents died saving me, too."

T'Challa leans his head against mine.

"I am sorry," he whispers. "How did you survive?"

I wince a breath. "It took me hours to get out. Hours of being buried in the dark. Everything was closing in on me. Even now, rooms just feel so tight, I can't stand it."

"Claustrophobia," he says, realization in his voice. "It all makes so much sense. No wonder you didn't want to sleep in the cabin on the ferry."

I nod. "So that's what my dreams are always about. I'm trapped under the rubble of our home . . . my parents next to me, and I'm not strong enough to save them." T'Challa takes my hand.

"It was not your responsibility to save them. You were just a child."

"I know this. Still doesn't change me wanting to do whatever I could to keep them alive. They were my entire world."

T'Challa exhales. "And you were their world."

Tears bubble up. I wipe a stray one away.

"And then, my world became much darker," I admit. "But I just keep thinking back to that last day. How I was about to cut all my hair off and my mom stopped me, telling me that I was meant to be a part of something bigger. I keep wondering if they knew about this thing . . . this power inside me. And if they knew, why didn't they tell me? Did they expect all of this to happen? Was that why they left New York and brought me to Cairo? Were they running from something?"

I sit up as the words start tumbling out faster, all the thoughts that have been trapped in the back of my mind gushing out. Now that I've started talking about them, it feels like I can't stop.

"I mean, what if the plane crash wasn't an accident? What if it was my fault somehow? And why weren't they close to my mom's family? Why didn't they want me to know them? Could they be dangerous? Am *I* dangerous?"

T'Challa looks away with a perplexed scowl.

"And did they know I would need someone like you to help me find my people? Someone who is all the things I'm not, and makes me want to be all those things again? And I guess . . . I don't . . . Is any of this even possible? What do you think?"

T'Challa stares into the fire, unblinking, and I just know I've said too much. I know he's judging me and thinks I'm completely mad. And, in some ways, he's right. Nothing has made sense in weeks. . . .

But he could at least say something rather than just sitting there like a damn robot.

"T'Challa," I say softly. "What do you think?"

He swallows hard, then finally speaks. "I think . . . I am going to kiss you now."

Sirens ring in my head. "Um . . . what?"

"I am going to kiss you. Because if I do not kiss you right now, I will regret this moment for the rest of my life."

I stop breathing as he shifts closer, arm wrapping around my waist, hand snaking up the back of my neck, into my hair, as if to keep me still, a fire in his eyes. He brushes the stray strands out of my face, cups my cheek, and holds my stunned gaze, pausing as if giving me a moment to decide.

My racing thoughts dissolve into a different type of panic. Because if I actually listen to that nagging voice inside me, telling me I'm not good enough to be kissed by a prince, I will run.

But I don't want to run. I want to kiss him. More than anything.

So I close my eyes, lean forward. The moment his lips touch mine, everything just fades . . . all my worries, all my panicking . . . melt like butter.

He draws back to gaze at me, amazed, and a rushing sensation takes over.

I pull him back to me, hungry for more. He smells like campfire smoke and leather; his lips taste like honey. His hands are everywhere, and I want more of him. All of him. Pressure builds in my chest and before I realize what it means, thunder cracks above us as a bolt of white light hits the ground near our feet, scorching the earth black.

We jerk away from each other with a scream, staring at the space by his foot in silence.

"Well," T'Challa says, catching his breath. "I have never had a girl try to kill me with lightning before."

I slowly turn to him before sucking my teeth and elbowing out of his embrace to stand.

"So you've kissed a lot of girls, I take it," I snap, stomping out the leftover flame.

He jumps to his feet. "A few," he admits, glancing back to where we sat in awe. "But that was . . . that was . . ."

I groan. This is not at all how I expected my first kiss to go. "That was nothing. Let's just forget this ever happened."

"Ororo . . ."

I whip around. "I almost killed you!"

"But you did not," he says, reaching for me. "And as you once so eloquently told me, 'almost is not enough.'"

I back away from him. "Now do you see why I need to get rid of this thing? I can't even kiss a boy without . . . without . . . Tah! What kind of life can I have, being like this?"

"An extraordinary one, if you ask me," T'Challa says, smiling. "These abilities of yours, if you learn how to control them, you can change the world. You just need to have patience with yourself."

"I don't want patience. I don't want to learn. I want to get rid of whatever this is so I can be normal!"

"But . . . what if you decide not to rid yourself of it?"

"And stay a freak forever?"

He scowls. "A freak to whom?" He waves his hands wildly. "To me, you are absolutely amazing!"

"Do you really think everyone is just going to accept me?" I pitch my voice higher. "'Oh, you can control the weather? Right, we're not scared of you at all!'"

"You are a terrible actress," he quips. "You could help so many people, save so many lives. Look what you were able to do for Ameen's village."

The praise chants echo through my thoughts. I shake them away.

"You act like this is all so simple."

"I believe you can learn how to control it. With patience and focus."

I know all about focus and I still find this to be impossible. I want to believe him. I want to believe that I can do something worthwhile. Be a part of something . . . bigger. But I can't let myself go down that road. To believe it, then to be proven wrong, it would kill me.

I shake my head again. "T'Challa. Who would want me to help them with anything? I'm nobody."

He closes the distance between us and grabs my arms, letting our foreheads touch. "You are not nobody. You are somebody to me."

Cool air fills my lungs and I shiver. His arms wrap around me tighter, lips grazing my forehead. Even after I almost killed him, he still wants to be near. I nuzzle into his chest, letting the relief flood through me. I haven't been this safe . . . this much myself . . . in a long time.

"I want you to come with me. To Wakanda."

I blink and reel back, positive I misheard him. But he only stares, his eyes warm and pleading, threading our fingers. I push him away.

"Tah! Are you mad?" Me, a street urchin, on the arm of a prince? In the most advanced country in the world, where poverty doesn't exist, where no one goes hungry?

"If you come, we can devise the best way to help you control your powers."

"I can't!" I say, my voice a little desperate.

"Why?" he shoots back, and I can hear the hurt in his voice.

"I have responsibilities! What about my brothers in Cairo?"

He frowns. "Is that really the life you want to go back to?"

I open my mouth and come up empty. My mind tells me yes, but my heart . . . my heart can't figure out what I want. To find my family. To stay with T'Challa.

But loyalty has me stuck. What would Moche and the boys think of me, leaving them for a life of luxury? What would they call me? A liar? A traitor? A freak? The American they always thought I was?

I sigh. "It's late. We should get some sleep."

T'Challa visibly deflates. "Would you at least consider it?"

He rubs his thumb along my knuckles and all I want to do is fall back into his arms, back against his lips. But I glance at the ground and hesitate.

"I'll think about it," I mutter. "Good night, T'Challa."

He smiles, kisses my forehead, and steps back to his mat.

"Good night, Ororo."

THIRTEEN

Nairobi is breathtaking. A gorgeous metropolitan city like nothing I've ever seen with lush trees, chrome buildings, manicured lawns, and stunning views of Mount Kilimanjaro in the far distance. Everywhere I look, there are people, so many beautiful brown faces, walking around in colorful dashikis and head wraps and the latest street fashion, their homes shaded by giant trees. The sun seems to shine brighter, and even the air smells crisper.

It's overwhelming. Here I am in my mother's homeland, where she went to university before flying to New York and meeting my father. I feel at home, knowing I'm closer to them, somehow. Here, I can remember the smell of her hair, the warmth of Daddy's arms, the laughter, the tears. . . .

All these years, I've been fighting the memories of them, too scared to face the fact that I miss them more than words can describe.

T'Challa drives around the city aimlessly. He, too, must be impressed by the colorful sights and sounds. Or maybe he's just buying more time. But that strange wall no longer sits between us. Maybe we both had things we needed to get off our chests. Maybe we both just needed to talk about what sat heavy on our hearts.

I snuggle closer to his back and rest my chin on his shoulder as we ride.

In any city, the best place to find information is a village's market. After stopping for lunch at an outside garden near the giraffe sanctuary, we chat with a few locals and are directed to Maasai Market.

T'Challa parks his bike at the gate of the massive open-air market, full of both tourists and Kenyans. No booths or stores, just long rows and rows of mini setups, merchandise laid on blankets or makeshift tables shaded under plastic tarps, tents, and beach umbrellas.

"This must be a familiar setting for you," he quips. "Perimeter walk?"

I nod and begin circling. Similar to the souks, vendors haggle over kikoy fabrics, paintings, woven bags, beaded jewelry, and leather goods. Once we make it back to the entrance steps, T'Challa grips my hand.

"Okay, I think it is time," he says, nodding at my head wrap.

I gulp. My palms suddenly begin to sweat. "Really? Right here?"

"It is the best place to do it. More eyes."

I look around at the bustling crowds, the chatter of the market filling the air. There are maybe more than a thousand people here. Since my parents died, only a handful of people have ever seen my hair.

"Maybe there's another way," I utter, taking a step back.

As if reading my mind, T'Challa steps closer. "This will work. I know it will."

What if someone recognizes me? What if the men back home find out that I'm here?

Here . . . in Kenya. My mother's homeland. I still can't believe I'm actually here. That I can maybe find my family and learn about where I came from. That alone is worth the risk.

I take a deep breath. Judging by the last time we've seen

anyone looking for us, we have at least three days' head start on any of the Shadow King's men. We should be fine.

T'Challa puts a hand on my shoulder, his tone encouraging. "Do not worry," he says with a small smile. "I will be with you, watching your back. Like always."

Clenching my jaw, I slowly unravel my head wrap, looping it around my neck, my hair braided down in one long ponytail over my shoulder.

"Beautiful," T'Challa whispers, and I can't help but smile. But when I look up, my stomach hits the ground.

"Everyone is staring," I murmur as we make our way through the rows of the market. Heads turn toward us as we pass, and I keep my eyes straight ahead of me, unable to meet a single person's gaze.

"That is what we want, right? For everyone to talk. To see if your hair jogs any memories."

I nod, feigning confidence despite feeling naked and ex-posed. Fighting the urge to just run away. Once again, I wonder if maybe I can stop running, stop trying to find out who I am and just . . . exist, with T'Challa, in Wakanda.

"What if we don't find anything?"

T'Challa frowns. "Come again?"

I twirl the bottom of my braid, clutching it like a rope that's keeping me from falling off a cliff. "We're low on money and options. Maybe this is the end."

T'Challa opens his mouth but seems to come up short.

"You! Young lady. Come!"

Just like Cairo, the vendors call to anyone passing by. T'Challa and I ignore them as we make our way through the market, our eyes peeled for anything out of the ordinary.

"Come!" another old vendor calls, gesturing to us. "Gold? Silver? I have many beautiful things, sista," he says in front of his spot, making a show of dusting off his collection.

"Not now, I'm busy," I mumble.

"Eh, eh! Busy? You work?" he shoots back with a tooth-less grin.

T'Challa bumps my shoulder. "We should start by talking to people." He juts his chin at the woman selling dresses under a blue tarp. "Divide and conquer?"

My panic spikes. "What? You're leaving me alone?"

He laughs, walking off backward. "Remember, you do not really need me."

I bite my tongue to keep from taking those words back. Now it feels like I need him more than anything. That he is my new home.

What am I saying?

I shake the fluttery words from my head and turn to the nearest vendor. His face brightens the moment we catch eyes.

"Ah! Welcome, my sista! Come! Maybe I can interest you in a necklace. A bracelet? Scarf? My sista over here sells beautiful paintings she has made herself."

"Oh. Really? Because I saw the same painting a few rows back."

The man pauses, then shrugs, still grinning.

"Ah, yes. Well, as they say, great minds think alike."

I can't help but let out a chuckle. Doesn't matter where in the world the market is, it's always a hustle.

"American?" he asks.

"By way of Cairo," I add. Just so he knows I'm not one to be swindled.

He snaps his fingers. "Ah, then I have the perfect thing for you."

He digs into a small tan pouch under the table and procures a pair of turquoise scarab beetle earrings.

"I was told this beetle is sacred in Egypt. It represents creation, resurrection, and rebirth."

I lean forward, drawn to the familiar image and colors of home. He's right. The scarab beetle means many things to Egyptians. Maybe they are a sign. Maybe I can start anew with T'Challa after all.

The thought of my brothers nags at me again, and I shift. Wind tickles my scalp, flyaway strands kissing my cheek as the sun beats on hair that hasn't seen the light of day freely in such a long time. Then that familiar tug pulls at my insides.

Come home.

I place the earrings in the vendor's palm. "May I ask you a question?"

"Of course, yes," he says, holding a hand out for me to continue.

"Have you ever seen someone who . . . looks like me?"

The old man gives me a once-over, confused.

"I'm searching . . . for my people," I offer. "They are from Kenya. I believe."

He measures my tone with a nod. "I am sorry. I have never seen anyone quite like you. I am but a young man," he jokes. "There are many elders who may have."

I nod. "Thank you anyway."

He turns, snapping his fingers. "Ah! What about this?" He ducks behind his table and pulls out a light blue cotton dress. "This color will bring out the ocean in your eyes. You can wear it to the party tonight."

I raise my eyebrows. "What party?"

"It is held on the last Saturday of each month. Everyone will be there. Maybe someone there will have the answers to your questions."

I glance down the aisle at T'Challa, who is now surrounded by a few young women flirting with him as he politely declines. He glances my way and gives me one of those smiles that can melt the moon.

The vendor stands by, waiting. "Let me see those earrings again."

He grins, placing them delicately in my palm.

T'Challa approaches, hands behind his back, seeming amused by something.

"What?" I ask.

He grins and reveals a black wooden comb, its handle curved and carved with intricate grooves. "The ladies thought you would like it."

I pluck it out of his grip, peering over his shoulder. The three women by the booth watch and giggle.

"Thank you," I murmur. "It's lovely."

He nods. "Any luck?"

I grip the earrings. "Let's not camp tonight. Let's get a real room."

T'Challa's eyes widen. "Really?"

I turn back to the vendor. "I'll take the earrings. And the dress."

X

The dress is absolutely ridiculous.

The silky material ties in a halter around my neck, stretching over my torso, stopping at the knees before fanning out into an asymmetrical shape. I haven't worn a dress since I was a little girl.

But the old man was right: the blue does bring out my eyes.

After the best shower I've ever had in my entire life, in a cheap motel with wide windows so the room doesn't feel so suffocating, I use my new comb to work through the tangles in my hair, leaving it big, loose, and wavy over my shoulders.

Trading my flats for a pair of cheap strappy sandals I found in a gift shop, I snap on the earrings and step back to take in my new look. I've become an entirely new human all in the matter of a few hours. I can practically hear Moche and the boys cackling at me, all prettied up like some American tourist. But I can't help falling in love with what I see in the mirror. Bright clothing, white hair exposed, a glint in her eye. She is me, but so much more.

You are more powerful than you know.

"Are you drowning in there?" T'Challa calls from the other side of the bathroom door. "The party will be over by the time you come out."

I chuckle before snatching the door open.

"You're so green. No one on earth goes to a party on time," I inform him.

T'Challa, standing by the desk, drops the water bottle in his hand, eyes flaring.

"Well, what do you think?" I ask, giving him a twirl. "No rain tonight, and it's the perfect temperature for this."

He swallows. "Wow." His stare skips from my hair to my knees, then back to my eyes. "I . . . well, wow . . ."

I bite back a smile. "That bad, huh?"

He stutters before finding his tongue. "Y-you look amazing, Ororo."

He stands there, staring at me like I'm made out of diamonds. We soak each other in for a long moment and my stomach does that little flip thing.

I clear my throat. "Are you sure tonight is a good idea? What if someone sees you fraternizing with locals and some white-haired girl? What would your fan club say?"

He steps closer, eyes raking over the dress once more before meeting mine.

"Let them see," he murmurs, taking my hand, and I feel myself melting to the ground.

We head out the door, and he can't take his eyes off me, and I try not to squirm at the attention. By the stairs, I stop to straighten my hair once more in the mirror, stealing a proper glance at T'Challa.

He is wearing a black shirt with black pants, hair freshly oiled, skin glistening, eyes blazing under long lashes.

"Black suits you," I say casually, trying not to sound lovesick.

He smirks. "It is my favorite color."

X

The Maasai Market is almost unrecognizable. All vendors are now gone, replaced with a DJ, a makeshift bar, a few high-top tables, and food carts as hundreds of people crowd into the space. The smell of roasted lamb and spices fills my nose. Feels as if all of Nairobi is now standing under a bright moon, listening to some of the same Afro trap I heard back in Cairo. It reminds me of the boys, and I wince at the thought of them sitting hungry in a decaying building while I'm out partying in fancy clothes with a real prince.

"What should we do first?" T'Challa asks, standing awkwardly by the gate.

"Act normal," I say, making my way across the dance floor, and he follows. I didn't go to many street parties in Cairo, but I watched plenty from afar and know the lay of the land.

We order two Cokes and lean against the bar, taking in the crowd. The older people sit in mismatched chairs near the grassy knolls while the younger people dance in the middle, dressed in every colorful, eccentric style you can think of. Purples, greens, and reds with gold jewelry, dark sunglasses, hats, Afros, even wigs. My hair doesn't feel like such a spectacle.

I breathe a sigh of relief and turn to find T'Challa's eyes on me. Again.

"Would you stop staring? Your eyeballs are going to fall out of your head!"

"Can you blame me?"

"We're on a mission tonight," I remind him. "We should be watching out for any suspicious men looking for us."

"All while searching for someone who may or may not know of your family." He nods solemnly. "Tough work, indeed. Maybe we should split up."

"No!" I blurt out, gripping his arm. "I mean, it's better that we stick together."

He squints. "Are you nervous?"

I tug at my dress. "No. I'm just . . ."

"Shall we walk the perimeter?" he offers, setting down his cup and turning away. But I grip his shirt, reeling him back.

"What are you doing? You don't just leave your drink out for anyone to drop anything in. Someone could try to drug you!"

T'Challa sighs. "I am beginning to wonder if this is street smarts or paranoia."

"A bit of both. I'm a girl, so I can't afford to be lax like you."

He measures me and grabs his cup.

"You are right, again," he says, offering his arm. My cheeks flush as I grip his biceps and we stroll around the party, making sure we pass slowly in front of the elders, hoping they take notice. But none of them seem to look at me with any recognition, just openly staring at my hair.

We make our way back to the dance floor, the cool night air doing nothing to relieve the sweaty bodies as they move. T'Challa studies the crowd, a little wide-eyed, intrigued and fascinated by the sight.

"Don't they have parties in Wakanda?" I ask.

"Yes. The best," he says defensively. "I have been to plenty of parties. But, well . . ."

I laugh. "Let me guess, none of them were like this. And you definitely weren't dancing. You're probably not allowed to party with commoners, are you?"

He rolls his eyes. "I cannot stand that word. There is nothing common about my people. I just have to practice a certain level of . . . decorum."

"Tah!" I snort. "I bet."

We stop in the corner by the DJ as he switches up the music. The crowd responds with a thunder of joy, hands up in praise.

"Oh, I love this song," I say, hips swaying.

But T'Challa doesn't move, just nods his head.

"What's wrong? You don't like Drake?"

"Drake?" he parrots, as if saying the word for the very first time. I stop moving.

"T'Challa, please tell me you at least know who Drake is?"

"Of course I do," he shoots back. "I just . . . did not recognize this song."

"You're lying!" I laugh, playfully pushing his shoulder. "I can't believe you. Does Wakanda not have internet?"

"We have that and so much more. You will see for yourself soon."

I swallow and turn away quickly so he can't see the fire growing across my cheeks. As I turn, a smile takes over my face when I spot a group of boys our age dancing with fancy footwork.

"Hey, you!" I shout.

The boys look up, and I push T'Challa toward them. "Can you teach my friend that dance?"

T'Challa balks. "What are you doing?"

The boys beam with pride. "Eh, eh, come, brother!"

The group drags T'Challa to the center, and he gives me a wary look. I wave, giggling, then find a seat by the bar and watch them try to teach T'Challa a few steps. He isn't the worst. Considering how light he is on his feet when fighting, it makes perfect sense that he would catch on to rhythm rather quickly.

"My boyfriend is an excellent teacher," a girl beside me says, jutting her lips toward the skinny boy instructing T'Challa on how to move his feet.

"He is," I agree, laughing.

"Your boyfriend is really cute."

"Oh no. He's not my boyfriend."

"Ha! Are you so sure about that? Because the way he has been looking at you all night . . . tuh!"

My heart swells. "So, everyone's noticed?"

"You are hard to miss," she says, laughing, glancing at my hair. "Why not make him your man?"

I stutter, searching for a response. How can I even begin to explain to a stranger? "He . . . It's . . . We're just from two different worlds, you know?"

"Seems like he is trying to have you in his world."

My eyes find T'Challa in the crowd, laughing with the boys, his eyes crinkling at the edges, and my heart softens. That smile . . . how can anyone resist him?

He is going to be a king, I remind myself. What would he be doing with a girl like me? My mind flashes back to the lightning that nearly struck him when we kissed. To the Shadow King and his men, probably not far behind me. This is no Cinderella story, I remind myself.

But what if it could be? You deserve a fairy tale after all you've been through.

I can't stop myself from imagining it. How it could be different, if I just stayed with T'Challa. And then, like clockwork, I think of Moche and my brothers. What would I tell them?

"Damn it," I grumble, and finish my drink, scanning the crowd. I've all but paraded myself around, and no one here seems to recognize me. What if this is all hopeless? Have I risked too much, exposing myself for no reason?

Lost in thought, I look up and lock eyes with T'Challa, who

immediately stops dancing. His stride is pure confidence as he prowls toward me. My tongue dries as he reaches me, a smirk on his lips.

"Um, you're not a bad dancer," I say, nervously sipping at an empty glass.

He takes the glass, places it on the bar, and tugs me onto the dance floor. My breath hitches, and any words I might have had die in my throat.

Fingers laced, he pulls me through the tight crowd, sweaty bodies bumping into us as we cross the dance floor, walking off to a secluded area just past the DJ table. My heart thunders in my ears.

"Where are we going?" I gasp, trying to control my breathing.

He spins around and pulls me against his body, his hands on the small of my back, gripping my hips, and for a moment, I forget anyone else is around.

"I wanted to dance with you," he whispers in my ear. "But there are many people, and I do not want you to panic." He leans toward me, his forehead touching mine as he stares into my eyes. "You are safe with me. Always."

"Oh," I mumble, my muscles melting yet again. My claustrophobia. He is always thinking of what's best for me.

At least someone is.

"What's wrong?" he asks, as if reading my mind.

"It's just that this whole thing . . . might be hopeless. I don't know what I was thinking, randomly coming to some strange country, hoping to find a family that may or may not exist. And if I don't find them, I'll be stuck like this for the rest of my life."

"You are not stuck," he says, giving me a warm look. "You can always come with me."

I let out an uneasy laugh. "And what? Return to Wakanda and be your queen?" I joke.

He cocks his head. "Why not? You already wear a crown so well."

I lean back, grinning. "Tah! That was pretty good."

He smiles and nods over his shoulder. "I got a little advice from the fellas."

I glance back at the crowd, the boys laughing and dancing.

"But I am serious, Ororo," he says, pivoting to face me. "If we cannot find your family, I will not leave you here alone."

Lost in his eyes, I suck in a breath, letting myself drown in him. "And I . . . don't think I want to be alone."

He eases closer to me, tipping my chin up, and I shift onto my toes, head lolling to the side as his lips graze mine. Then my mind catches up and I reel back.

"Eh, eh! What are you doing?"

He raises an eyebrow. "Uh . . . kissing you?"

"Are you insane? Here?" I gesture wildly to the dance floor. "Don't you remember what happened last time? Don't you think enough people are staring? You want me to strike someone dead, too?"

He laughs, arms roping around me, heat in his hands. "Just focus and keep your thoughts on me. I have heard that I am very nice to look at."

"That soda has really gotten to your big head," I grumble. "T'Challa . . . I could *kill* you."

He looks at me, dead serious. "It is worth the risk," he whispers, bringing me closer. "*You* are worth the risk."

My heart surges. He would be willing to risk everything, just for me. He tucks a piece of hair behind my ear, letting his fingers linger on the nape of my neck as he pulls me forward.

"Just focus on me," he whispers right before our lips touch and that same magic pulses through me, sharp and stinging, but in an irresistible way.

Think of T'Challa. Think of T'Challa.

His lips taste sweet, and I'm caught in the warmth of our bodies together. Pressure builds in my chest, floating to my head, my hands tingling, but I manage to push it all down.

I break our kiss to take a breath, amazed that we're both still standing. Hungry for more. T'Challa's eyes are dark as he sighs.

"I have wanted to kiss you ever since I held you in my arms in that tree," he says. "It was all I could think of." He leans his forehead against mine. "Tell me you are still considering."

"You mean Wakanda?" I whisper. "You are asking the impossible."

"With us, nothing is impossible." He blinks. "Unless you don't want to . . . because of me?"

"What? No. That's not it at all."

"Then what is it?"

"It's just . . . what would people say if they saw me with you? All the things I've done . . . who would respect a girl like me?"

He chuckles. "Who would not respect a girl with your powers?"

I want to believe this. But I have no clue about my powers. I would be such a burden for such a brilliant country.

"But I . . . could hurt someone, T'Challa. I'm dangerous. I'm—"

"I don't believe it! It is really you."

We jump, spinning toward the small voice behind us. A girl, maybe a few years older than me, stares at us. Or, more at my hair, her hazel eyes wide in sheer disbelief.

"I am so sorry to intrude, but . . . is that really your hair?"

"Uh, yes, it is," I say.

"Wow. And you were born with it?"

My neck tenses. "Why do you ask?"

She shakes her head, grinning. "I've heard rumors of your kind. But to see with my very own eyes . . ."

My heart nearly leaps out of my mouth.

"You know someone who looks like me?"

"No. But . . . I've heard the legends. Your people were a tribe who could control the weather."

The world suddenly stops spinning.

T'Challa grips my hand. "Who told you this?"

"My grandmother. She used to tell me these stories of blue-eyed women with white hair who lived in the forest."

The forest!

I lunge toward her, suddenly worried she'll disappear right before my eyes. "Where is your grandmother? Is she here?"

"Oh no. She's not here. She's nearly a hundred years old. She is safe at home."

"Where is home? Are you from Nairobi?"

"No. I was born in Mombasa. It's on the coast, the most beautiful beach city you have ever seen."

"I have heard of it," T'Challa says, nodding. "It is said there are many caves by the beaches. Some even have restaurants inside."

"Yes!" she says, brightening. "I used to hang out in the caves all the time. Well, until . . . I wasn't allowed to anymore."

"So, your grandmother is in Mombasa?" I try not to wince, but the coast is another day's journey from here.

"Oh! Uh, no. She lives in Caribou, just a short drive from the market."

I bite my lip. "Do you think we can talk to her? I'd love to learn whatever she knows."

The girl nods excitedly. "I can bring you to her. Meet me by the market tomorrow morning at nine. My grandmother will be so thrilled to see one of her stories in real life!"

I look at T'Challa, hope blazing in my chest.

"We will be there," he says proudly, hand around my waist. "And you are?"

"I'm Zawadi."

"Thank you, Zawadi," I say, my voice cracking. "Thank you so much."

"Though I must warn you," she starts as we head toward the dance floor. "Caribou is quite different from this place. Different from my home, too."

"Do you have a lot of family nearby?"

"No," she admits shyly. "My parents died when I was very little. It has just been me and my grandmother."

I nod. "I understand exactly what that is like. Are you here alone?"

"Uh, yes. I'm supposed to come, make friends." Zawadi nervously glances at the crowd. "This is all wonderful. But . . . I miss home a lot. There is nothing like the sound of the sea."

To feel so alone and miss home, I know the feeling all too well. I grab her hands and she looks up at me. "Then you'll party with us!" I say, gently pulling her back toward the crowds. "Now, please, tell me more about this beautiful city."

X

We partied with Zawadi for the rest of the evening, ending the night by snacking on roasted corn and laughing endlessly over T'Challa's terrible jokes before hopping into our respective cabs. I never thought my life could feel so open and free—being with friends, my hair out for anyone to see. I almost forgot we were on a mission.

"I can't believe it!" I sing for the millionth time as we return to the motel. "We really are going to talk to someone who knows about my family! Or has at least heard of them!"

T'Challa smiles. "Yes. It is amazing."

I can't stop smiling. "But this is a start! I didn't think it would ever be possible, yet here we are!"

T'Challa locks the door, slipping off his shoes. "It is good to see you so happy after traveling all this way."

I yank off my sandals, happy to be free of them, and glance at the one bed. This is the first night I've shared an actual room with T'Challa since we met. Our nightly routine in the desert had become somewhat comforting. But this arrangement makes my pulse spike.

"So, uh . . . ," I start.

"You take the bed," he offers. "And I will take the sofa."

"Right. Okay." I sigh. "Well. Good night, T'Challa."

He winces a smile. "Good night, Ororo."

I swallow and head to the bathroom, closing the door.

"Um, Ororo?"

I swing the door open. "Yes?"

He twists his lips, as if debating how to phrase his thoughts. Then he says, slowly, "You once asked me if I was scared of anything."

". . . Yeah?"

"There are many things that scare me." He folds his hands. "Back in Sudan, when that man held that gun to your head . . . my heart stopped. I do not think I have ever been so afraid." He looks at me, and my heart stutters. "When you jumped into the lake, I was afraid. I watch you sleep because I am afraid that something may take you when I am not looking."

I drift away from the bathroom door, slowly closing the distance between us, needing to be closer.

"I have never met anyone like you, Ororo," he whispers, shaking his head. "I do not think I ever will. I did not realize how deep my feelings for you have grown. And that scares me, too."

He stares with a pained expression, as if revealing all these truths about himself cuts deep to the core. The sight of him, so open and vulnerable . . . it guts me. He's been afraid of losing me the way I'm afraid of being with him.

Fear has ruled over us this entire journey, and now that we are so close to the end, I don't want him to feel fear anymore. I just want him to feel an ounce of the comfort he has provided me.

So I take his face in my hands and kiss him, pretending that he isn't a prince, and I am not some girl off the streets. Pretending that we are made for each other. That we are just two lost souls in search of each other's comfort.

I take his hand and pull him toward the bed.

His eyes flare and he draws back, legs moving stiffly. "I . . . I . . . Are you sure?"

I give him a soft smile and cup his cheek, the light stubble tickling my fingers. "I'm sure about you."

FOURTEEN

As the sun rises, I roll over to find I'm alone in the bed with a note on T'Challa's pillow.

Training outside. Will bring back breakfast. You slept well. :-)

I grin, already missing the sound of his heartbeat in my ear, missing his warmth, his honey scent, and the pressure of his arms wrapped around me.

I gaze out the window, thinking about the day ahead, snuggling deeper into my blanket. The weather will be beautiful, warm but not too hot, zero chance of rain. The perfect conditions to learn about my family. There are so many questions to ask Zawadi's grandmother, but right now, I feel something closer to peace than I've felt in a long time. This nightmare will soon be over. I'll find my family's tribe and rid myself of this curse. If all goes well, I could be back in Cairo by next month.

I know it's wishful thinking, as my entire hope lies in an old woman's hands. Still, I find myself at ease in this moment.

Well, you can always go to Wakanda. . . .

I allow myself to briefly imagine what life would be like with T'Challa. Maybe it is possible that I could gain control of my powers. I didn't hurt him or anyone last night, after all. But I catch a glimpse of my white hair in the mirror and sigh. What would I look like in his royal court? They'd probably laugh in my face.

Always a black sheep with white hair.

After I've showered and dressed, T'Challa returns with two cups of coffee and a box of fried dough. He smiles at me.

"Big day!" I announce.

The light goes out of his eyes a bit. "Yeah. Big day."

At this point, I'm too riled up to think too much about T'Challa's reaction. We're about to meet someone who's actually heard of my mother's family. For the first time since Mommy and Daddy died, I'm so close to their stories again. Like a part of them is still with me, rather than a faraway memory.

Maybe . . . I still have family out there. Maybe I haven't been so alone after all.

When T'Challa and I reach the market, all has returned to normal from last night's party. The vendors are already set up for the morning rush, the streets humming with energy.

We sit on a bench by the market gate as we wait for Zawadi. She's over thirty minutes late. My eyes keep tracking every new person who walks through the gate, every girl who appears as I fidget with my pants, wondering if I should have worn something nicer.

"Do not be nervous," T'Challa says.

"I'm not nervous," I snap.

He points to my tapping foot. I huff and take to unraveling my braid.

"Everything will be fine," he says, but his voice is missing its usual warmth.

I turn to him. "Is something wrong?"

He doesn't look at me, and I can tell he's considering lying, but thinks better of it. He shakes his head with a chuckle.

"I want to help you find your family. But I also . . . selfishly . . . do not."

A war of emotions takes over—a flash of anger, a bit of sadness, some excitement and disbelief. But then I look at T'Challa and feel that wave of peace between us.

He makes me believe that anything is possible. Reminds me of how I want more from life.

Maybe we *could* be more together. After all that we've been through, it isn't so hard to imagine a future with him now. I've never seen anything like the holograms T'Challa showed me of Wakanda—a country that's just so *normal* to him and his people. But if his country is so advanced, and his people are used to the unknown, then perhaps they wouldn't see me as someone who's so different.

For the first time, I can truly picture myself in Wakanda with T'Challa, walking down those streets with the unreal skyscrapers. My hair free from its scarf. Maybe I wouldn't fit in with the prince in his throne room, but I could find a place in Wakanda, nonetheless. I could make a place for myself there, just like I did in Cairo.

Once we learn more about my family—once we *find* my family—what's stopping me from just . . . doing what I want? Of course I would miss Moche and the boys, but the thought of leaving T'Challa makes my heart ache like nothing else. And with my powers gone and the Shadow King off my back, there would be no reason for his men to stay in Cairo. My brothers would be safe. I could visit them from time to time. It's a solid plan.

Besides, I'd have to be a real idiot to turn down a prince.

"Okay," I finally say. "I'll come with you."

T'Challa whips around, beaming. "Do you really mean it?"

"Yes. I do."

His grin is infectious as he wraps his arm around my waist,

squeezing. I find myself smiling in return. The happiness that fills my chest . . . I've never felt anything like it.

He touches his forehead to mine. "Okay. But first . . ." He nods over my shoulder at Zawadi walking in our direction. But she doesn't look like the glowing girl we met last night. Her eyes are puffy and red, skin ashy, her clothes crumpled and dusty, as if she slept on the sidewalk.

I jump up. "Are you okay?" The words fly out before I can stop them.

Startled, she glances up at us and winces a smile.

"Oh. Hi. Yes. Of course I am. Just a long night."

T'Challa and I share an uneasy look. Even her voice sounds different. Distant and raw. I try not to read too much into it. I should be grateful. She is about to bring us to someone who knows about my family, so I paint on a smile, despite the gnawing in my gut telling me something is up.

I gesture beyond the market gate. "Shall we go?"

We quickly find a cab to Caribou, Zawadi riding up front. I roll down the windows to take in the city sights as we drive out farther and farther, my heart thrumming in my chest. I catch quick glimpses of Zawadi in the passenger mirror; her eyes seem far and distant—cold, even, before she catches me staring and smiles.

Finally, the cab pulls up beside a tall, rusted fence that seems to stretch for miles.

"Here, we go by foot," Zawadi says, climbing out of the cab. "It is a long walk."

"Why not drive?" T'Challa asks, pointing to the entrance.

"Cabs do not enter this part of the city." Her laugh is full of spite. "Welcome to Caribou!"

I nod as I take it in. Caribou is a sprawling labyrinth of tiny houses made of tin siding and scrap wood. No bathrooms. No running water. Just narrow roads layered with trash, and gutters overflowing with sewage. Wind kicks up the rotting stench of water.

Face pinched in a frown, T'Challa's eyes roam, taking in the makeshift city. I can almost see the wheels turning in his head. He slows to a near crawl before standing in the middle of the road.

"It's . . . a slum."

"T'Challa," I snap.

"You are not wrong," Zawadi says. "This is the largest slum in Nairobi."

"The place is contaminated," he mutters.

"It is safer here than out there," she says, nodding toward the way from which we came. That is something Moche would say, I think.

I fall back, letting Zawadi walk ahead of us, and grab T'Challa's arm.

"Can you quit gawking? You're embarrassing me."

"People really live like this?" he says, astonished.

"When you have no options, you take what you can get."

He shakes his head. "This is no way to live."

I shrug. "Home is a roof over your head."

"Home should be much more than that." He turns to me. "Is this how you lived in Cairo?"

I cringe, thinking of what he would say if he ever came to Garbage City. What he would think of me. Would he finally see that I'm not good enough for him?

"Not exactly. We have apartment buildings. But the circumstances are similar."

He closes his eyes and shudders.

"There are so many sustainable ways to build homes, with better infrastructure. . . ."

"With what money do you expect them to do all that?"

"Their governments should pay."

"I say again, with what money? You expect corrupt politicians to magically pull money out of their pockets? For Black and Brown people? They'd rather see us starve, or not see us at all. I mean, look how far we are from the city."

T'Challa's frown deepens, as if my words made no sense at all.

"We have so many advancements in Wakanda," he mutters. "There must be a better way. Everyone in the world deserves clean water."

"There is no clean water here," Zawadi says, clearly overhearing the last bit of our conversation. "We are in the middle of a terrible drought. The reservoir is nearly dry. If only you could . . . Well, never mind. It is not important."

"No, please, continue," T'Challa insists.

"Well." Zawadi looks at me. "It was said that your tribe can control the weather. The wells are dry, and the nearest is miles from here." She stares, her eyes full of—something, as she continues, unblinking. "So, maybe you can help . . . by bringing water to us."

It takes me a moment to catch her meaning, and I blink. "You mean . . . make it rain?"

"Yes!" Zawadi beams. "You could refill the dry wells. Help wash some of the soot and pollution away. It would be wonderful!"

T'Challa turns to me excitedly. "Yes! You can do it. You did it before. Think of how it helped Ameen's village."

I hesitate. "But that was an accident. I don't even know how I did it."

"You just need to focus."

I snort. "Oh. Is that all?"

"It is worth a shot. You could really help these people."

"We would be so grateful if you would call the rain for us,"

Zawadi adds, her tone level and cool. Nothing like the bouncy girl we met yesterday.

"But in front of all these people?" I blanch. "I'm trying to keep a low profile."

"No one will say anything around here," Zawadi says. "We are good at keeping secrets."

How can I trust that?

I look around us, at people poking their heads out of their homes, giving us curious stares. But it's the kids in stained clothes, kicking around an empty Pepsi bottle, that give me pause. Makes me think of the kiddies. A pang of sadness hits my chest. If I have the power to really help these people. . . .

T'Challa slides his hand into mine.

"Just try," he says. "I will be here to tell a bad joke when necessary."

I stare up into his soft eyes and fold. "Um," I say softly. "Okay."

Zawadi smirks, as if satisfied with herself.

"Please," she says, ushering us toward the alley. "Take all the time you need."

I step away from them, standing between two tin homes, my back to the road, trying not to think of everyone watching me like a circus act. I clench my fists a few times, shifting in place, feeling awkward in my own skin.

Call the rain for us.

Is it that simple? Just dial it up on the phone?

Maybe. I think of all the times that I've made the weather change in the past. I take a deep breath, close my eyes, and imagine reaching inside myself, pulling at that rubber band. I grip hold of it with my mind and pull it forward.

Rain.

For a moment, nothing happens. I linger on the thought, unsure, until I'm about ready to give up.

But then the wind shifts.

"Ororo," T'Challa says. "I think you are doing it!"

I look up. The sky is a slate gray, thick with heavy clouds.

I'm doing it. I'm doing it!

A thunderous roar cracks, and water crashes down in buckets, dinging off the tin roofs. Behind me, people cry out in joy.

I gasp. "I did it! I can't believe I did it!"

"Yes! You did," T'Challa says, laughing.

The cool rain feels so good on my skin, and a wide smile stretches across my face. Maybe T'Challa is right. Maybe I can control . . . my powers. Maybe my people can teach me how.

I shake my hair out of my eyes, laughing. "Where is your grandmother?" I ask Zawadi.

"She is this way. Come!"

We follow her down the road, watching everyone in Caribou joyously play in the rain, filling jars, bowls, and bottles. I swell with pride.

As we walk farther, rain comes down harder, slowing our steps. Soon it is heavy, almost blinding. Zawadi takes a left, then right, then another left. The city is a deep maze, and it feels as if we've been walking for miles.

"Are you sure this is the way?" T'Challa shouts over the loud chorus of water drumming on the tin roofs. "I think we've passed this house before."

"No, it is this way. Come on."

The rain continues pouring down. As we walk, the dirt roads turn into muddy lanes. Trash begins sliding down mini creeks. The laughter around us starts to die down and turn into anxious muttering.

Where the hell is she taking us?

"This is a lot of rain," T'Challa says to me.

"You think?"

"It's okay. We need it, remember," Zawadi says, smiling.

I glance back the way we came, my sense of direction askew. "Maybe we should—"

"Hold on," T'Challa says, stopping short. "What is that sound?"

We stop and listen until a wave of water veers around the corner, smacking into our legs, almost knocking me over. T'Challa stands me upright.

"What is this?"

"The dam! It must be filling up."

People are shouting now. It suddenly hits me—no one was prepared for rain, and this place isn't equipped to handle weather like this.

T'Challa turns to me, as if having the same thought. "Can you stop it?"

"I . . . I don't know how." I try to call to the pressure, but my mind is racing. There are so many voices and noises. . . . It's all too distracting.

"The houses are flooding," Zawadi shouts, turning to us. "I need to get to my grandmother!"

"We'll come with you," I say. Maybe if I'm inside somewhere, I can focus better.

We wade through the water as people stumble out of their small homes, using cups, bowls, and pieces of wood, trying to push the water out. My stomach lurches at the sight of men, women, and children fighting to save their homes.

This is all my fault.

Up ahead, I can see the concrete wall of the dam, no taller than T'Challa, water cascading over its edges, pooling at the bottom.

"She is over here!" Zawadi waves us toward a house not far from the dam. "She is in there. Be quick!"

She rushes inside and we follow, water flooding the small tin home, and as we step through the door, I immediately feel as if we're inside a dark shoebox, with only enough room for one twin bed, a bucket, and a pot. My anxiety explodes, and I'm ready to run back out the door.

Until I realize who is on the bed. My heart stops.

"Moche?"

There, gagged and handcuffed to the small wooden head-board, is my best friend.

"Moche!" I spring for him, yanking the muzzle off his mouth. "What are you doing here? How did you get here?"

His mouth opens, but no words come out.

"He came here with me, of course."

I stiffen at the husky voice behind me. I turn around slowly.

Zawadi's eyes are now fully black, red veins stretching like roots of a giant tree across her face.

My blood chills. T'Challa backs into me, slack-jawed.

Zawadi cracks her neck and grins. "You didn't think I'd let you go that easy, did you?" She sighs, spreading her arms. "Ah. What a lovely family reunion."

The rain rages outside, muffling the screams of the city. T'Challa stands, arms arced, knees slightly bent, as if waiting for an attack.

"How did you find me?" I whisper. It is all I can think of to say.

Zawadi smirks at Moche.

"Your friend told me where you were headed. It didn't take long to convince him to trust me. Once I told him what you really were."

Moche . . . betrayed me?

Moche shakes his head.

"I'm sorry, Ro," Moche coughs in a weak voice. "He made me tell him where you went, or he was going to hurt the kiddies. He got inside my head. That's how I got here."

Realization nearly brings me to my knees. The Shadow King jumps from body to body. Somehow, he possessed Moche. But why didn't he stay in Moche's body? And why is he using Zawadi now?

"Come now, Moche," Zawadi says. "Be honest. You wanted this. You see, Ororo, it doesn't take much to convince street urchins to turn on one another. You just have to name a price." She jerks her head toward Moche. "He wanted to be the new leader. But he couldn't lead with a freak among his rank."

Moche's eyes toggle between Zawadi and me. He doesn't deny it, and I feel the knife twisting in my back.

T'Challa readies himself, muscles flexing. "I do not know what you are trying to do, but you will not succeed. You will never take possession of her!"

Zawadi ticks her head to the side with a grin. I whip around to T'Challa. "Wait, you *know* him?"

He gives a curt nod, not taking his eyes off Zawadi. "I have heard stories. He is a demon."

Zawadi throws her head back and barks a laugh. "I'm not here for you, Little Prince. I'm here for Ororo."

T'Challa nearly lunges at her before I grip his shoulder.

"Don't hurt her," I whisper.

Outside, more screams. The rain is coming down harder now. Water rushes by the open door like an angry ocean.

"The dam is flooding," I say, trying to find the right words to buy myself time. "I need to stop the rain!"

"Maybe we don't want it to stop," Zawadi teases. "Maybe we want it to flood."

"But these people will die!"

"And whose fault would that be?"

The air is ripped out of my lungs. They'll die because of me. Because I can't stop him. There's nothing I can do.

Then Zawadi slaps her own face. Again. And again. Nails scraping her own cheeks, her skin turning red.

"Stop it!" I scream. "Leave her alone!"

The Shadow King's laugh echoes in the tight tin home, and I'm tempted to cover my ears just to escape it.

"What do you want?" I cry.

"You know what I want," Zawadi hisses. "Let me in, Ororo. Let me into your soul. Let me in and I'll spare your little friends."

Spare them? From what? How can I trust anything he says?

Moche bucks, tugging at his cuff. Zawadi measures my hesitation and shrugs. "Or don't. The choice is yours. But the clock is ticking, dear one."

I glance at T'Challa, unsure of what to do. He shakes his head.

"Do not give him what he wants. Your power would be too dangerous in this monster's hands."

She smirks, slowly backing out of the house.

Oh no, oh no no no! He is kidnapping her. I jump off the bed, lunging for the door.

"Where are you going? Come back!"

T'Challa grips my arm. "No! Do not follow. It is a trap. He is trying to distract us."

"But Zawadi—"

"Look at the water," he shouts, pointing to the floor. The water laps against the bed, soaking the mattress. "If you cannot stop it from raining, we need to save as many people as possible. Starting with your friend."

We both turn back to Moche. His eyes jump between us, face unreadable. He gives a hard yank at the handcuffs.

"I need to help get everyone to safety," T'Challa says, heading for the door.

"What should I do?" I yell desperately.

"You have to make it stop raining."

I almost argue, then remember: I'm the one who started it all. I'm doing this to us.

"Focus on stopping it, Ororo," T'Challa insists.

I can't. I can't focus. I can barely think.

He cups my face, and as if reading my thoughts, says, "You can do this."

And then he's gone, racing up the road.

I turn back to Moche, who only stares, eyes ablaze. I reach into my hair and come up empty. No head wrap. No needle.

"Damn," I grumble, spinning around the room, looking for anything I can use to work on the handcuffs. But almost everything is underwater.

"Here," Moche huffs, holding up a piece of thin metal.

I snatch it out of his hand.

"Why didn't you get out of this yourself?" I ask as I start working on the cuff. He glares at me, leaning up.

"You don't think I tried?" he sneers.

I say nothing. Because we both have always known I am better at locks than he is. I slip the metal into the keyhole, digging for the latch.

"The rest of us are fine, thanks for asking," Moche hisses. My stomach sinks. In all the chaos, I didn't think to ask about them.

"And Achmed?"

"He was released. But . . . not the same. Glad to see you're doing so well without us."

My cheeks burn with shame. I glance up at the door, eager to get outside and help T'Challa, then find Zawadi. I don't understand. Why is the Shadow King using Zawadi? Where does she fit into all of this? She's just some girl from a village. What is his angle?

Click. The cuffs pop open.

Moche rips them off, rubbing his wrist.

"Come on," I say, trying to help him off the bed, but he snatches his arm back.

"I got it," he snaps as he stands, storming out of the house. Without me.

"Moche?" What's wrong with him?

I run out after him, wading through the water, and the streets are like a mudslide.

"Moche!" I call, but he ignores me as he heads down the road.

The Shadow King's laugh echoes over the water, and I spin around.

Zawadi stands a few houses down, the skin around her eyes crinkling, wet hair matted to her face.

"Don't hurt her," I shout. "Please! This is between you and me. Leave her out of this."

"You've made your choice!" The Shadow King's voice bellows from the small girl. "Now you suffer the consequences."

I'm at a loss for what to do. How do I stop him and save her at the same time? Or what if I can't save her? What if there's no hope? Shouldn't I still try?

I begin wading through the water toward her but freeze as she looks up at the sky, letting the rain pummel her face. "How amazing it is that I don't have to hurt anyone. You have already done it for me."

What does that mean?

Zawadi cups her hands, then slams them on the muddy ground like a sledgehammer. There's a rumbling explosion, a gunshot under our feet. I stagger, losing my balance as others scream. A crack forms in the ground, splitting the earth, snaking its way up the road, toward the dam.

Oh Goddess.

Zawadi watches her work with a satisfying smirk. She slams the ground again, her muscles flexing, and I see a golden flash of light under her skin. This isn't the Shadow King's power. This is Zawadi.

The crack creeps up the dam wall, and it takes nothing for the water to burst through the concrete, racing down the road, knocking down houses and leaving destruction in its wake. Zawadi laughs before she climbs on top of a roof and disappears.

I stand, stunned. *That's why he wanted her. For what she can do.*

"Ororo!" T'Challa screams, and I can see him up the road, helping children run from the incoming tidal wave.

He hesitates, as if he's about to come back for me.

And then I see Moche standing in frozen horror in the middle of the road between us, watching the wave approach.

"Moche!" I scream, sprinting for him.

"Ororo!" T'Challa shouts. "Don't!"

The pressure builds in my chest until I can barely breathe, it's so strong. I jump in front of Moche and hold my hand out to the oncoming water.

"STOP!"

A large gale of wind swoops in, stopping the wave in its tracks. The water cascades around us like a raging river around a rock. I push the wind harder, until it forms a small bubble around us. But it does nothing to stop the rest of the water from tearing down homes.

I push, harder and harder, until the water slows, the dam drained, and the rain suddenly stops like a shut-off sink faucet.

Panting, I nearly collapse on my face and turn to Moche. "Are you okay?" I cough.

Moche's chest heaves. He backs away from me, his hands held up, wet hair sticking to his stunned face.

"He said . . . he said you were dangerous," he mumbles, his wide eyes panicked. "I didn't believe him. But now . . ."

I take a step forward, and Moche flinches.

"Moche, it's hard to explain. This thing I have, I inherited from my family. That's why I came here. To find a way to get rid of it."

"But you didn't," he snaps. "We were all so worried about you, and the whole time you were screwing around with him!"

The hurt in his eyes, the pain in his voice. . . . Somehow, being with T'Challa made it all so much worse for Moche. Then it hits me. . . .

I think of that night on the roof. How he mentioned wanting to travel together, to be the new bosses . . . together. The way he looked at me, the way he held me before I ran off . . .

Moche has feelings for me. How could I have been so blind?

I open my mouth, but the rage in his eyes almost leaves me speechless.

"I . . . I wasn't screwing around," I say, hiccuping breaths. "I really was trying to get back to you. Please, Moche, you have to believe me!"

"No, Ro, just admit it. You abandoned us to find your real family, when you *were* my family!"

My body seizes at the word *were*. Past tense.

He shakes his head, scanning the muddy road, the collapsed tiny tin homes, his eyes landing on me once more. "Just . . . stay away from us, Ro."

My stomach drops, and the world stops moving.

"Moche, I can fix this," I cry desperately. I reach out for him and he flinches from me.

"How?" he shouts. "How can you fix any of this when you can't control yourself? Ro, think of our brothers. The kiddies. They can't be around you like this. Everywhere you go, people would know who you are. How would we live? Eat?"

Just the mention of the kiddies nearly brings me to my knees. The thought of something like this happening where we lived . . . It would break me.

Moche shakes his head again, and my heart cracks as he walks past.

"I love you, Ro," he mumbles without looking at me. "But don't come back to Cairo. Ever."

FIFTEEN

T'Challa is waiting for me at the Caribou gate, where hundreds of now-homeless people are gathered, standing around in soaking-wet clothes, combing through the ruins of the city.

I've made their already-dire situation much worse. I've stolen what little peace they had.

"Are you all right?" T'Challa asks.

I don't slow as I pass him. "What do you think?"

He follows. "Ororo, this was not your fault."

"Of course it's my fault!" I scream. "I listened to you. I tried to help, and it blew up in my face. Look what I did! I could've killed them. They almost *died*." I shake my head, delirious from the shock. Moche is gone. We were all fooled. I ruined these people's lives, and I'm no closer to finding my family than before.

"I'm such an idiot," I say, throwing a hand up, rage building. "Messing around with you, I'm completely off my game. I *know* how to read people. I should have recognized the way Zawadi was playing me. I should have known something was wrong."

"So, this is my fault?" he balks.

"You should have stayed with me," I snap. "Told me one of your stupid jokes."

He shakes his head. "Jokes are just Band-Aids. There was

221

always going to be a day where I would not be with you, and you would have to control it on your own."

"Did that day have to be TODAY?"

"Ororo," T'Challa says, keeping his tone even. "You cannot give up. We are so close."

"I just . . ." I cough a shuddering breath. "I just lost my best friend, the only family I've known since my parents died, and ruined an entire city, all in one day. And for what? To chase down my ancestors. To see where I come from." I bend over, chest heaving. I can't seem to draw enough breath, but I keep going. "I'm no closer to finding out who or what the hell I am. So, no, we are close to nothing!" My voice cracks, tears streaming down my face.

T'Challa tries to take my hand and I slap his away.

"I am done. I'm never using this power ever again."

He doesn't stop trying. His tone is soft when he says, "I know today was quite hard, but you will learn and improve with training and practice. And then you will be able to help so many people. It is the right thing to do."

I whirl back to him. "What do you know about the right thing to do, or helping others? You come from this magical castle with all the techy bells and whistles, and yet your people never once tried to help anyone. You selfishly sit on your pot of gold and watch the rest of the world suffer. So don't you dare lecture me on what's the right thing to do. You want to talk about me, about my duty to help other people, but what about *you*?"

T'Challa leans away as if I struck him. "Ororo . . ."

And all at once, something dawns on me that stops me in my tracks. "You knew all along the Shadow King was after me, didn't you?"

T'Challa freezes, which is the only answer I need.

"Not completely," he mumbles. "I figured it out once you

asked about the Astral Plane. There was only one I could think of who would want your type of power."

I shake my head with a chuckle. "You lied to me."

His eyes bulge, nostrils flaring. "And you did not trust me! After all we have overcome. I am starting to question if you trust anyone, even yourself."

The words slap so hard that my eyes sting from the pain.

I shut them and sigh. "Like I said, I'm done."

I turn away and T'Challa jumps in front of me. "Where are you going?"

"Get out of my way."

"Look, I am sorry. But maybe we should—"

"I said MOVE!" I scream, and a crack of thunder echoes overhead.

Children in the crowd behind us cry out, a rise of concerned voices peaks. There's fear in their eyes as they all stare, clutching to their parents, lips trembling.

They're scared of me.

T'Challa stands, at a loss for words, fighting the urge to stop me. My heart breaks open.

"Don't follow me," I hiss at him. "And I mean it."

He lowers his head, solemnly stepping aside.

And I let my legs do what they've wanted to do this entire time—walk.

X

I trek through the night in soggy clothes down the highway. A few cars stop, offering rides that I refuse. I don't deserve help. I just want to be left alone.

Somewhere in the pitch darkness, I make a left and keep walking. Passing trees, through bushes, before reaching the savanna, the city noises long gone and only the stars to keep me company. But I can still hear the screams of the people in Caribou, water rushing by the open door, the heartbreak in Moche's voice.

The sun rises and I keep walking, passing small lakes and narrow rivers. No direction. No guidance. No purpose.

Nothing matters anymore.

Sweat drips down my back, my hair a tangled ball of string. I wet my tongue at a few nearby lakes.

But by the third sunrise I give up on that, too. And as the sun scorches the earth, I stop looking for shade and just walk wherever my feet want to go. None of it matters. I have no home, no family, nothing. I am nothing.

I close my eyes instead and let whatever is pulling me through the dark continue. Maybe this is my end. Maybe I should just let the Shadow King take me.

Sun again. The horizon begins to blur, waves of heat ebbing. My clothes drenched with sweat, my shoes stuffed with cement, I somehow keep moving. The sun seems so far away, yet it feels like it hovers right over my head like a halo. Maybe it'll burn whatever is left of me.

My knees begin to shake before I finally slump to the ground and the world goes black.

Come home, Ororo.

My eyes flutter open as the ground moves beneath me. Something that smells awful huffs through the heat, my limbs swinging below me. I close my eyes and pass out once more.

Come home, Ororo.

SIXTEEN

Drips of water cool my chapped lips. I catch the scent of mud and damp wood. An unfamiliar voice cuts through my sleepy fog.

"Drink."

"Huh," I moan, struggling to peel my eyes open. An older, brown-skinned woman in a red kaftan and a colorful beaded bib smiles down at me.

"Drink."

My neck tenses and I sit up too quick. The room spins.

No, not a room—it's a small home, a hut of some sort, the roof made of sticks. I squint through a small glassless window at the brutal sun beating the plains. More huts outside.

I take in the woman's shaven head, long neck, and thin wrists with strong hands as she tries to push me back on the cot.

"Where am I?" I croak out.

"Drink," she says again, pushing a ladle up to my lips.

My dry tongue cries to take a sip, but the memories of the dam come rushing back. I shove her hand away with what little strength I have left. "Who are you?"

"Drink," she insists. "You are severely dehydrated."

I try to focus my blurry vision and look her in the eye. She could be the Shadow King. The water could be poisoned!

"What's in it? What are you trying to do?" I say, my voice reaching a terrified pitch.

She shakes her head, trying to force the ladle down my throat. "Drink."

I squeeze my lips together, refusing.

"Drink, stubborn child," she grumbles, grabbing my chin.

Hair sticks to my sweaty face and neck. My hair isn't wrapped; everyone can see. My hands begin to tingle. Panic surges through me.

"No, wait, get away!" I shout before I quickly turn, directing the shooting light to the ground, striking a nearby wooden stool. Smoke fills the small hut.

I freeze, too frightened to move, to see her reaction.

The woman waves smoke out of her face, staring at the blackened, charred remains of her seat.

"Well. That is very interesting," she states, her face expressionless. She sets the bucket down next to the bed. "Okay. Drink. Don't drink. It is up to you. Life is always in your own hands."

She walks out of the hut, leaving me alone.

The frantic, hushed voices outside tell me people either saw the lightning or heard it and are freaked out. I don't blame them.

I breathe in, my lips cracking as I open my mouth. The hut feels like the inside of a cooking pot. I glance at the bucket of water beside me and immediately bring it to my lips, guzzling it, water dribbling down the sides of my mouth. I flex my feet and pain shoots up my legs. How far did I walk?

And where am I?

I pull broken twigs out of my hair, glancing around the hut. No bathroom, no mirror. I can't begin to imagine what I look like right now. I try to tie my hair into a messy bun.

There is another small cot covered in cowskin on the opposite side of the room, a few weatherworn books stacked beside it. Near the door are metal bowls, spoons, and a small stone firepit. Cups of herbs sit on the windowsill. On a bench are wooden bowls of loose beads, string, and gold wires.

I look back at the charred stool. I could have killed her. And yet, she said nothing.

I emerge from the hut, wincing at the bright sun, and find the woman sitting on a chair just outside with a bowl of beads in her lap.

"Ah. She has risen," she says without looking up from her work.

A few dozen men and women, all dressed like her, gather by their huts, excitedly chatting in Swahili. The village is small, only a few huts and cordoned-off cattle. Not a city skyline in sight. Just pristine forest and rocky ranges in the distance.

"Where am I?" I croak.

"You are in Uzuri. One of our hunters found you deep in the savanna, close to the Serengeti, clutching to life."

I take a staggering step toward her, my body still weak.

"You could have been killed by many animals," she continues. "Lions, leopards, hippos, warthogs . . . but none touched you. It is as if they sensed something very interesting about you. As do I."

I swallow hard. Maybe she's seen my kind before.

Come home, Ororo.

I attempt to stand straighter. "Do you know . . . what I am?"

The woman smirks. "What you are is a long way from home."

I sigh. It was worth a shot.

"Tell me, girl," she says. "What were you doing walking through the savanna alone?"

My breath feels labored and heavy. "I was . . . Well, it doesn't matter anymore."

"Tell me anyway."

Her face is expressionless, and . . . I'm just too drained to bother with a made-up story. So I tell her the truth.

"I don't really know. I was just walking. Letting my legs do the thinking. It always feels like something is telling me to walk this way or that."

"Or maybe your soul . . . your intuition, was telling you where to go, yes?"

"Maybe," I offer. But my intuition told me to go to Kenya, and it was wrong. I take a step and wince. "Well, thank you for saving my life. I'll just . . . get going."

The woman turns back to her bowl, focusing on her work. "If you walk away right now, a lion will eat you in your weak state. You will stay for dinner. Then we shall talk about this 'leaving.'"

I lean against the hut, knees threatening to give out, and squint at her. Then I blurt the only thing I can think of.

"Who . . . who are you?"

"My name is Ainet." She stands. "And you will clean up the mess you made inside my home."

X

Night falls on the village. I guzzle several jugs of water while Ainet roasts meat on an open fire. Her hut stands off to the side, away from the others. As most of the villagers lie sleeping, it feels as if we are all alone, engulfed in the dark.

"You are in luck, child," she says, dumping a porridge-like substance into a bowl. "I just made some ugali before you arrived."

I take in her features in the firelight—thin arms, wide smile, almond eyes, high cheekbones, a shock of white hair with black roots that stops just at her shoulders, pulled back by a beaded gold headband.

"Your English is really good," I note, then wince. "I mean . . . I didn't mean it like that."

She smiles, taking the pot off the fire. "I went to university," she says. "A long, long time ago."

"Really?" I glance around the village. "And you . . ."

"Are you asking me why I chose to live in Uzuri?" She chuckles. "Well, because it is my home."

That I can understand. More than she will ever know. My heart aches at the idea of never seeing Moche, the boys, or the kiddies again.

"And where are you from, child?"

I hesitate. "Cairo. But I was born in New York City."

She offers me a bowl of steaming broth. "Mmm . . . Long way from home."

I take a sip and the spices burn down my throat, but I can feel my senses starting to come back to life.

"I came here, to Kenya, to find a cure for . . . what you saw earlier. But there is no cure. I'm stuck like this . . . Stuck like this forever."

Ainet holds my gaze and rubs her hands together.

"Mmm. Forever is a mighty long time when you do not know what you are doing. Perhaps I can help you?"

I scoff. "How?"

She passes me a plate of roasted goat and steamed greens, along with a slice of the ugali.

"Here, in this village, I am a healer. I fix broken bones and broken souls." She meets my eye. "I see a lot of pain in you. And though I may not have a cure, perhaps there is another way to overcome your ailment. By learning how to control it."

"Tuh. You sound like . . . Never mind." I poke around at my food, staring into the fire, wondering what T'Challa is doing at this very moment. Did he already make camp? Did he leave Nairobi and head back to Wakanda?

I take a nibbling bite of the ugali. The grainy texture melts on my tongue, immediately bringing me back to my mother's kitchen.

"I've . . . I've had this before," I utter in pure shock. It's the snowball—the one my mother used to make us for dinner!

Ainet nods. "Of course you have, child. Ugali is quite common in all Kenyan kitchens."

My breath hitches. Energy springs new life into my veins as I dig in. I savor each bite, overwhelmed with thoughts of my parents. It feels like they are with me again, laughing at our small table by the kitchen window, overlooking the city, the fire like the warmth of the too-hot oven. I close my eyes and relish the memories I tucked away long ago.

I notice the awkward silence and realize Ainet is watching me daydream. Heat rises to my cheeks, and I clear my throat. "Um, sorry. It has been so long."

She nods. "So. Do you accept my offer to help?"

I laugh harshly. "Thanks, but there really is no hope for me. And I don't want to hurt anyone. Again. I'll just leave in the morning."

Ainet stares at me, her body still, face expressionless. "Hmm. Where will you go?"

"I . . . don't know yet." I shrug, and something about her makes me feel like I have nothing to hide. There's nowhere left for me to run. "I have nowhere to go, really."

The enormity of the statement suddenly hits me. I haven't felt this alone since . . . since my parents died. I glance down at my empty plate, hot tears threatening to bubble over.

"And what will you do when you get to 'I don't know'?"

I sniff. "I don't know."

"Hmm. Seems to me like you have more don't-knows than knows. Running from your own shadow rather than learning how to live with it."

I sigh, turning to face her. "Ainet, I did something . . . really terrible. I tried to give people water, and I lost control. People got . . . hurt. I ruined everything."

She frowns. "Give them water by . . ."

I gulp, gazing at my worn-down shoes. "By making it rain."

Ainet stares at me, then nods. "Hmm. Very interesting indeed."

I squirm under her silent judgment. I don't need some strange woman in the desert telling me what I already know—that I'm a bad person, a freak, a monster.

My chest tightens as images of racing waters, screaming people, shacks toppled by swelling waves, flood my mind. I did that to them. No one else.

"It's . . . complicated," I say, my voice hoarse. "Anyway, I'll be gone in the morning, so you won't have to worry."

Ainet sets down her bowl and begins clearing our plates. "Do you know about the natural order of nature?"

I shake my head.

"Everything has a reason and a purpose, even the droughts," she says, waving her hand as she speaks. "It is very much a circle of life. When one thing disrupts that circle, there are consequences. You interrupted Mother Nature's plans, and she responded accordingly."

"But . . . I was just trying to help," I say, my voice cracking.

"Yes. And it was a kind thing you attempted to do, but it was not fully thought through. Mistakes are mistakes, flickers in the past. Nothing you can do to change them." She hums thoughtfully. "But a mistake made twice is a decision. And this is how, perhaps, I can help you. . . . Understand the natural order so that you can better understand your capabilities and never make the same mistake twice. You'll learn to instead control it."

"Control it?" I shake my head. "There's no controlling this. I've tried."

She gives me a pointed glare. "Have you truly tried? What

do they say, 'practice makes perfect'? Yes? You just discovered this; it is still fresh. You could not have possibly given yourself room to try and try again when you don't even know what you're dealing with."

I start to counter but then think of T'Challa, training every morning for a challenge that is a year away. And he's doing it for Wakanda, the country he loves and knows. I only tried once or twice to make rain, and only just learned what my mother's snowball is called.

This entire journey I've been ignoring my power, running from it, trying to free myself from it. But what if learning where it came from—where *I* came from—helps me figure out what it is and how to control it? Would it hurt to really try?

Ainet reads my silence, then reaches out and holds my bouncing knee. "Will you trust me to let me teach you what I know?"

I swallow, thinking again of Caribou, the children's screams haunting me. "But . . . what if I hurt someone?" I whisper.

She regards me with a laugh on her lips. "You let me worry about that."

I glance around the dark village, then off into the distance. Nothing. There's no pull of any kind. No dreams. For the first time since the sandstorm in Cairo, the call inside me is quiet. The rubber band is . . . not gone, exactly. But lying still. I didn't think I would miss the feeling. Now I find myself frightened by its absence.

I have no money and nowhere to go. I really am out of options. And wherever we are, we're a long way from the Shadow King's watchful eye. At least I think we are. Maybe I can stay and hide. What do I have left to lose?

"Okay. I will trust you. But only if you teach me how to make this ugali."

X

"Wake up, child."

I blink awake. For the past three days, Ainet has fed me healing goat broths and bitter tea, letting me rest to regain my strength. But today is the first day of my training, and I'm to wake up with the rest of the village.

All night, I could barely sleep, wondering how she will pull this off. Unless she has powers or magic that I don't know about, how is she going to relate? How can she even understand?

Ainet stands over me, the sky behind her an ombré blue, stars still twinkling. "Is the bed not suitable for you?"

I rise to my feet, kicking my makeshift bed of hay, and stretch. "I like sleeping outside."

"Hmm. Come," she says, offering me a cup of tea, and I follow her. Ainet stands in front of her home, closes her eyes, and inhales deeply. "Breathe. Like me."

I watch her chest rise and fall, then follow.

"Every morning, we breathe in the air and thank the Gods for another day. Every bit of air that enters our lungs connects our bodies with nature so that we may be its servant. You try."

I breathe in deep, my lungs struggling, feeling the tingling pull of the rubber band ever so slightly, wrapped around every organ, squeezing tight. I let out a gasp.

"You will do this every morning. Before every chore, we breathe. Before every meal, we breathe. Breath is the key to life." She glances at me and smiles. "Come. Let us walk."

She walks toward the village, and I scurry after her. We stroll toward the center, the villagers slowly rising, men heading out to the field where the livestock is gated off. I can smell tea brewing in every home.

"Our people have been in this village for many years," Ainet says, nodding. "We live in harmony with the land and the animals. Everyone here is a warrior. We back away from nothing. You are now a part of that."

Outside a larger hut, a little boy sits, staring at my hair. A woman, I assume his mother, quickly grabs and yanks him inside.

I push a strand of hair behind my ear. I should be used to the gawking, but it still unnerves me.

"Everyone earns their way around here," Ainet continues.

"I definitely know how to do that," I reply. "That way of life is nothing new to me."

"Hm." Her grunts are often loaded with judgment that I can't yet make sense of.

We reach the fence, where a tall, brown-skinned man is clicking his tongue at a few of the cows. Ainet waves him over.

"This is Mukami. He will teach you how to care for the cattle."

He nods at me with a gummy smile. "Nice to meet you."

I raise an eyebrow at Ainet.

"I taught him some English," she says with a smirk. "Go now, lunch will be ready at noon."

Mukami gives me the rundown: Each morning, the cows are milked before they are herded with the goats for grazing, and their stables are cleaned and prepped. Then the cattle are slaughtered for food or milked again before they are put away for the evening, sheltered at the center of the village so they are protected from lions and other predators. He seems hesitant with me at first, but I assure him that hard work doesn't bother me.

As I clean the stable, I watch the village come to life—women working on their homes, cleaning, cooking, fetching firewood and water. I'm just about finished shoveling all the poop into the corner when Mukami leads a giant brown and white cow in my direction.

"This is Kioko," Mukami says, patting her side. "She is the most prized here."

Kioko whips her tail around with a grunt. Mukami hands me a metal bucket and ushers me toward the cow.

"Oh. You want me to milk her?"

He nods.

I've never milked a cow or handled any animals on my own in my entire life. But it can't be that complicated.

I approach Kioko from the side and stoop to my knees, reaching for her udders. Kioko shifts away.

"Uh, huh?"

I look to Mukami, who only stands by with a knowing smile.

Okay, let's try that again.

I reach for Kioko, and she stomps away. I step toward her again, and still she runs away. Soon I'm practically chasing her around the fence. She's rather quick for something so big.

The next day is more of the same. Kioko just about does everything but spit in my face as she avoids my grasp. I spot Mukami and the others laughing at me.

The following day, Kioko gives me a dry look before swinging around, bumping me with her backside, causing me to fall into a pile of cow dung.

But today I've had enough. I'm going to milk that damn cow or make steaks out of her.

As the villagers prep to take the cattle out for the day, I corner Kioko, cutting her off from the others, using two long sticks to block her path. Kioko spins around and cries out before charging full speed to shove by me, and I hit the fence.

"Ugh! Would you just hold still!" I scream.

A tingle zips up my arms, and I drop the sticks to quickly ball my hands into fists.

Oh no.

But it's no use. A crackling light slips out of my fingers, and I hold my hands toward the ground, sizzling with a loud pop.

The cows scream and break out of the fence, creating a small stampede toward the fields. Shouts ring out; the villagers scatter to capture and herd the animals back home.

All except for Kioko, who only stares at me, unblinking.

"Ah, I see you've finally met your match."

I turn to find Ainet, watching on from the fence, a laugh on her lips. "You cross the savanna, only to be defeated by an old cow. Very interesting."

The rest of the village women stand in horror, murmuring frantic whispers.

I sigh. "I am sorry I scared everyone."

Ainet regards me with pursed lips. "Breathe. Now."

I take a deep breath, filling my lungs with the stench of cow dung.

"Your frustration turns into a weapon when you are not in control of your emotions," Ainet notes.

"It's just . . . this cow is stubborn. Animals usually love me."

"Hmm. What is it that you need?"

I give her a pointed look. "Milk, of course. Unless she has some money I don't know about."

She chuckles. "Well. Did you ask her?"

"Ask her?"

Her smile grows. "Yes. Did you ask her, or did you just expect her to read your mind?"

"She doesn't understand English," I counter.

"Respect is a universal language." She motions toward Kioko. "Cattle will respect what you command if it has direction. Ask and you shall receive. You can't always take what you want in this world and expect nature to respect you. Respect is given as it is earned. It makes me wonder how much respect in your life was not properly given."

I think of Moche and the boys. No matter what I did or

236

how much I proved myself, I was always just going to be a little American girl.

Cheeks burning, I turn back to Kioko, who begins back-pedaling, as if she knows I am coming for her. I creep closer, gently rubbing her side.

"We need milk. Please," I whisper softly.

Kioko shakes her head, as if clearing out her ears.

"Milk," I say again.

Kioko snorts.

Milk. Please.

Kioko rears around and headbutts my arm. But then she stands perfectly still, as if waiting for me. I'm so shocked that I almost forget what I'm supposed to do.

I fall on my knees, place the bucket under her, and squeeze her udder. Milk splashes into the bucket with a ping.

"Ha! Yes! I did it!"

Gushing with pride, I look over to Ainet, who only nods and heads back to her hut.

SEVENTEEN

After a week, I've just about mastered asking Kioko for everything but the meaning of life. Meanwhile, I've learned nothing more about my powers, not to mention controlling them. I want to believe there is some method to Ainet's madness, but I haven't seen much proof.

Ainet is stirring a pot of rice for lunch when I ask, "Um, Ainet. When are you going to start helping me figure out how to use my powers?"

She hums, adding a few mystery seasonings to the rice. "Hmm. We need more water."

"Ainet, really?" I balk. Why isn't she taking this seriously?

She strolls outside, and I follow.

She picks up a wooden bucket with a rope handle. "You do not believe I am training you now?"

"I don't see how."

"Hmm. Close your eyes. You see too much."

I sigh and do what I am told. Ainet shuffles forward and ties a piece of fabric over my eyes, blindfolding me.

"There. Now walk. And fetch us some water."

She shoves the bucket into my stomach and I grip the handle.

"What? But I don't know where I'm going. I've only been once."

"You will figure it out."

"How? What if I get lost?"

"You must learn to stop seeing with your eyes and start seeing with your soul. You and Mother Nature are very connected. If you listen to her, maybe she will start listening to you."

"I . . . I don't understand."

"You will, once you start walking. And don't forget to breathe."

I breathe in deep and start walking the way I remember, hands outstretched in front of me. I walk slowly, feeling my way one step at a time, until I can no longer hear the village. Quickly, I go to take the blindfold off and then I stop myself.

What if Ainet's watching?

I think of the day in the bar with the professor and shake the thought away. I take another deep breath and keep moving, stumbling over a rock. And more rocks. And plants. After another tumble, I stop to stand still, my lips aching for water. Yet I have no idea if I'm closer to or farther from the river.

How the hell am I supposed to find water like this? I'll be out here for hours, maybe days. That's if a leopard doesn't find and eat me first.

See with your soul.

"Okay, okay, okay. Listen. Must listen," I remind myself. Soul is internal. I must go inside myself.

With another deep breath, I take stock of my emotions. Past the panic, frustration, and confusion, I catch the faint pull of something tugging at my chest. The familiar feeling cools my skin. Much like water.

If you listen to her, maybe she will start listening to you.

"Um . . . water," I say aloud, feeling insane.

A breeze slips through my hair, and I turn to the right to face it, letting it kiss my cheeks. I lean forward as my legs start walking. The breeze doesn't leave me as I trek farther, farther out. It pulls and swirls around me.

I let out a gasp and walk faster, catching the familiar scent first, and then I hear it—trickling splashes over rocks.

I stop short, ripping off my blindfold, gazing at the river in awe.

X

Ainet sends me to fetch water every day, blindfolded. Sometimes she asks me to look for certain herbs and plants along the way. As a test, I turn myself around at times, heading in the wrong direction. But I always find my way to the river, then back to the village before sundown.

Despite all my attempts to pull my weight and prove myself, the villagers still look at me as if I have twelve heads, mumbling in Swahili with wary eyes, keeping their children far away from me. I can't blame them. But the loneliness, the isolation, feeling so . . . unwanted is starting to weigh on me. The stares make my skin crawl.

A solution comes to me on my walk back from the river one day—maybe if I look more like them, I'll be easier to digest.

I walk inside Ainet's hut and begin searching through her few belongings.

"Is there something I can help you with?" she asks, amused.

"I need scissors. Or a knife."

She frowns. "For what?"

"My hair."

"What?" she snaps, and her anger catches me off guard.

"It's . . . distracting," I try to explain. "Everyone is staring."

"And what is wrong with that? What is wrong if people stare at the gift you have been given?"

"Gift?" I balk, grabbing a fistful of hair. "This is not a gift! None of this is a gift. More like a curse!"

She narrows her eyes. "You dare to consider your gift a curse?"

"I can't believe anyone would think this is anything other than a damn curse." I sigh. "Ainet, it would just make my life . . . easier if I at least try to fit in. I can try to dye it with some clay from the riverbed. Dress like you."

She sucks her teeth. "Eh, eh. I do not know why you are so set on making yourself small when you were not born for that purpose."

"So you'd rather me be arrogant? Flaunt this in everyone's face?"

"I would rather you be confident! Walk with your head held high, and be proud of who you are. Being humble does not mean to shrink into oneself. Rather, it is to be exactly who you are, unapologetically."

I shake my head, looking away. "You don't understand. You look like everyone here."

"Do you think the zebra has never wanted to change its stripes? Or the giraffe has never wanted a shorter neck? They know they cannot, and yet they continue to walk tall and carry on. They do not sit in the grass complaining." She stomps closer. "You said the women in your family have your hair, your eyes, yes?"

I swallow. "Yes . . ."

"So your powers must be from their tribe, correct?"

"Well, yes, but—"

"Then why would you want to throw away the one gift your mother has left you?"

The gut punch lands so hard I almost buckle over. I have . . . never thought of my hair that way. My eyes fill with tears as I look to Ainet.

"You must change the way you speak of yourself. Words have power. And to call this power a curse is an insult to the very person who gave it to you. Your mother's greatness was passed down not just in your features, but in the very essence of your soul. Where your power lies."

EIGHTEEN

We fall into a steady morning routine: just before dawn, I take several breaths, then sit by Ainet as she prepares breakfast while I boil water for tea, readying for the day's work. Yesterday, I heard Ainet mention something about the moon in passing, and I realized the worm moon must be approaching. I haven't given much thought to the Shadow King since I've been here. I feel at ease here, as if I'm unreachable by his grasp. But at night, when I look up at the changing moon beginning to peek behind the black blanket of sky, that sense of impending dread creeps in.

A part of me wonders what would happen if I just let life go on without anyone knowing I'm here. Do I really need to know how to use my powers if I stay hidden? The Shadow King would just be forced to live without me. It's better this way; I'm too harmful to people I love.

I sit on my cot, eating a small bowl of rice for breakfast. Ainet sits on her stool, sipping tea, staring at me from across the room.

"What's up?" I ask, holding a spoonful to my lips.

She slowly stands, picking up a bucket of water. "It is time that I kick you out of my home. You are cramping my style."

"Okay," I say with a chuckle. "So where am I supposed to stay?"

"How everyone else lives. Come."

Outside, a woman carrying a large pile of sticks under one arm and three stacked bowls in the other smiles as she passes us and walks to a spot just beyond Ainet's hut, where a large pile of black dirt sits.

"What is she doing?" I ask as we approach.

The woman sets down her sticks and starts digging up the dry earth, creating a hole next to a pile of rocks.

Ainet nods at the woman. "This is Osunda. She is one of Mukami's wives."

Osunda smiles, nervous eyes shifting over to Ainet. Of course she's scared of me.

"What's all this?" I ask, gesturing to the different piles.

Ainet sets the water bucket down and Osunda immediately pours some into the hole.

"These are the materials for your enkaji, your new home."

"Really?" I tiptoe closer to the pile of dirt. "It smells awful!"

"The best homes are made with the freshest cow dung Kioko can offer."

"Wait . . . this is . . . no." I stare at the massive pile, floored. "You expect me to build my own home . . . with this?"

"All of our homes are made of mud, sticks, grass, cow dung, rocks, and ash."

Mukami carries over two more buckets of poop, dumping it next to Osunda, who begins combing through it with her bare hands.

"Ew. Gross," I say, gagging. "There is no way I'm touching that!"

Ainet holds a steady gaze. "The home that has provided you shelter was made of these very materials. So is everyone's home. No one complains. Are you too good to live in our homes now?"

Shame bubbles up, my cheeks on fire. "No."

Ainet regards me with a skeptical eye, then continues. "Osunda will teach you how to build your home." She walks in a large circle. "I believe you can build something right here." She stomps her sandal in the ground. "I would start soon, before it gets too hot."

Ainet grins and walks back to her hut. I stare at the empty space, then look to Osunda, who smiles at me, and I can only wince a smile back. With rocks, we outline the small circular shape of what will be my home. Mukami, Osunda, and I begin building the skeleton of the hut with sticks lying on top of one another. Ainet watches us from outside her hut on a wooden stool, a bowl of beads in her lap as she works on a new necklace.

Once the structure is up, Mukami heads back to the cattle and Osunda ushers me toward the buckets. Osunda doesn't speak English, so we communicate through hand gestures and nods as she gives me the recipe for cow dung plaster. First, we start by mixing dirt with water to create a muddy soup; then we add the mashed cow dung, kneading all the ingredients together until it has a thick consistency. Then we mix in sticks and grass, followed by ash from the firepits. Once it's ready, we pat it against the sticks, like frosting a large cake, so it looks like a mound of black hummus. Or just a big pile of poop, but I try not to think about that part too hard.

She pats more mixture against the sticks, building upon it. And as it dries, it cements and takes on a light brownish color. Once Osunda finishes with the first batch, the hut starts to take shape. Then she wipes her hands and waves with a smile as she walks away.

"Wait, you're not going to help me finish?"

"All the women build their own homes here," Ainet answers for her. "You do not need help. You only needed guidance."

I glance back at my house materials.

"It's fine," I mutter to myself. "It's just another test. I got this."

I start making a new batch of plaster but can't replicate what

Osunda did. It's soupy and doesn't seem to thicken, despite all the ash I mix in.

The next day, I try another batch, adding leaves and grass, hoping it will hold. It works for a moment, but by the time I start laying it against the siding, it drips to the ground. I make another batch and think I've nailed it, but by the next morning, I find that half of the plaster has softened.

"It keeps melting," I shout over to Ainet. "I don't think I'm doing this right."

"Sounds like you have a problem," she says without looking up from her beading.

"Can Osunda maybe write down the measurements of stuff?" I huff. "Ainet, this will take me forever!"

"Forever is a mighty long time. Good thing you like to sleep outdoors."

I suppress a shiver. "Being inside is too . . . restricting."

"A roof can keep you safe."

"Not always," I grumble.

Ainet looks up at that comment, but I don't meet her eye as I snatch a bowl and head to the village to collect more ash. On my fourth batch, I have to return to the stables and collect more of Kioko's poop, and I hold my breath to fight the rancid smell.

I ask Osunda for help, but she signals that she is busy. Everyone is. I can't tell if they're trying to avoid me or if this is all a part of my "test."

X

Night falls on the fourth day. I'm almost sure this is just a big, elaborate joke, as I've barely put a dent in my new home. My back aches, my legs are stiff, and my fingernails are permanently stuffed with muddy poop plaster.

But while the rest of the village sleeps, I keep working, unable to stand the thought of failure, of not being able to unlock the key to this one simple task. I'm on my sixth, maybe seventh, batch of plaster, and I'm out of water, so this batch has to work until I can retrieve more in the daylight.

Ainet walks over from her hut, standing a few feet away. I can barely see her in the pitch-black dark, but I feel her watching me slab the plaster against the sticks with my hands, letting it drip down my arms.

"It's late," she says.

There's a taunting laugh in her voice. I glance over my shoulder, seething.

"You think this is funny, don't you?"

She doesn't answer. Just stares down into my latest bowl of plaster. "I do not believe that you paid any attention to what Osunda showed you. Instead, you are just throwing things in a bowl to see what sticks."

I turn and shake the plaster off my hands. "You know what," I snap, kicking the bucket over. "I'm done!"

"Hmm. How can you be done when you still do not have a roof, girl?"

"Does that really matter?" I shout. "I'll be gone in the morning."

"Hmm. So you are quitting?"

"You said you would teach me how to control my powers. And all I've learned is how to beg a cow for milk, fetch water, and build a house out of sh— Poop! This is all useless to me!"

Ainet rocks back on her heels, her stare steady, her face expressionless.

"I can't believe I was so stupid to think even for a second that . . . that . . . that I could control any of this," I say, waving my arms around. "That you or anyone could help me!"

"So you are giving up? Without even trying?"

"Did you hear a word that I just said? I've *been* trying! All my life, I've tried!"

"Hmph. That remains to be seen."

I stomp away from her. "You don't even know me. You don't know what I've done or been through!"

"If there is still air in your lungs, is life truly so terrible?"

"Ha!" I whirl back to her. "First I'm born with this ridiculous hair. Then my parents die, and I'm left to live on the streets, stealing anything I can get my hands on just to survive. Now I've turned into some freak shooting lightning out her hands. I've lost my brothers, my home, and T'Cha—I've lost everything. It's just not fair. All I want is to be normal! I don't want whatever you think this stupid gift is!"

The air tenses, wind kicking up, but Ainet seems unfazed by it.

"So you still think the gift given by your mother is stupid? Why?"

"Because she's not here to teach me how to use it!" I scream, bursting into tears as thunder rips through the sky overhead. "None of them are! They're all dead, and I'm still here. I don't want a gift; I want HER. I'd give all this up to have her again. To have my father again. Even for a moment." I crumple to my knees, sobbing. "My life would have been so different. I wouldn't have been left in the streets to die. I wouldn't be alone!"

Ainet's eyes soften. "Alone, you say? Silly girl. You have never been alone. The ancestors seek to be one with you, but you refuse to listen. Too obsessed with what you lost." She steps forward as tears stream down my face. "A terrible thing has happened to you. Something was stolen that you will never be able to steal back, something you wanted to hold with both hands. Life is unfair. It will always throw crap at you. But you must learn to take that crap and build a new life with it. The smell will eventually fade. And you will go on. You cannot let what happened yesterday keep you from tomorrow."

I blink and let out a breath. "I'm going to be honest with you, Ainet. I wasn't expecting you, of all people, to say *crap*."

She smirks. "They say I am full of surprises."

I bow my head. "I just . . . The things I've had to do . . ." My mind flashes to houses collapsing, water roaring down streets, Moche jerking away from me in horror. "I don't deserve whatever gift you think this is."

She shrugs. "You did what you needed to do to survive. But you must learn to let go of what no longer serves you. If not, it will always be what weighs you down, what keeps you from greatness."

I slump, hair billowing over my shoulders. "But what good is it all if I can't control it? And who the hell am I to have this gift? I'm no one. Just some street rat. It should go to someone good. Someone who's worthy."

She steps forward and grabs my arms. "You are more than worthy of such a gift," she whispers. "Close your eyes."

Emotionally drained, I let go and listen.

"Now breathe."

"Ainet, I don't want to—"

"*Breathe!*" she says sharply, and I inhale. "Deeper. Breathe from the core of your belly."

I breathe in deep, then let it out. In, out. In, out. The winds begin to calm.

"You have an emotional block that is affecting your ability to control your power," she says. "It is why you have been struggling. *Breathe!*"

I jerk and let out another breath.

"Your breath controls your nervous system, much like the systems of weather here on Earth. If you can control your emotions, then you can control your powers. Even without your powers, if you can't master your mind, then you'll give anyone or anything control over you without even trying. It all starts and ends with you."

"I don't think I can," I whimper.

She grips my hands. "What is a storm made of?"

"Um . . . wind?" I reply. "Rain, thunder, lightning. Sometimes ice, snow, and hail."

"And where do storms come from?"

"The sky. The atmosphere."

"Can you make a storm?"

"Huh?"

"Think of the way Osunda builds a hut. How does she make her plaster so that it stands? She has all the materials she needs, but what does she do with them?"

I think hard, back to watching Osunda mixing the plaster, trying to remember every step she took, her method. The memory blurs, but I realize . . . she wasn't following any hard rules; there was no measuring as she mixed. She was following her instincts.

"Do you see it now?" Ainet says. "Now breathe and imagine a storm the same way, just in your mind. What would go first to create it?"

"You would need clouds," I whisper, feeling a pull inside me.

"Then?"

I lick my lips. "Then . . . rain? Maybe wind. Lots of wind. Um, thunder. Moisture, water for rain. Then lightning."

"Do all storms have lightning?"

"No. Not every storm."

"Only if Mother Nature is so inclined?"

Wind whips around my hair, the air electric. "Yes."

"You and Mother Nature have a lot in common. Both of you can create the very things you think of. You can decide what you want in your own storm. So think hard, girl. Listen to your soul. Imagine it, then be it. Ask for what you want. You can build a storm as big or as little as you want. And it is yours to control."

I think hard, bearing down, trying to feel for that light when I realize what she means.

I don't have to look. I just have to ask.

But I shake my head, a sob bursting from my lips. "But . . . what if I can't stop it? What if I fail? I'll hurt people."

Ainet grips my hands tighter. "You are not the same girl who arrived in this village all those days ago. You are something stronger, wiser. Now ask for exactly what you want. As long as you respect the order of nature, she will respect you."

Trembling, I bear down on the rubber band pulling inside me. *Rain.*

At that very moment, water hits my eyelid and I look up. A small cloud has formed just over our hut, rain sprinkling, not as heavy as the rains in Caribou. Ainet kicks a bucket under the cloud.

"This is the gift your mother gave you," Ainet says. "The gift your people blessed you with. No one can steal it from you. It is in your hands alone."

Her words ignite a fire within me. This is *mine*. My mother gave this to me. And I won't let anyone take it.

I widen my arms, let the clouds bloom wider and the rain fall, heavy like a waterfall, but never overwhelming. I let it pummel my face, and I breathe.

"Enough," Ainet says.

I draw my arms back in, and the storm evaporates as quick as it came. Panting, I turn to Ainet.

"Very good," she says, picking up the filled bucket of water and passing it to me. "Now go wash off. You smell like crap."

X

It's like a switch flipped. For the first time maybe ever, it feels like I can breathe. Actually, truly breathe.

I complete the walls of my hut the very next day, with plaster I make on my own. When I return from my walk to the river a few days later, I have two buckets of water and a handful of leaves that Ainet requested.

She takes one leaf from my grip and lays it on the floor.

"Here," she says, motioning. "Make this leaf dance."

I take a deep breath and call to the wind, feeling it tug at my chest, and hold out my hands toward the leaf.

"Concentrate," she orders from against the wall. "Imagine it, then be it."

"Imagine it, then be it," I repeat to myself. I must imagine being a leaf dancing in the wind.

But every time I stretch my hand, a puff of wind shoots out so fast it takes the furniture with it. I slump. We've been trying this one challenge for days.

Ainet looks at the leaf and sniffs the air. "Hmm. There is a wedding tonight. You will attend."

I balk. "I can't go to a wedding! Everyone will stare at me."

She picks up a bucket of water and heads for the door. "And that is exactly why you will go."

I rush out to follow her. "Ainet, I get it. You want me to stop being so . . . self-conscious. But let's not push it. I don't want to ruin anyone's wedding."

"Tuh. You are so worried about what other people think of you that you do not have time to think about yourself."

"It's just . . . someone's wedding? I don't want to be a distraction."

Ainet stops and turns to me, sunlight beaming on her face. "What if you did not know anyone was watching? What would you do?"

I bite my lip. "I guess I would just . . . exist."

She raises an eyebrow. "Just existing can be so underrated, can it not?"

I sigh, shrugging my shoulders.

"What anyone thinks of you is not your responsibility." She picks up the end of her dress and continues toward her hut. "Come. Let us find something for you to wear."

X

The wedding is between one of the women I've seen around and a warrior from another village. The bride is dressed in red, with the beautiful necklace and headdress I saw Ainet working on, the beads blue, yellow, and green. The bride and groom grin brightly as the elders bestow blessings, and something inside me feels peace. They remind me of the happiness I've only felt with T'Challa. Could I ever have something like that again?

After the ceremony, the village gathers for a large feast of stewed goat, rice, milk, and steamed pumpkin leaves. Ainet cornrowed my hair with black beads, and I wear a royal purple shuka with a yellow headband. The people from the other village stare, mumbling to one another, but I keep my head straight, solely focusing my attention on the beautiful bride . . . just like everyone else should be doing.

As night falls, the villagers sing and dance around a giant bonfire, children clapping along. Men high-jump to beats of the drum, the muscles in their legs taut and sharp. Women's hips roll, rhythmic and mesmerizing, their dresses flowing, their wrists rotating, bracelets jingling, and I find my own hands moving along with them.

I can't help but think of the last party I was at . . . . with T'Challa.

Focus on me.

My skin flushes at the memory of our kiss, the way our

bodies seemed to curve around each other. He must be back in Wakanda by now, cursing my name along the way. My heart sinks.

I drape the shuka over my shoulder and drift out onto the plain, walking farther and farther away from the light of the bonfire. I sit on top of the ridge and stare off into the valley, watching swirling blue-black clouds hover in the distance. Lightning crackles, a dazzling light show, booming thunder echoing across the savanna.

I could make a storm like that.

I laugh. A month ago, you couldn't get me to even acknowledge I had power. Now look at me, competing with Mother Nature, making it rain, controlling winds . . . well, almost. I wish T'Challa could see me now. As much as I try not to think of him, he always seems to creep into my thoughts.

He'd probably be so proud of me. So why can't *I* be proud of me?

A familiar pain gnaws at my insides. Maybe it's because I still feel guilty for leaving the boys.

My whole goal was to rid myself of this curse and make it back to Cairo, where I thought I belonged. But how can I belong in a place where I have to hide who I really am? I've done everything I can to be normal. Kept myself hidden, barely seen, hardly heard—but it made no difference. Going back now, I would never be able to use my powers . . . the boys would never let me. Moche would never let me.

And if I'm honest, I feel more at home in Ainet's hut than I did in all my years in Egypt.

A half-moon peeks through the clouds. The worm moon is almost full. The Shadow King must be desperate by now. And desperation can lead to many lives lost. What kind of person am I to hide away from it all? But who am I to stand up to something so . . . unknown?

"Ah. There you are! I was looking for you."

Ainet treads up the hill, holding the hem of her robe, ankle bracelets swishing as she walks.

I jut my chin at the horizon. "There's a storm coming."

"Ah, yes. The short rains. Must be quite beautiful to you." She sits beside me on the rock, looking out on the plain, expression content. "The dancing was quite beautiful, too, yes?"

"Yes," I mumble.

"I take it you do not like weddings?" she quips.

"I've never been to one. It was nice. There's just a lot on my mind."

Ainet rests her hands on her knees, pursing her lips toward the building storm.

"You know, you and storms have much in common. Unpredictable. Chaotic. Full of light, roaring thunder, furious winds. Powerful beyond measure . . ."

I sigh. "And feared."

She glances at me and chuckles.

"Ah, yes. Fear. Fear is often one's first perception of anything they cannot control or understand. But it is not the storm people fear. It is the inevitable change a storm brings."

My breath hitches up into my throat.

Ainet taps my thighs and stands to leave, her beads jingling. "You know what else people fear about them? That no one can change a storm's path. Only the storm can do that for itself. A storm, like you, can never be controlled. Because a storm has a destiny."

X

Later that evening, I walk back into my hut and find the leaves still on the floor where I left them. I stare at them as I unravel my braids. I can still hear the drums in my ears like an echo, like a whisper of voices calling my name, and I picture the way the women moved their arms to the sky.

I square my shoulders, take a deep breath, and hold my hands out, letting the breeze glide through my fingers. My hair billows around me, and I round my arms, dancing like the women to a song only I can still hear.

The breeze gently scoops the leaves up, twirling them into a slow twister that remains perfectly centered in the middle of the hut. Leaves dancing as I tell them to.

NINETEEN

"Jambo, Kioko," I say as I walk over with the bucket. Kioko whips her tail, gnawing at the ground. "I thought you'd be sick of me by now."

Kioko snorts, pushing her head at me, and I laugh. "I knew you liked me."

Well, at least she does. Even after all this time, the villagers still don't entirely trust me. I don't take the rejection personally anymore. I've fallen into a comfortable rhythm here with the people. Doing chores and practicing my powers in the safety of my hut. But every now and then, I test the waters outside.

Spotting a pile of leaves in the corner, I check my surroundings to see if anyone is watching. I extend my fingers, twirling them, and a breeze kicks up, lifting the leaves. I wiggle my pinkie, and the leaves swoop and dance around one another.

"Oh, I see someone is being brave today."

Ainet stands by the fence with a satisfied grin. I never see or hear this old woman move!

"I swear you have catlike feet."

She enters the pen and pats Kioko's side, nodding at the leaves. "I would like to see you up there someday."

"What do you mean?"

She shrugs. "The winds carry leaves. Why can they not carry you?"

I pause for a moment and laugh. "You're very funny."

She doesn't break her stare, and I'm just about to confirm that she is, indeed, joking, when I feel something shift in the air and turn.

Dust kicks up on the horizon. I shield the sun with my hand, watching an army-green jeep drive in our direction.

"I think this safari tour might be lost," I say with a laugh.

"They are not lost," she says as she heads back to her hut.

The jeep pulls up by the fence. An older, bald man hops out the truck and is greeted by the other villagers. He gives me a warm smile. Ainet emerges, holding something in her fist.

"This is Absko. He will take you to the city. I need you to pick up a few supplies."

My heart drops. "But . . . why can't Mukami do it? Or someone else?"

"If you have not noticed, we are all very busy here. Besides, you know the city well, don't you?"

I can sense this is another one of her challenges. The one I'm most terrified of. "I don't think I'm ready to face them yet."

Ainet chuckles.

"That is the problem, is it not? You're thinking rather than just doing. Here, this is what I need."

She gives me a small piece of paper and I scan down the list.

"These are medications," I say, head popping up in surprise.

"Yes. Sometimes we cannot always rely on our herbs. Science helps, too."

I want to ask her more, but Ainet plays her hand close to the chest, and I respect that.

"I'll be back as soon as I can," I say, and walk inside to grab my bag and head wrap. Ainet snatches the wrap from my grasp.

"You do not need it. You no longer need to hide who you are."
I tug back at it. "But everyone will stare at me."
She leans closer. "Let them."

x

The trip back to Nairobi is much shorter in a jeep than it is by foot. We reach the city by afternoon, and I'm transported back in time. I almost forgot what it was like to be around so many people. Absko drops me off at the pharmacy near Maasai Market.

But the pharmacist needs at least four hours to fulfill the request. Absko has to run a few errands, so we agree to meet back at the market by four.

I plop down on a bench outside the pharmacy and take in my surroundings. The street clothes, cars, and technology . . . it's comforting in a different way. Familiar. But here, I look over my shoulder every few minutes, feeling everyone's eyes on me, staring at my white hair, blinding in the hot sunlight. My heart ticks faster.

"Breathe," I tell myself, trying to dry my clammy hands.

Let them stare. There's nothing wrong with me.

But I can't just sit here like an animal at a petting zoo. I think maybe I'll take a walk in the park or a garden, until I spot the line of cabs outside the market gate. I dig into my wallet, pull out the last of the backpacker's money, and know what I have to do.

x

When the cab drops me off in front of the entrance to Caribou, anxiety rears its ugly head, and it takes everything in me not to vomit.

But I hold my breath and walk through the gates, carrying

bags of sweets, cakes, and fresh fruits I bought from a vendor, ready to accept whatever wrath I deserve. They'll probably throw trash at my head, chase me out of their city. I sort of deserve it. I owe everyone an apology.

I walk through the labyrinth to the main road and gasp at the sight.

There are brand-new tiny homes, made with seemingly stronger materials, painted in red, gold, green, and purple. Less trash on the roads, even flowers planted in clay pots. Kids in clean clothes playing with proper toys. Everyone is smiling and laughing, a joyous sight, and I'm left stunned.

"You must be Ororo."

I jolt at the voice behind me and slowly turn to a man standing outside his small green home, maybe in his thirties, dressed in slacks, a white button-down, and sandals.

"I am," I mumble.

"I am Thomas," he says, smiling. "Welcome. As you can see, there have been many changes and improvements since we last saw you."

"I . . . didn't think anyone would want to see me again. After what I did."

"After you saved Caribou? We should all be singing your praises!"

I blink. "Saved?"

"You tried to give us water. And when the dam overflowed, you helped keep us all from drowning. You are most welcomed here, sista."

My eyes flood with tears. My heart feels like it's on the verge of exploding. "I'm . . . so sorry."

Thomas reaches for my hands and takes the bags, giving them to a young girl standing behind him.

"Look what Ororo has brought us! Make sure everyone has some, okay?"

The girl scurries off with the bags as Thomas turns to me.

"Come. Would you like to see?"

I nod, unable to form words through the trembling tears.

We stroll down the road toward the dam as he points out all the major improvements. The dam has been fortified with metal and stone, built taller than the previous one. A few of the homes even have solar panels for electricity.

"How did this all happen?" I ask, in awe.

"We received some help," Thomas quips.

The transformation is astonishing, but I can still see myself standing in the rain, begging Moche not to leave and yelling at T'Challa. My throat aches with the guilt.

"Have you . . . I mean, did you see the boy I was here with?"

"The one who saved the children?"

I nod with a sniff.

"Yes, I did," he says, heading back toward his home. "After the dam broke, he stayed and help us rebuild. I think he was waiting for you. He often looked toward the gates, in search of something."

My heart skips. "Where is he now?"

"I believe he was called back to his country. But he left something for you. In case you were ever to return."

"Of course he did," I mutter under my breath with a chuckle. T'Challa thinks of everything.

Thomas walks into his house and returns with a box wrapped in a purple scarf, similar to the one I had in Sudan.

"Here," he says. "He asked me to give this to you. He did not want to leave without giving you a way to contact him."

I slowly unwrap the box, swallowing at the scarf that smells like him. Inside is my blue dress, the beetle earrings, the comb . . . and a cell phone. But it's unlike any phone I've ever seen. Not the same bead thingy T'Challa wore. It's sleek black marble, shaped like a narrow shell.

Of course he would leave some contraption with no instructions. I press a side button and the screen lights up purple. There are a few apps and games, but in the contacts, only one number saved: T'Challa So Green.

I smile. The corny jokes never end.

X

After I say my goodbyes, promising to visit again, I pick up Ainet's medications and wait for Absko at a café near the pharmacy. At a table near the window, I palm my new phone, finger hovering over the number. Should I call? Tell him that I am okay? He's probably worried sick. After all he did to help me.

Would he still want me to come to Wakanda?

"Strong earthquakes continue to hit the coastal city of Mombasa. . . ."

My head snaps toward the TV set sitting above the bar.

"Seismologists are perplexed by the strange earthquakes rattling, as there are no reports of tectonic-plate shifts in the area. . . . Citizens are asked to stay away from the beaches and caves. . . ."

That's where Zawadi is from.

It's Zawadi's powers making those earthquakes, that much I'm sure of. Or the powers that the Shadow King is wielding inside her. But why would he take her back there? What is he trying to do? What if it's another trap?

The air in the room tightens. There is a strange energy . . . like a toxic smog. The hairs on my arms prickle. Suddenly, the rubber band thrums to life. I glance up at my reflection in the café window and notice two shadowy figures by the door behind me.

I take a deep, calming breath before spinning around—just as a man reaches for me.

I shove both my hands out. Wind scoops him up and throws him out the window, glass shattering.

People in the café scream and scatter, running over broken glass. I leap to my feet, whipping around to get a better look at him, but on my right, the other man charges for me.

The light blooming in my hand blinds him before I zap him in the chest and he slumps to the floor. I stand over him, sneaker at his throat, holding one hand over his face like a loaded weapon. His eyes widen, lips stiffening, sweat dripping down his brow.

I recognize his face. It's the man I saw in the market in Sudan with T'Challa. The one who smashed the vendors' stands.

"Tell your boss I'm done with his cat-and-mouse games," I hiss. "Go find someone else to use!"

The man shakes his head, relentless. "No. He wants you," he croaks in a thick accent that reminds me of Cairo, of home.

I press my palm closer to his temple, and he strains away. "Why? He can have anyone!"

The man peers at me, his eyes hard. "You are Mother Nature. Why wouldn't he?"

"That's ridiculous. I'm not Mother Nature. I'm not . . ."

And then, like a puzzle, it all clicks. I can't believe I didn't realize it all this time—he doesn't want to inhabit just anyone. He wants to inhabit a person more powerful than himself. He wants me because of what I can do. He wants to take over the world with my powers. With Zawadi and me combined, he could start floods and tornadoes, create hurricanes in an instant. He could kill millions.

But if he can't capture me, he'll stay in Zawadi, and even then he'll never leave me alone. He'll keep coming after me, Moche and the boys, the village . . . all in retaliation for not getting exactly what he wants.

A crowd forms around the café, people staring inside at us.

The man I threw outside comes to and stands shakily. I raise my hand toward him, eyes narrowing.

"Go! And don't come after me again."

His face pales, torn about what to do.

"Save yourself," I tell him, nodding below me as I take my foot off the other man's neck. "And your friend. Come after me again, and I won't be so kind."

The man rubs his jaw as he stumbles to his feet, walking out of the café, retreating with his friend.

I glance up at the television. The portal must be there in Mombasa; that's the only explanation for him returning. If I don't face him, I'll be hiding from him forever. He'll never stop. Not unless I give him exactly what he wants.

But how can I stop him and save Zawadi and myself at the same time?

T'Challa's words come slipping back:

One first would have to find an opening, a portal, which is like finding a very small needle in a vast universe. Then that opening would only last for a brief stretch of time. Minutes, a couple of days, maybe weeks . . . If the spirit does not find a body to inhabit before the portal closes, it will cease to exist entirely.

Wait a minute, what day is it? How long have I been gone?

I turn to the stunned woman standing behind the register.

"You!" I bark. "When's the next full moon?"

She holds her hands up, eyes wide. "Uh, tonight, I think?"

It took me ten days to get to Kenya. Weeks with Ainet. That means the worm moon is tonight. The portal will close today! This is my chance to stop him for good.

"How do I get to Mombasa?"

TWENTY

It takes ten hours to make it to Mombasa by bus. I know I should've waited to tell Absko where I was going, but time is of the essence. One more night and the Shadow King will be in Zawadi forever. He'll use her to keep hurting people, as revenge. He'll never stop.

I wrap my hair to maintain the element of surprise. But he must know I'm coming for him by now. He planned it this way. My plan in comparison isn't so concrete—I need to lure him out of Zawadi somehow, even for a moment, and then use my lightning to send him back into the portal.

Once I reach Mombasa, it isn't hard to find the caves. They're located in cliffs by a giant white-sand beach on the shore of a crystal-clear ocean that goes on for eternity. I breathe in the fresh ocean air as the ground trembles with aftershocks. I snake around authorities roping off access and tourists fighting to have their time in the sun, then climb down the rocky cliffside.

I'm pulled toward one cave in particular, and I follow the feeling. As I near it, I sense a shift in the air and glance at my palms. I have one shot at this.

Holding my breath, I inch closer to the mouth of the cave, peer in, and nearly fall in shock.

The portal is a small sliver of choppy white light, like a crack in a building's side, embedded in the wall of the cave, with a kaleidoscope of colors swirling inside it.

One first would have to find an opening, a portal, which is like finding a very small needle in a vast universe.

I watch as Zawadi props rocks around it, grumbling to herself as each one falls soundlessly into the crack.

What is he doing?

Suddenly, Zawadi's back tenses. She whips around, her eyes still black, staring directly at me.

"Ah! There you are," she says, her voice raw and husky. "I was wondering when you'd show up."

I glance around the cave, uneasy. "What are you doing?"

"Ensuring that no one will ever send me back," Zawadi growls.

Zawadi bangs her fist against the rock, skin glimmering gold. The ground ripples as far as the ocean.

Heart racing, I stand outside the cave, unable to move. I eye the portal. One wrong step, and it will swallow me whole.

"You wanted me, right? Let her go!" I shout. "Come on! She has nothing to do with this. This is between you and me!"

Zawadi turns in my direction. "Let me into your soul and I'll let the girl go."

"Let her go first! Then we can talk."

She shakes her head, eyes dangerous. "There will be no negotiations."

Zawadi pounds at the ground, and the earth rumbles beneath my feet. Massive rocks tumble down the hill. I shriek, dodging the avalanche, stumbling back. I peer over the cliff's edge, watching the rocks rain down on the beach below.

Look at what he's doing with Zawadi's power alone. He would cause even more destruction if he had mine.

I swallow. "Let her go, and I promise, I'll give you what you want."

She stares at me with those soulless eyes, as if considering.

Suddenly, her head snaps up, and she looks out at the sea with a hideous grin.

"You have saved some before, but there will be more blood on your hands again."

"What?"

She slams her hands against the ground. More rocks fall, some even hitting Zawadi, cutting her shoulder. But she doesn't move—the Shadow King doesn't care. He's just using her.

I think of Moche, the guilt-stricken look on his face when he admitted he let the Shadow King use him to get to me. He saw everything, sitting in the passenger seat of his own body.

Which means . . . Zawadi is still in there! And there must be a way to lure her out.

I take a deep breath and inch into the cave.

"Zawadi," I start, keeping my tone light. "I know you can hear me. You need to fight him."

Zawadi lets out a hoarse laugh, drool dripping down her chin.

"He's using you," I insist. "Just to get to me. He used my friend Moche, too. He uses everyone, and they all end up hurt. Don't believe a word he says. He's a liar!"

"Stop talking to this girl," Zawadi snaps.

"I know you opened the portal by accident. And now he's using you to close it so he can't be sent back where he was banished to."

Zawadi's face screws up; she shakes her head. "Banished? I wasn't banished."

I see a flicker of hope. "Yes, he was, Zawadi. I saw it myself."

"Shut up, stupid girl!"

"Think about it," I insist, creeping closer to her. "He used you to trap me. Because my power is what he really wants. He doesn't want anything or anyone else." I extend my hand. "You think he'll need you after he has whatever he needs from me? You'll be alone again!"

Zawadi's face crumples a touch, her eyes briefly turning back to normal. "No!"

"I don't know what he told you," I carry on, pulse racing. "But I do know what it's like to feel different, to feel like you don't belong, to want to be like everyone else." I swallow. "But people like you and me, we're not meant to be like everyone else. We're destined to be more! We're special; we've been given a gift." As I say the words, they course through me like a thudding pulse. What I'm saying is right and true, and I believe it with my whole heart.

"You are extraordinary, Zawadi. Your abilities, your powers, they are not in vain. Do not let him rob you of your gift. You need to fight. Fight with all you have!"

Zawadi stomps her foot and the world shakes. "NO!"

I stagger back, clutching the cliffside, but she just pounds the ground with two fists, arguing with herself. The gold under her skin crackles like a malfunctioning light bulb.

"Stop this . . . no . . . stop . . . You said you would . . . NO!"

The cave begins to rumble, a terrible quake. My heart leaps into my throat as I back up, the rock crumbling around us.

A rock hits Zawadi in the head, and she falls.

"Zawadi!" I scream, and dive on the ground for her. She's knocked out cold. Blood trickles out the side of her head.

A cluster of red dots hovers like soap bubbles, flying through the falling rocks, and I look up, momentarily stricken by the sight. My heartbeat spikes. And before I can run out, the cave collapses inward and a thick dust cloud blinds me.

TWENTY-ONE

Sparks flicker in my hands in short spurts like a match striking, and then light blooms from my palms. I cough through the dust and raining dirt. I hold on to the light, raising a hand to see the entrance to the cave completely walled in by massive black rocks.

Oh no. Oh no.

"Zawadi!" I shriek, shaking her shoulder.

She is still breathing, but the gash on her head is deep. I turn and find that the other side of the cave is a narrowing passage, so narrow my legs won't even allow me to walk through it. The dim light of the portal glimmers.

The cave is spinning. Or is it me?

"There's no way out," I wheeze, and shake her shoulder. "Zawadi, wake up!"

Zawadi moans, her eyes fluttering open. I hold the light to her face and look into her hazel eyes.

She's back!

"Oh, thank Goddess," I cry.

"What . . . happened?" she whimpers.

"We need to get out of here," I say, unable to hide my panic. "Is there another way out?"

"Huh?" she groans, then notices the jagged pile of rocks

blocking our way. She sits up, holding the gash on her head. "Oh God . . ."

My body is buzzing, the walls of the cave are pulsing, the air too muggy . . .

I'm going to die in here.

"We're trapped!" she cries.

"I know!" I scream, trying to suck in a breath. "Can't you break the rocks?"

Her eyes scan the cave, shaking her head. "If I make the earth move again, the rocks will bury us."

My nerves shatter. That is the absolute last thing you want to tell some claustrophobic girl.

"Stop talking. Just please stop talking," I say. I pace in a circle as my mouth dries, sweat dripping down my face. The walls of the cave are closing in on us. My heart jumps into overdrive as I realize that my lungs won't take in oxygen.

We're going to die.

"I tried to tell him, but he wouldn't listen," Zawadi carries on. "He wasn't trying to close the portal. He was trying to keep it *open* so he could buy more time . . . so he could find you!"

But I can barely listen as my vision blurs, my breath turning shallow . . . and in the fog, I can see a hand sticking out from under the rocks.

Momma?

"No, no, no . . . ," I whimper, trembling.

"Ororo, we don't have enough air in here," Zawadi says, sounding winded. "Why can't you use your power to break the rock?"

"I can't breathe," I gasp, leaning my head against the rock. The cave is spinning.

Wind wisps under me, whipping through my hair. Sand and rocks kick up. Hands on my knees, I hunch over, wheezing, tears dripping down my face.

Zawadi scoots away from me. "Ororo . . . what are you doing?"

I can't. I can't. I can't . . .

The wind whips around like a violent tornado, and I register the fear in Zawadi's eyes. I'm losing control, but I can't stop. I . . .

BREATHE! Deeper. Breathe from your belly, and let it out.

Ainet's words rip through me, snapping me back to the village. I can almost smell the herbs in her hut.

If you can control your emotions, then you can control your power.

In, out, in, out, my lungs about to burst. I manage to lean against the rock until my vision sharpens.

Breathe. *Breathe.*

Focus.

Lungs aflame, I straighten my back, stomach aching, hands itching for a release.

You are more powerful than you know.

The voice echoes in my ears as I face the rocky dam, pulling power to my fingertips.

You are a part of something bigger.

Wind howls in my ears as the cave shakes, a rumble around us. But I am bigger than this cave. It cannot hold me.

"Zawadi," I shout over the wind, "stand behind me!"

Zawadi moves quick, her hand on my back. I push harder, calling all the light, feeling the power pool in my palms. I pull back and launch it at the rocks with everything I have in me. Light shoots out of both hands with a blue hue like a massive waterspout, busting through the rocks. Sunlight streams through, but I barely have time to take it in.

I grab Zawadi's hand, and we run through the new hole before the rest of the boulders come tumbling down.

TWENTY-TWO

Panting and coughing, I gape at the collapsing cave behind us. Chest heaving, I inhale big gulps of the ocean air and fall on my back. I've never been so happy to see sunlight in my life.

"You did it," Zawadi mutters in astonishment. "You saved us."

I did. But now the entrance to the portal is closed, and the Shadow King is still on the loose. We're not out of the clear just yet.

"Damn," I grumble, and jump to my feet, wiping the dust off my face. I scan the mouth of the cave, bracing for an attack. But there is no sign of anything or anyone.

Where is he?

Zawadi sits crumpled on the ground, eyes far off, shaking her head.

"I thought . . . He said he would take care of me," she mumbles in a daze. "He said he would be my new family."

Blood trickles down her forehead. I crouch beside her, ripping the sleeve of my T-shirt and pressing it to her wound.

Anger rages in my belly. *He will hurt so many more people.*

I whip around. "We need to find him. Where is he? Where would he go?"

Zawadi winces, holding the rag to her cut. "He would most likely look for another body," she says. "If he does not find a new host within minutes, he will be lost and forced to return to the plane."

"But the portal to the plane is now closed."

Zawadi turns to meet my eye. "So what does that mean?"

As if on cue, T'Challa's words come back to me. *If the spirit does not find a body to inhabit before the portal closes, it will cease to exist entirely.*

"Come on! He can't have gone far," I say, racing for the beach. But as I climb down the boulders, a goat shoves past us, climbing up. Two more goats follow.

Something shifts in me, drawing my attention toward the ocean. A flock of birds caw overhead, flying away from the sea.

Birds of a feather . . .

I glance down at the beach and notice the water receding farther and farther, exposing the ocean floor, fish flopping in the sand in desperation. I stare out into the ocean, my mind swirling as dread fills me.

"I think your earthquakes . . . might have traveled farther than we thought," I say slowly. I close my eyes to listen. In the distance, there is a roaring like a loud train . . .

. . . or a massive plane heading into our home.

"Something is coming," I say, voice quivering.

Zawadi follows my line of sight and gasps. "A tsunami . . ."

I whip around to the beach full of people. "We need to get everyone out of here. Now!"

Zawadi stares at the open sea. "This is all my fault," she whispers.

I grab her arms. "You didn't know what you were doing! But now you know better and have a chance to make it right."

"How?"

I point to the beach. "By saving these people!"

Eyes full of tears, she nods and runs in their direction. "Tsunami!"

Some people glance at her in confusion, while others ignore her shouts.

I clap my hands and thunder booms, drawing everyone's attention.

"Tsunami!" I scream. "Everyone, run!"

"Head to higher ground. Now!" Zawadi hollers.

Startled, the crowd jumps, grabbing their belongings and children, racing for the hills.

We run down the beach, helping others up, leading them to a set of wooden stairs toward the main beach entrance as others climb up the boulders. The roaring of water grows closer, racing. If only we had time to slow the water down, or if there were some type of dam, like in Caribou. . . .

A dam!

I turn to Zawadi. "Get everyone to safety. I'll hold off the wave."

"How?"

"I'm not sure. But you need to help everyone in case I fail."

Zawadi grips my arm, her eyes wild. "Do not be foolish, Ororo. Save yourself!"

I shake my head. "I can't leave people to die. Go. Now! I'll stay and make sure everyone is off the beach."

Zawadi hesitates before running past, grabbing a child, and climbing up the rocky cliffside.

I scan the beach, hoping we've reached everyone we can. But by the shore, a white man in a tropical shirt and shorts stands facing the water, his hands in his pockets, as if waiting for the wave.

"Hey! You!"

I run down to the shore and tap the man's shoulder. "What are you doing?"

He slowly turns, his eyes pure black.

Air sucks out of my lungs, my mind going blank with fear.

But before I can remember how to defend myself, the man backhands me, and I fall face-first in the sand. The man arches his hands up, preparing to thrust them into my stomach. I spin onto my back and leap to my feet, steadying myself. I throw one hit, then another. My elbow connects with his jaw, and he stumbles on his feet. The Shadow King roars with anger.

"You think you can just get away," the man snarls. "You don't deserve your powers, Ororo! You're no more than a little street rat!"

The ground rumbles. I glance at the sea, and my stomach plunges. In the distance, a ferocious wave looms, making its way to shore. And in those few seconds I turn away from him, the Shadow King tackles me. He grips my throat, shaking me in the air toward the water.

"Look at it!" he cries, mad. "It's perfect! You can't save anyone! Everyone here will die because of your stupid insolence. Believing you are worthy of such power, when you are worthy of *nothing*!"

I claw at his fingers, tears streaming as I watch the water tower over the beach.

"No prince to save you, no family. You are all alone. Let me in, and I will use your powers to save these people, something you will never do."

Panic surges, my heart cracking.

"Okay," I croak. "You win."

He yanks me back to his face and hisses the words: "Now I will have you."

His eyes bore into mine as they change from black to a glowing red, his grip on my neck tightening. I beat at his hand for air, the edges of my vision fraying.

This is it. I'm going to die and he's going to take me.

But he can't take something that was never his.

Power pools into my hands and bursts. The man's eyes flare

before he loses his grip. Another low rumble hits, and the sand suddenly plummets beneath us.

We fall into a deep pit in the sand, hitting the bottom with a thud. The Shadow King stumbles to his feet with a moan, as if momentarily forgetting himself. But then he spots me and dives for my neck. I swing-kick him off, sending him flying to the other side of the crater.

In that moment, I realize how tight the space felt. Scrambling, I crawl out of the hole and see Zawadi standing at the bottom of the stairs, a hand on the ground. She gives me a nod.

"Ororo!" the Shadow King bellows just as he clambers to the top of the pit, wet sand covering his enraged face. I throw lightning at his chest, tossing him toward the receding water, and he hits the wet sand. I slap the air twice, and a small tornado whips up, tossing the man again. I throw lightning once more, and he falls flat on his face.

"Uhhh," he groans, fish flopping around him. His body stills. Red particles drift out of his skin, floating above us.

"No you don't!" I shout, shooting light at them with a sizzling zap. The red particles short-circuit, my lightning zapping between them as if playing a game of Ping-Pong. The particles drift drunkenly away.

I dive for the Shadow King's most recent host.

"Zawadi!" I call, turning the man onto his side, tapping his cheek.

The man lets out a small groan, and I exhale a sigh of relief. He's still breathing. I didn't kill him.

Zawadi runs toward me, dropping to her knees. The massive wave races closer.

"Get him off the beach!" I yell, helping to lift the man to his feet. "Hurry!"

"Come with us!" she says desperately. "The wave . . . You won't survive!"

I turn back to the sea, the wave barreling toward us. I push the man onto Zawadi's shoulder.

"Go, now!" I order. Then I turn, facing the wave. And I walk toward it.

The sound of water grows louder, like a stampede of antelope through the savanna, heading straight for me. I take a deep breath.

Imagine it. Be it.

I spread my arms wide, palms up, and I stare down the wave. The air around me stills; I can see the tiniest bits of water floating in slow motion. I call on the wind, pulling it toward me. My body shakes, trying to stay rooted to the ground as the wind builds into a solid invisible wall. Fingers splayed, I stretch the wall wider, as far out as it can go.

The wave—it's massive. The wall of wind needs to be taller, higher.

A dream so big that it may scare you. That's when you learn just how brave and powerful you can be.

"Goddess, help me," I mutter, sweat building on my brow, my muscles trembling, palms growing so cold they almost burn. I bear down, pushing harder, my jaw quivering against the mental weight. I take another step toward the incoming water.

Higher. I need to be higher.

Suddenly, something inside me cracks, a thunder so loud it's deafening, and I'm blinded by an explosion of colors. Brilliant blues, greens, golds, and purples tint my vision. My body jerks as all my power comes pouring out of me, as if it was trapped by a wall. A wall of doubt I could not break until this very moment.

The power unfurls in waves. I can feel every atom shift, every strand of hair sway. Air rips through my lungs in the form of a scream, a battle cry, before my vision sharpens behind foggy white eyes.

The wind swoops under my feet, dancing up my sides to my arms, and I'm lifted off the ground. My hair comes loose and coils around me. I'm too busy staring the wave down to notice how high up I really am.

Focus, Ororo. Focus.

I take a deep breath and shove the wall of wind toward the wave like a shield.

The water crashes violently into the wall and I push forward, teeth bared, flexing my muscles. The water pushes harder, as if it refuses to believe it can be stopped.

"You will not get past!" I scream, pushing back, flying closer, shoving my wind-made dam into it.

Then, suddenly, I'm no longer struggling. I'm just existing.

I glance down the beach at my wall in wonder and notice the red particles, weakly struggling down the shore, and remember Zawadi's words . . .

If he does not find a new host within minutes, he will be lost and forced to return to the plane.

I lower one arm, letting a sliver of the water tip over my wind-made dam and dump on top of the red particles, stopping them in their tracks.

The giant wave swirls and pipes into itself, slowly losing its anger until it begins to calm and shrink.

I lower my arms, letting the dam down, and watch the small remainder of the wave rush onto the beach, never making it far up the shore. The wave scoops up the particles and pulls them into the sea. And then they are gone.

As I watch, I realize I'm still floating in the air.

Because I want to be.

The thoughts come crashing in. I wanted to save T'Challa, to rescue the children from war, to help the villagers, to save the people on the beach. . . . It all begins to make sense. Who I *am* is more important than who I thought I was supposed to be.

Still floating, I spin around and spot Zawadi by the steps.

I sail over to her and try to touch down on the beach but stumble, falling on my knees with an "Oof!"

My landing isn't the best, but it will get there.

I glance up at Zawadi.

"You were . . . you were flying," she utters in disbelief.

"Yes," I agree, breathless.

"But . . . how?"

I glance back at the sea. "Because I wanted to."

X

Zawadi and I sit on the boulders, looking out at the sea, the water returning to its normal gracefulness. My body buzzes with an intoxicating energy that I never want to go away.

"You saved me," she says.

I nod, not looking at her. "Yeah."

"You were willing to give yourself up . . . for a stranger. Why?"

"I told you. . . . We're a lot alike," I say, nodding to the caves. "We can both do things no one else can."

Zawadi twists her fingers. "You know, I had never been to Caribou until that day," she admits.

I figured as much. "And your grandmother?"

She shakes her head. "My grandmother died last year. She was my only family. She knew I was . . . different. I was trying to keep my secret about what I can do to the earth. But sometimes . . . I was tempted to try. So I went near the caves, where I thought no one would see or hear me, and I touched the ground. The cliffside cracked, and the Shadow King came out in this red light." She laughs harshly. "I thought he was an angel. He told me that I was special. That he could provide for me what no one could—protection, a family, the chance to belong to something.

He had a great big plan, and I helped him. I'd been so alone, and it all seemed worth it."

I think of Moche and the boys in Cairo, and how familiar I am with wanting to do anything to feel like you belong. Even trying to be everything I am not.

Her eyes well with tears. "I wanted to be a part of something. But now . . . no one will take me after what I've done. I don't belong anywhere now."

I glance back at the sea and smile. "You know what's amazing?"

She frowns. "What?"

I scoop up a handful of sand and wiggle my fingers, whipping the wind into a mini tornado.

"We actually can belong anywhere we want."

TWENTY-THREE

I glance up at the sunny sky, palming the phone in my hand. I take a deep breath before dialing the number.

T'Challa answers on the second ring.

"Ororo?" he gasps, and his voice sends all those silly butterflies to my tummy.

"Hello, my king."

He sputters out a quick chuckle. "I would tell you to not call me that, but I will let you call me anything if you keep talking. Are you okay? I heard what happened in Mombasa. You were flying!"

I wrap a strand of hair around my pinkie. "Indeed. It was . . . amazing."

"Are you back in Nairobi?"

I look out from Thomas's tin house in Caribou at Zawadi, playing soccer with a few of the children, laughing and giggling.

"Yes."

"Stay there! I can be there in a few short hours."

I steel myself for this next part. "T'Challa, I have a favor to ask."

"Anything!"

"I know Wakanda doesn't like outsiders. But Zawadi . . . she's all alone."

There's a pause before he says, "You . . . want me to bring her here?"

"Yes."

"And will you come as well?"

I hold my breath for a few seconds before releasing it. "No. I'm afraid not."

There is a long silence. I can almost picture his thinking face.

"You are going to look for your family," he says, but not as a question. He knows me too well.

"Yes. I'm not ready to give up the search just yet."

"But I can help you. We have tools here. . . ."

I twirl a strand of my frizzy hair and sigh. "Wakanda sounds amazing, T'Challa. It would be an honor to be there with you. But I respect that Wakandans are not fully ready for the outside world to know of their existence, and you're not king just yet. Letting in two outsiders might be too much, and I won't have you jeopardize the start of your great reign for me." I pause, letting my voice soften. "Let Zawadi take my place. She has no friends or family, no place to call home. My family is still out there. And my home is here, in Egypt, in Sudan. My home is the world. The way I felt when I saved all those people on the beach, or in Caribou . . . I just have this feeling that this is a part of my destiny. Or something bigger."

T'Challa sighs and clicks his tongue. "You have always been wiser than me."

"You've finally seen the light!"

He laughs and I smile. I've so missed the sound of his voice.

"There must be others like me and Zawadi," I say. "I don't think the world is ready for people like us, so we need to get ready for the world. Will you help her?"

"I will send a ship to pick her up. She will be in good hands."

I glance out the door at the new and improved homes, the

solar panels and potted plants, so different from how I first left things.

"T'Challa . . . I'm sorry for what I said to you in Caribou. This entire time, you were only trying to help me. And I was being an ass. An ungrateful one, too. I would have never gotten this far without you."

"No, I am the one who is sorry," he says. "I pushed you to do something you were not ready for. You told me and I did not listen."

I breathe a sigh of relief. "So, forgiveness all around."

He laughs, then exhales. "Ororo, you have given me a lot to think about. About the type of king I want to be. About the future of Wakanda. Our privacy has made us blind to some of the suffering around us. But we are hoping to change that. So, I hope, one day soon, you'll reconsider. There are lakes with no crocodiles here."

My heart is ready to burst out of my chest.

"Well, we'll see," I say, trying to play it off. "Well, thanks again."

"You are most welcome."

The line goes silent, but I sense he is still on the other end.

"What are you waiting for?" I ask.

"For you to wish me good night. So I know that I will see you again. Soon."

I glance up at the high sun and grin so hard my face splits. "Good night, T'Challa."

And I can just picture his deep dimples before he says, "Good night, Ororo."

X

"T'Challa is sending a ship," I announce as I walk out the house. "You are going to Wakanda."

Zawadi's face turns up as if she's smelling something rotten. "Wakanda? That little place?"

I laugh. "Trust me when I say you're gonna want to be there. And they'll be able to help you."

She kicks the ball to the kids and walks over to me.

"And I should be helping you," she says. "I was not lying about the stories my grandmother used to tell me. She told me a story about a tribe with a white-haired priestess who wielded magic and could control the weather. She said they were descended from the rain god, who knew how to ride the winds and lived in the Forest of the Lost Child."

My eyes flood with tears. I grasp her shoulders. "Thank you."

"Ororo!"

I spin around at the familiar voice. "Mukami! What are you doing here?"

Mukami rushes toward me, the sight of his red robe both alarming and welcome.

"You must hurry," he says, out of breath. "Ainet is ill."

A blade pierces my heart.

The medications! I never brought them back to her.

I pull Zawadi into a quick hug. "I have to go. Stay here and look out for a ship!"

She nods as I run toward the dam.

Mukami points to the road in the other direction. "The car is this way. . . ."

"Yes, but flying would be faster," I yell back, and take to the sky.

TWENTY-FOUR

Ainet is a stubborn woman.

"I can get water fine on my own," she snaps, tugging at the other side of a bucket.

"Ainet, you've only just gotten back on your feet," I say, pulling at the handle. "Let me help you."

Whatever illness came over Ainet, it passed within a few weeks. But she still seems feeble and a little out of breath at times. I helped nurse her back to health, cooking her stews and broth, taking over her beading duties. But now she's up, dressed, and being ridiculous.

"This is not up for discussion," she scolds outside her hut. "Now let it go."

I pull the bucket closer to me, meeting her eye. "You can either let me get it, or I'll have the water come to you."

Ainet's eyes flare. She knows I mean business. She sucks her teeth and releases the bucket.

"I am quite tired of your little rain clouds and wet clothes," she grumbles, plopping down on her stool.

I smirk, slipping off my sandals, and take to the air, the wind wisping under me, my blue dress fringed at the hem. I twirl, my hair wild and free.

"I'll be right back in no time."

She groans, lips set in a hard line. "You know, I think you just like using any excuse to fly anywhere."

"Maybe." I laugh, and turn just in time to see a few villagers drop their buckets and each fall to the ground in a full bow.

"Mungu wa kike!" they shout.

Not this again.

"Would you tell them to stop that?" I say, floating just above Ainet's head.

Ainet juts her lips at the people. "What do you expect them to call a flying white-haired girl?" I sigh and head for the river, passing over the grazing cattle, grass now plentiful since I've been watering it with a few quick showers. I wave to Kioko, pretending not to notice the other villagers fall to their knees, shouting.

"Mungu wa kike! Mungu wa kike!"

Goddess. That's what they started calling me the moment I came back from Nairobi. From the second my foot touched the ground, the villagers broke into hysterics, hollering at the gods, performing ceremonies of praise and sacrifices. I was too busy caring for Ainet to correct them. Now they've made me their deity. In the mornings, I wake up to offerings at my doorstep. Food, jewelry, cow's blood, even once a baby. That made for an interesting day.

I skip across the water, toes tapping the cool surface, and land by the rocks at the river's bend. Hippos eye me curiously but continue to hunt for their next meal while the zebras gather around and stare. I think of all the animals I've encountered, especially the dogs in Garbage City, and smile.

Ainet is right: I'm a miraculous being, and this is my new normal. But could I live the rest of my days here being known as a goddess? What kind of life would I have here? Making it rain during droughts, protecting them from the elements? Shouldn't I be doing more?

Where else could I go?

I gaze into the mirror at my reflection and pause, admiring the girl before me. The golden, rich copper skin, the sparkling blue eyes . . . the beautiful white crown of hair. Everything about me has somehow heightened since I started using my powers.

"I was there all along," I muse, poking at my reflection's nose, letting the ripples spread out.

As I dip the bucket into the water, a breeze ruffles the nearby reeds. Pulse spiking, I straighten with a gasp.

That's not the wind. Something is coming. And fast.

I ditch the bucket and shoot up to the sky, speeding back toward the village, dropping down in front of Ainet's house with a loud thud.

"Eh, eh. That was quick," she says, amused, her hands busy working on a new necklace. "Where is my water?"

"Something's coming," I mutter, focusing on the sky. Taking a deep breath and tapping into that thrumming pulse, calling in the energy of the wind. I feel my eyes change to white orbs. In an instant, dark clouds roll in, a fog shielding the village.

"Rain," I command, and the clouds gather closer. I'm letting lightning build in my hands when I hear a voice in my head that I haven't heard in years.

Ororo, I'm just here to talk.

I gasp and lose hold of the building clouds. They evaporate as a glimmering silver ship pierces through the fog, hovering low in the sky.

"What is that?" Ainet says behind me as the villagers scatter into their huts, others grabbing weapons, prepared to fight.

The ship lands near the far field, cows crying in response to the disturbance. It's twice the size of planes I've seen before. I hold my hands out, letting the lightning crackle in my palm and stand at the ready. This could be a trick.

The back hatch of the plane opens and a mechanical ramp

lowers. A chrome wheelchair glides down the ramp as if skating on ice, and the sight of the sun hitting his head makes my mouth drop.

It's really him. . . .

His chair hums as it rolls in our direction over pebbles and patches of grass, parking right in front of me.

"It is very good to see you again, Ororo," the man says. "I believe you have something that belongs to me."

Too stunned to speak, I dig into my pocket and retrieve his wallet, fumbling to pull out his ID, just to make sure.

"Professor Xavier?"

X

Inside Ainet's hut, we sip on water as the villagers crowd around. The hum of their excited chatter bleeds in through the walls.

Meanwhile, I can't stop staring at him. He looks exactly as I remember. Pale skin, intense blue eyes, bald head, and a pleasant, knowing smile. Feels like I'm nine years old again, being in his presence.

"You use a chair now." I can't help but state the obvious. "What happened?"

"It's a long story," he says, straightening his red tie.

"How did you find us?" Ainet asks, her voice a little detached. Almost cool.

Professor Xavier gives her a warm smile.

"Years ago, I took a trip to Egypt, thinking I would do some exploring, when I ran into a young girl with white hair sticking out of a scarf, who was trying to procure my wallet."

He waves the worn leather, and Ainet gives me a pointed look. I grimace.

"I'm . . . sorry about that," I mumble.

He holds up a hand. "Water under the bridge. Anyway, as

we spoke, I could sense a strange presence nearby. A dangerous presence. It's why I sent you away so quickly. He clearly sensed something in you the same way I did." He brings his hands together, steepling his fingertips. "He was hunting you. He had been hunting you from the moment you two met at your school gate."

Memories come flooding in, jabbing my chest, stealing my breath.

"I remember that day. I wouldn't look at him," I gasp, clutching my stomach. "I felt violently ill."

The professor nods. "Though your powers may not have manifested until now, your keen instincts were always there."

Even my mother's instincts sensed his poison. She was trying to protect me, even then.

The professor folds his hands. "That day, in the bar, I killed the Shadow King, banishing him to the Astral Plane. But somehow, he found his way back."

"A girl named Zawadi opened up a portal in the rocks," I explain. "That's how he came back. She didn't know what she was doing with her . . . powers."

"Yes, Zawadi." He says the name with reverence. "She is a mutant as well."

"A mutant? What's that?"

"A mutant is a person like you and me, born with a specific genetic makeup, an X gene, that gives us certain unexplainable capabilities." He sighs. "I'm afraid you are not quite the rain goddess this village has made you out to be."

Ainet shifts in her chair. It's slight, but I notice.

Hope squeezes at my heart hard. "There are others . . . like me?"

He smiles widely. "No one is exactly like you. But there are many others who have the mutant gene. We are making efforts to keep track of us all around the world."

"Why?"

He leans back. "After that day in the bar, I realized how dangerous mutant powers could be if they fall into the wrong hands. When we battled in the Astral Plane, I saw the Shadow King's intentions. If he were able to manipulate you, he could possess you, kill thousands of people. I knew he needed to be stopped at once." His brow furrows as he continues. "But there are also others, like the Shadow King, who want to use mutants for their abilities."

I swallow, remembering how the Shadow King made Zawadi slap herself, the manic look in her eyes back in Caribou.

The professor continues. "Which actually brings me to the reason I'm here. That moment with the Shadow King inspired me to start a school, in the hopes that humans and mutants can learn to live in harmony." He tips his head toward me. "The school is for individuals such as yourself. We help train and educate students on their unique capabilities."

My mind whirls, trying to process it all. I've feared going back to school for years, unwilling to relive the torment. But a school for people like me, a school where I'm not the only one who is different . . . can there really be such a place?

"You know more than anyone how cruel school can be for people like us. That is why I need your help. To not only protect your fellow mutants, but to protect us all from any evil that tries to destroy humanity." He nods to Ainet graciously. "I'm sure you've done a lot of training here with Ainet. But at our school, you'll have the opportunity to learn even more. You'll be able to talk to scientists and meteorologists who can help you better understand your powers and use them in different ways."

I rub my thumb into my palm, turning the prospect over in my head. It all sounds so promising.

But I look at Ainet, whose face has not changed since Professor Xavier arrived. It's not like her to have nothing to say.

"I'd like to talk to Ainet alone if you don't mind," I say, nodding at the door.

Ainet's brows pinch, lips set in a tight line.

Professor Xavier smiles. "Of course. I'll be at the ship. Take all the time you need."

He rolls out of the hut, leaving us staring after him, overwhelmed by all he dropped into our laps.

I take an uneasy breath. "Well. What do you think?"

Ainet stares at his empty space for a long moment, her shoulders rigid. She turns to me with a tight expression.

"Never let anyone belittle your greatness," she says sharply, index finger stabbing the air. "Who is this little white man to tell you whether you are a goddess or not!"

I snort. "Ainet . . ."

"And how dare he just fly in without warning like some church missionary, telling you who you are, what to believe in, and what you must do? As if you needed his help defeating the Shadow Man when he couldn't do it properly the first time!"

"Ainet." I laugh, shifting my stool closer to her.

"He is mistaken. You are not a mutant. You are from a long line of goddesses! Let no one tell you otherwise."

I sigh with a giggle. "Yes. I know, Ainet."

She straightens with a huff. "Oh. Well. Then what are you worried about?"

"I am not worried at all. I just wanted a moment alone with you to say thank you."

She cocks her head back. "Eh, eh! Whatever for?"

"For helping me find my home."

"What?"

I take her hand in mine. "I feel more at home in my own skin here than in any other place I've ever been. My family has always been with me, just like you said. But I've been so worried about finding them and not worried enough about finding me.

Without you, I would have never realized just how powerful I am. So powerful that even some American man needs my assistance."

Ainet's face softens.

"Goddesses have always helped mortals, despite themselves," I continue. "So maybe this is a part of my destiny, to help these mutants. Maybe this is the 'something much bigger' my family has been hinting at all this time. It's about time I start listening and not being afraid of what is meant for me."

She pauses, her eyes raking over me, before a big smile takes over her entire face. She brushes a strand of my hair back and cups my cheek.

"Yes. That is exactly it."

✕

I change back into my harem pants and T-shirt, packing the few items I own—a scarf, the blue dress, my beetle earrings, the comb, and a beaded necklace Ainet made me. I finger-comb my hair to fluff up my curls. My hair, which hangs down to my butt, is thick and voluminous. No more braids, no more scarves, no more hiding.

The villagers walk me to the ship, dancing and chanting behind me. I hug them all, promising to visit when I can. I save Ainet for last.

"Make sure someone takes my hut," I say.

She waves her hand. "No, no. We will save it for you. For when you return."

I glance back at my hut, the humble home that felt warmer, safer than any place I've been since my parents died.

"Thank you for saving me," I whisper.

Ainet's eyes fill with tears. "Remember everything I ever told you, girl."

I laugh. "No pressure."

She gives a reassuring smile and pushes me toward the ship. My knees falter as I get closer. A plane, the very thing that pivoted my life in this direction.

My stomach clenches. Last time I boarded a plane was with Mommy and Daddy. Now I'm setting out on a whole new adventure. I grip the railing, trembling.

"Breathe," I tell myself, and take the steps up one at a time. At the top, I wave at Ainet as the door slowly closes.

Inside, the ship is sleek and state-of-the-art, full of more computers and fancy technology than I've ever seen. My eyes widen as I take it all in.

T'Challa would love this.

Behind me, someone clears his throat, and I turn around to a young boy with dark turquoise skin, jet-black hair, pointy ears, and yellow eyes. He motions to the empty seat next to him.

"Hi!" he squeaks.

Another mutant. Like me, but not.

Too nervous to speak, I nod and plop down beside him, fumbling with the seat belt. He leans over and snaps me in.

"It's kind of tricky," he says, his lizard tongue clicking.

I trace the *X* symbol in the middle of the belt with my pinkie. The engine purring beneath us hiccups; wheels retract. I grip both seat arms, swallowing hard.

The boy grins, his fangs showing. "Afraid of heights?"

I think on it, my nerves easing. I'm not afraid of heights. Whenever I fall, I can always catch myself.

I shake my head. "I haven't been on a plane in a very long time."

"Oh! Well, it's not that bad once you get used to it," he says. "Professor said you can fly. Is that true?"

I blink a few times. "Yes."

His long tail flicks up. "Sweet! My name is Nightcrawler. What's yours?"

Again, I note his hue and glossy jet-black hair. That is not his real name, the name his family gave him. It's one he must have chosen for himself, a name that represents who he is. I look out the window at the villagers watching and waving as the ship rises higher. In the crowd, I spot Ainet's red robe dancing in the wind. She is not waving, just smiling proudly.

No one can change a storm's path. Only the storm can do that for itself. A storm, like you, can never be controlled. Because a storm has a destiny.

"Storm," I mumble, pressing a hand to the window. "My name is Storm."

ACKNOWLEDGMENTS

Let's give a round of applause to my outstanding, patient editor, Tricia Lin. I literally could not have written this without you and have learned so much about fantasy. Thank you, Tricia, for being so understanding and trusting me with this story. You deserve all the praise. Thanks to MARVEL for giving me this amazing opportunity. I'm still speechless.

To all my tour guides in Cairo, Luxor, and Nairobi, I know I bothered you with my weird questions, but thanks for helping me make Ororo's world come alive!

After experiencing a slew of health issues over the last two years, I want to thank my doctors for patching me together. I do NOT thank my pain-in-the-butt health insurance.

Much love to my family, friends, agents, and readers for holding me down and sending much-needed light.